Reckoning from the Shadows

Puja Guha

Book IV of The Ahriman Legacy

Reckoning from the Shadows
Puja Guha
www.pujaguha.com
pujaguha@pujaguha.com

Praise for The Ahriman Legacy Series

"It is a fast-paced read that is powered by non-stop action and a taut, emotional narrative, elevating the story beyond the usual hijinks of the genre novels. It is sure to entertain and please spy thriller fans."
— **RECOMMENDED by the US Review of Books**

"Most thriller writers depend on reference books and the Internet to do their research for their novels. But Puja Guha has 'been there, done that.' She's traveled throughout the world from remote poverty-stricken nations to the boardrooms of high finance in the world's richest cities, and it shows in this excellent novel. Fans of high-paced and action-filled thrillers won't be disappointed."
— **Brendan DuBois, bestselling mystery author, three-time Edgar Award nominee and James Patterson collaborator**

"Resurgence of the Hunt is both a gripping thriller and a nuanced character study. Puja Guha writes with real authority and authenticity."
— **Lou Berney, Edgar Award-winning author of November Road**

"Taut, pacy thriller, with well-drawn characters, believable relationships, and a satisfying plot."
— **Cathy Ace, award-winning author of The Cait Morgan Mysteries, and The WISE Enquiries Agency Mysteries**

DEDICATION.

For the people of Burundi,
who emerged from trauma with spirit and joie de vie.

Prologue

Veronica Salazar reached under her pillow to grab her Colt pistol when she heard a noise by the window. Instead of overtly reacting, she pretended to be asleep, listening intently for any further noise. It could be nothing, but her instincts told her otherwise. For the last three months, she'd been moving between Agency safe houses and her nerves were starting to run awry. How long would the FSB be hunting her?

She slid out of bed with a quiet sigh, she had been in the spy game long enough to know that there was no end date in sight. A year earlier, she had infiltrated the highest levels of the Russian government by posing as an aide to then president Ilya Rasskazov, and he had been hunting her ever since. When Rasskazov had been booted out of the presidency a month earlier, Veronica had hoped the hunt would abate, but so far it had only escalated—apparently, Rasskazov retained secret control over the FSB, including a special division that ran off-the-books black ops. Veronica would have been protected from the investigation through a series of cover identities, but all of the Agency's protections had fallen apart when her colleague and ex-boyfriend, Kevin, had turned out to be an FSB mole.

Thinking about Kevin still felt raw even though she had been coping with his betrayal for the last several months. Veronica forced herself to focus—she had to be sure that she was alone in her apartment. Holding her gun outstretched and ready, she checked her bedroom, then walked the hallway into the living room and turned on the lights before inspecting every corner. She checked the bathroom before switching off the lights and returning to her bedroom a few minutes later. Taking a deep breath, she leaned against the wall by the doorway, feeling a mixture of relief that the area was clear and annoyance at her paranoia. *Guess it's kept me alive so far,* she shrugged and set the pistol on her bedside table.

She was about to get back into bed when she heard a brief squeak on the wooden flooring just outside her doorway. Reacting on instinct, she stepped to the side and sent her right elbow backward with as much force behind it as she could muster. As soon as it made contact, she pivoted around to face her adversary, simultaneously sending her left foot out in a front kick. Without waiting for a glimpse of her opponent, Veronica sidestepped back into the bedroom, reaching forward for the pistol at her bedside. As she grabbed the gun, she once again heard movement by the doorway and sent her left leg wide in a side kick. The combination of the kick and her stretch made her stumble, but she brought the gun to bear, her other hand grabbing the edge of the bed behind her. Once she'd caught her balance, she reached for the wall with her free hand and flicked the light switch, keeping the pistol trained on the doorway as light flooded the room.

The person she saw standing there made her do a doubletake. She squinted, perhaps the bright light had blinded her into thinking he could be there. Her jaw dropped when she realized that she wasn't imagining things, Kevin was indeed standing just a few feet away from her, with his gun outstretched. "Give me one reason I shouldn't shoot you right now," she fought to keep her voice stern and steady, she had no intention of letting him see that he had put her off-balance.

"Veronica, please don't shoot."

"What the hell are you doing here?"

"I'm here to warn you. Please, I'm putting my gun down." Kevin released the hammer and let the gun roll backwards in his hand before bending and setting it on the floor.

"Slide it over—no funny business." Once the gun was at the base of the bed, Veronica slowly stood, making sure to keep her pistol trained at his head while she secured the weapon. She felt her shoulders relax after placing it at her back, held in place by the waistband of her shorts. "It's about time you stopped hunting me. I'm taking you in." She frowned, "How the hell did you find me anyway? The Agency got an all-new set of safe houses after you... after you left."

"You can take me in if you want, but I came here for you. I had to warn you."

Something in his tone caught her attention, and Veronica found herself wanting to believe him. He had handed over his gun—he had to know that she would take him in.

He could have killed me earlier. She was tempted to chastise herself; clearly, the first noise she had heard hadn't been her imagination, but somehow, he had eluded her. She'd have to address that later and check the next safe house for security holes. Veronica sighed, hopefully she would have a chance at another safe house... *at this point, I might as well let him say his piece.* She silenced her doubts, she had him in her sights now anyway. Still, she decided to remain cautious, he had duped her and the Agency multiple times. He might have given up his gun to lull her into a false sense of security. "First, handover your other pieces, then maybe I'll hear you out."

She watched quietly as he removed another pistol from a secondary holster on his shoulder and slid it over to her. "I know about your ankle holster and the knife you keep in your left boot," she said, her voice deadpan.

Kevin caught her eye for a moment before retrieving and following the same procedure with both munitions. When they were safely in her grasp, Veronica met his gaze, unsure whether or not trusting him would backfire. She wanted to believe there was a smidgen of good in him, that their entire relationship hadn't been a lie. "On your knees, hands behind your head—you know the drill."

Veronica waited for him to kneel with his hands clasped. "Out with it, what are you doing here?" she blurted, her tone wavered, but she focused on keeping her pistol steady.

"I had to tell you—the FSB is after you."

"I'm aware. Why else would I be in a safe house?"

"They're not going to stop, Veronica."

"Don't you mean *you're* not going to stop? Last time I checked, you'd joined up with them."

"I left."

Veronica rolled her eyes, *That's it?* He could have at least come up with a better lie. No matter how much she wanted to believe him, she wasn't going to be tricked again. "Please."

"Why would I come here and put myself at your mercy? You already have all of my weapons."

"Tell me something I don't know then."

"This is serious. Rasskazov is determined to catch you, and nabbing an Agency operative would go a long way to getting his credibility back in Russia."

"Getting his credibility back? What are you saying?" Did he mean that Rasskazov was setting the stage for a coup?

"Isn't it obvious? You can't have expected he would just go quietly into the night. That's hardly who he is." Kevin paused, "That's why I left—at least in part."

"You expect me to believe that after years of serving him in secret, you suddenly grew a conscience and decided to jump ship? Come on, what kind of an idiot do you think I am? You can't exactly up and quit the FSB." *Fool me once, shame on you, but fool me twice—*

"This is serious. If I could find you, it's only a matter of time." His gaze strayed toward the window, "You have to let me go. I shook my tails, but I don't want to take any chances, not with you anyway. They knew I'd be able to find you, so I have to disappear." He looked back at her before continuing, "I'm not asking you to do anything to help me. I have to run, I can't let them find me, but I couldn't disappear without warning you—not without seeing you one last time, anyway. All I can say is they're coming for you. They don't have this safe house yet because I sent them to that bogus apartment you used to have in Jersey. Otherwise, they would have already found you. Go on, call it in—they're following your trail instead of taking us both into custody right now."

"The apartment in Jersey?" her throat quivered. She and Kevin had set up the decoy apartment while they were still working together, long before anyone at the Agency had realized his betrayal. If it was true that he had sent the FSB there, then he was indeed working against them—why else would he send them to an obvious decoy?

Unless this is some kind of elaborate ruse... Still, that didn't explain why he would hand over all of his weapons or why he hadn't taken her in when he'd had the chance. Her grip on the gun wavered, but she stopped herself from lowering it. Even if he'd given her enough to merit a modicum of trust, she was hardly ready to let him go. Releasing one hand from the grip panel, Veronica reached for her phone and tapped onscreen— she still had the decoy apartment under surveillance. Once the surveillance app opened, she caught a glimpse of the clock that she had specifically hidden in the corner of the camera frame as a trick to pick up on whether the feed had been looped. *He's right,* she realized, the second hand remained on the four-second mark. *Damn it.*

"You can trust me, V. Why else would I send them there?"

The emotion in his voice made her resolve crumble, but she steadied herself against the bed. "You sent them to Jersey, so what? Why? I still can't trust you."

"I loved you, V, I promise you that wasn't a lie. I betrayed the Agency, but I never gave you up. You have to know the FSB would have found you months ago if I had helped them, but I couldn't let that happen. I could never let them hurt you, but I can't protect you anymore."

"Have you lost your mind? What do you think this is, some kind of romance novel? Do you really think I'm that naïve or lovesick? You turned your back on everything that we believed, everything we worked and stood for. You held Petra and Carlos at gunpoint for God's sake, and you almost let a bomb go off in the middle of D.C."

"We had to wake up the American government, there was no other way. Besides, I was never going to let the bomb detonate, and I never wanted Petra and Carlos involved in the first place. I didn't have a choice."

"You didn't have a choice?" Veronica looked down at her gun, her grip once again solid. She could end this, once and for all. *Could I even do it?* She wasn't sure of the answer to that question—he wasn't an immediate threat, more than anything, she was angry. He had shared her home, shared her bed, and they had talked about sharing a life together. Did knowing what he'd been hiding erase all of those moments, all of those feelings?

"My feelings for you were—are—real, you can trust in that." Kevin got to his feet, "I didn't come here to hurt you, but you have to deal with this threat once and for all. The FSB will come for you, and I can't help you anymore. You have to run, get off the grid completely… or neutralize the threat." He straightened up and took a step toward her, "They're coming for me, V. Either shoot me now or let me go."

Veronica winced at his repeated use of her nickname, a term of endearment from their time together. She stared at him, attempting to read the micro-expressions on his face. The look in his eyes, the emotions, the words, it all seemed real. *It seemed real before when we were together.* The reminder struck a nerve, and she shuddered.

He took another step toward her and stopped when her pistol was pressing against his chest. The seconds dragged by as the debate in Veronica's mind raged. Their eyes remained locked as he placed both hands on hers, then slowly but surely extracted the gun. She resisted, twisting her hands in the opposite direction, a maneuver that she knew well, that had been drilled into her at training. Against a normal adversary, she would have been in the clear, the gun would have been back in her control within a second. But the strength in her hands faltered, and it started to slip from her grip. She brought her right leg up and around to hit him with a roundhouse kick, but her reflexes were too slow and all she hit was air. He took a step back, lowering it toward his waist, but turning it to point back toward her.

Veronica gawked—how had she let him turn the tables like this? There was no reason he should have been able to overpower her so easily; before she had seen who the adversary was, her blows and kicks had landed like clockwork.

"I really do love you," he leaned forward and kissed her on the cheek, the pistol making contact with her belly as he reached around her to simultaneously retrieve his revolver from the back of her waistband.

Kevin withdrew to the window, opened it, and stepped out onto the fire escape, setting her pistol on the ledge. When he leaned in to close the window, he looked as if he was about to say something—in a movie, he would have waxed poetic about how love transcends all, about how they could still have a life together. *In a movie, I could have forgiven him.*

"Goodbye, V," he whispered, then disappeared down the stairwell.

Veronica kept her eyes fixed on the window, imagining what might have been as she secured the window latch from the inside. If someone had asked her what she would do if Kevin confronted her, she would have assured them that she'd take him in, no questions asked. Clearly, she had a different reality to contend with. She stepped backward and slid to the ground with her back up against the bed. This wasn't a movie, but she had still let him go.

* * * * * *

Chapter 1

Petra Shirazi stretched out on the couch, putting her feet up on the armrest as she spoke to her old friend and mentor Carlos on video chat. "I can't wait to see you and Diane," she said with a grin. "We'll see if you're still as much of a lightweight as last year."

"I blame jetlag—you try drinking a whole bottle of wine on two hours of sleep with a fourteen-hour time change."

"Touchy, touchy," she chuckled. "When do you get in?"

"Diane's conference here finishes on Friday, and we'll spend a couple of days exploring Munich together, then take the overnight train on Sunday."

"Awesome. How do you like Munich so far? I'm guessing that you aren't spending a lot of time at the conference."

"Only as arm candy for the evening events. More than that, and I just get in Diane's way—I may be many things, but an expert in medical device tech is not one of them," Carlos answered. "Munich's great—not the first time I've been here, but definitely much more pleasant than the last."

"Right," Petra caught the hint—Carlos must have gone to Munich with the Agency, back when he was still an operative. "Well, I'm glad you're getting the chance to enjoy it this time."

"Absolutely. Speaking of enjoying it, kiddo, I better get going. Besides, don't you have to get ready for your big dinner date?"

He made a show of winking to tease her, and Petra rolled her eyes. "I've got plenty of time, don't worry. It's nothing fancy, just a fun date night at a restaurant he wants to try."

"I wouldn't be so sure—I bet Kasem's itching to propose. It could be anytime now."

"Don't get ahead of yourself," she countered, trying to play it cool, although she felt her face flush.

"Nice to see you look happy about it, kiddo, and not nervous. It's about time. When he does do it—tonight or some other night—I expect to be in your first five calls."

"All right, old man, if it happens, you will be. I'll talk to you later." Petra hung up and looked up at the ceiling, *Could he be right?* Despite all of their relationship's ups and downs, she finally felt like she and Kasem were in a good place. They had dated years earlier while she was on an operation in Iran— officially, he'd been her asset, although she had rarely gathered intel from him. Her post as an Agency operative had cost him everything, though. Because of her, he'd been captured and held prisoner by a rogue Iranian general, then been duped into serving as an assassin to ensure her ransom. In reality, Petra had never been captured, and she'd been immediately evacuated out of Tehran. After months of searching, the Agency had pronounced Kasem dead, and she had spent months in therapy to deal with her guilt and post-traumatic stress disorder. Years later, she had discovered that he was alive and continuing to work for General Majed as the infamous international terrorist and assassin the *Ahriman,* named for the Persian spirit of destruction.

Since then, they had begun a working relationship that had rekindled their friendship and romance over the last three years. Petra had struggled to trust him, to forgive him for his past, and to forgive herself for the role she had played in that past. She had left her career as a spy behind and was now teaching

Security Law at a master's program in Paris under the name Ana Zagini, an identity with which she now felt quite at home. After their last operation working together, she and Kasem had decided to return to Paris—to build their relationship out in the real world rather than in a long-term vacation bubble. Petra's fears about whether they could last in the real world had turned out to be wrong—Kasem was able to fit in well with her life and friends in Paris. The one thing that was missing was a real career for him, it was too risky for him to work in finance as he had before his capture in Iran and working as the Ahriman yielded few legitimate career prospects. Despite her best efforts to let him move his career at his pace though, it bothered her that he hadn't figured something out yet. He could at least try something out, see if he likes it. Anything would be better than doing nothing all day. She'd been helping him to look at different types of non-profit and other work, but so far, he hadn't found anything that resonated. Still, he seemed happy, and their life together as a couple was solid. That said, she had to question whether he was solid as an individual. She pushed the thought aside, it was normal that Kasem was still dealing with the aftermath of his imprisonment in Iran, the nightmares and anxiety were normal. He was in therapy and would get to the other side.

Petra stretched out, dragging herself off the couch. The muscles in her legs were sore from a hard gym workout the day before, and she winced as she made her way to her closet. She examined her collection of dresses, unsure of what she should wear. Despite her attempt to play it cool on the phone, Carlos' suggestion that Kasem might propose made her heart flutter. Her gaze wandered to her left ring finger, and she imagined a diamond sparkling there. *I'm ready,* she smiled to herself. After all the roller coasters they'd been through, this was what she wanted.

* * * * * *

Chapter 2

Veronica resisted the urge to bang her fist onto the table, "What you're saying is that we've managed to track down one of the Agency's most notorious moles, but we can't initiate an op to go and grab him?"

Her boss Chris McLaughry raised his eyebrows and answered in his dry Scottish accent, "I'm saying that we can't just go in guns blazing. First of all, we don't know what Kevin is doing in Burundi, other than some kind of freelance work— probably for the Chinese. Besides, you know as well as I do, if we storm in there, he'll be gone before we get within a half mile of him. How do you think he's managed to elude us for this long? This is the closest we've come to real-time intel on where he is. We'll blow this shot if we move too quickly."

Why on earth did I let him go? Veronica kept that fact to herself, although it had been raging in her mind all week since she had watched Kevin climb out of her apartment window. All she had told Chris was that he had shown up at gunpoint and had gotten away before she could get the jump on him. "Fine," she sighed. "What do you propose?"

"For starters, we need to gather more intel—find out what he's doing there. If I had to guess, I'd say it's got something to do with the power contract that the government's about to award. There are three bidders vying for the deal, each trying to one-up the others, a Chinese consortium, a French-American JV, and an Indian-British JV."

"Since when is the power scene in Burundi that important? When I worked in East Africa, they could barely furnish power to their population."

"That's true," Chris nodded, "but since then, their politics have stabilized. They opened up three new solar plants in the last four years, but this one is major—they plan to build a mass solar farm with most of the power sold to neighboring countries. Looks like both Congo and Rwanda have already committed to buying about forty percent of the power generated."

Veronica leaned forward and zoomed in on her tablet screen to skim the executive summary of the current Agency brief on Burundi's economy. The document made mention of the new power plant but failed to provide any solid details. "Is this all we have on Burundi?"

"Basically—it hasn't been an Agency priority until this deal started to get traction."

"Wait, are you saying it's an Agency priority now? This deal, I mean, not catching Kevin."

"Just Kevin, at least for now."

"Then why do you care about investigating the deal? We should let the government deal with that—as you said, it's not our priority. Let's just get Kevin," Veronica frowned.

"I agree, but we can't exactly catch him without more intel—we need to know if he's actually on an op in Burundi or if he's just hiding out from the Russians since they have such a small presence there. You know the protocol—we can't be responsible for an international incident if Kevin's doing something halfway legit for the Chinese. And frankly, I think we need someone else on this—"

"Excuse me? No one knows him better than I do. You need me on this if we're going to catch him."

"I wasn't saying that I want to exclude you from the op, Veronica, but you're too close to this. We need someone else, someone who could be more objective."

Veronica stopped herself from reacting with a stream of suitable expletives. *Don't you dare take this away from me.* With a deep breath, she asked, "Who exactly did you have in mind?"

"I don't know, we have to go through his old personnel file in more detail. Any ideas?"

"There's a couple of people that went to training with him, but I'd guess they're out on ops." She opened up Kevin's file and paged through it onscreen, "He did an op with Vik, but obviously that doesn't work, Aaron Cole was at training with him, but he's on an op in Thailand. Dev Patel worked with him in Kenya but he's in India right now, Rafael Suarez did an op with him in Venezuela, but he left years ago. Carlos and Petra both worked with him, but they're gone too. I don't know, I've got nothing." They didn't need anyone else, she knew him better than all of them put together.

Chris reached over to examine the list himself. "Slim pickings, indeed," he said a moment later. "We'll have to come up with something. I'm not letting you do this on your own."

Are you serious? "Petra would be our best bet if she were here," Veronica said, hoping to underscore the point that Chris needed to let her do this on her own.

"True, but I need to talk to her anyway."

"Didn't she ask you to stay away?"

"We haven't spoken in a few months, but things were better last time we did speak. She was grateful that I helped her and Carlos out in Madagascar."

"Right," Veronica couldn't keep the skepticism out of her voice. "Isn't that well dry by now? She came out of retirement to help us a few times already."

"I might have something we could use to convince her."

"What do you mean, you might have something? Something on Petra? Really?" Veronica looked at him in confusion. While she was still sore at her old friend for abandoning the Agency, she didn't love the idea of blackmailing her. Besides, even if Petra did do something wrong, she'd bet it was Agency-sanctioned.

"Not on her, exactly, but I'd bet she still wouldn't want it to come out."

"Care to share?"

"It's not need to know," he shook his head.

Veronica considered what Chris had said and thought back to who Petra was close with. If he didn't have anything on her, this would have to be about her boyfriend, or maybe Carlos. "Fine," she said, pretending to acquiesce—Chris wouldn't reveal sensitive intel just because she asked. She'd have to find out on her own. Pondering further, she could recall a few brief details on Petra's boyfriend, the most important of which that he had served in Iranian intelligence under General Majed. *And he worked with the Ahriman.* If Chris had something, she'd wager it was on him. "I'll stay out of it, I promise. When can you bring her in?"

"My intel's not solid yet, but we can use the time to figure out what Kevin's up to."

"If you think we need her, why not bring her in now?"

"I'm sorry, Veronica, no can do."

"Then why not let me go to Burundi?"

"I don't need to explain that again. We can revisit this in a couple of days. I've got another meeting now," Chris waved at his office door.

16

Veronica gritted her teeth but managed to keep silent. On her way out, she passed Grant, an old Agency tech operative who now did occasional freelance work for Chris. She paused, glancing back as Grant shut the office door behind him. Chris only used Grant for off-book work… and Grant used to date Petra. Maybe he knew what Chris had on her? Her right hand curled into a fist as she pictured herself bringing Kevin in rather than letting him walk out onto her fire escape. Whatever Chris had, she had to figure it out. She wasn't going to let another chance to grab Kevin slip by her.

******

Chapter 3

Paris, France

Kasem Ismaili checked for the ring box in the inside pocket of his blazer for the third time that evening as he waited for Petra to emerge from their bedroom. He was surprised that she was taking so long to get ready—normally she was quite fast—and the waiting so far had only served to increase his nervousness tenfold. When he'd mentioned that he wanted to go out on a date night, he'd been as nonchalant as possible, not wanting to spoil the surprise, but now he wished he'd told her that he'd made a reservation instead of their more typical spontaneous plans. *We're going to be late,* he glanced at his watch with a sigh.

The bedroom door opened, and he looked up to see Petra wearing a bright green floral sundress. Her hair was down, falling to her shoulders in soft black waves, just the way he liked it. Kasem smiled at her, "You look lovely."

"Sorry I took so long," she said. "I couldn't decide what to wear since the weather's been so unpredictable."

"It's okay. We should go—the place gets full early, so I made a reservation."

Under normal circumstances, the fifteen-minute walk to the restaurant along the Canal Saint-Martin would have been relaxing, but instead, Kasem found himself sweating and short of breath. The more he tried to relax, the more nervous he got, and with each step, he worried that Petra would pick up on his mood.

She paused at the canal bank, "This time of the evening is my favorite. Dusk in the springtime, before it gets too hot."

He gave her a quick nod, and she asked, "Kasem, are you okay? You seem distracted or something."

"I'm fine." He exhaled and took her hand, forcing himself to join her in taking in the scene. *This is a happy moment, we're doing so well.* Putting his arm around her shoulder, he pulled her in close. She had to say yes—this relationship was the most important thing in his life now. In the back of his mind, he wondered if it was the only thing in his life these days, what with his difficulties finding work that he was remotely interested in, but he dismissed the notion.

A few minutes later, they turned onto *Rue de Lancry* and walked into the *Le Verre Volé* restaurant, a wine bar with a small but renowned food selection. The waiter led them to a corner table situated with a large picture window on one side and the extensive wine rack to the other. Petra peered over the window ledge to her right, "It's fun to watch the people go by along the Canal. Thanks for picking this place—it's really charming."

"I'm glad you like it." Kasem sat down and for the first time that evening, or rather that day, felt his shoulders release some of the tension that had built up. "It's just one of those Parisian finds—I've walked by the Canal a million times and never noticed it, but as soon as I did, I knew we had to come here. It reminds me of one of the places that you took me to when we first met."

"Oh, of course."

Petra turned her head, and Kasem kicked himself, he shouldn't have brought up how they had first met, she still felt guilty that they had met when she was cultivating him as a potential source. He'd fallen for her immediately, although he wasn't sure when it had happened on her side. *Sometime later, I guess...* "I hope I didn't bring up a sore subject," he reached across the table to grasp one of her hands. "I know things were different back then, but I like those memories too. They're part of us, part of what got us here."

"Thank you for saying that."

The rest of the evening moved more smoothly as they ordered dinner and both relaxed, working their way through a bottle of Côte du Rhone wine. After sharing an appetizer and a heaping plate of fresh bread, Kasem ordered a hearty entrecote steak, while Petra chose a mixed seafood dish. They chatted about random stuff, Petra told him a funny story about one of her colleagues, and he recounted his day, which he'd spent wandering along the Seine, followed by a visit to the Bastille Farmers Market and an hour at a nearby outdoor gym.

"I was doing dips on the bars, and I saw this girl on the high bar doing pull-ups—she kind of reminded me of you since it's not something you see often. On the other high bar, there was this teenage boy who kept looking at her, trying desperately to do a pull up himself. His friend was trying to teach him and mock him at the same time. Meanwhile, I think she did almost ten in a row," he chuckled.

"I'm glad you had a good day. I get worried sometimes that you end up spending too much time at home."

"Sure... do you want to order dessert?"

"I don't know. I'm guessing it's good here, but I kind of want to go sit by the Canal instead. It's still early, and it's Wednesday, so it's not party central," she answered, referring to the large groups of students who would often set up picnics on the banks of the Canal so that they could get drunk on cheap wine and liquor.

"You can't blame them for wanting to picnic out there, it's such a great spot—" Kasem's jaw dropped as a mouse ran across the floor, straight through the middle of the restaurant. A woman at the table next to them shrieked and jumped up, pointing at the ground. Petra wheeled around, her knife in hand, only partially concealed by the napkin from her lap as the waiter chased after the mouse. Before he could catch it, the mouse scurried away and darted out into the road.

Kasem was still reeling as he settled back into his chair, "Well, that just happened." He felt dazed, had his plan to propose just been ruined?

Petra shifted in her seat, "I'm glad we already finished eating. Let's go somewhere else for dessert. Maybe get some ice cream and sit by the Canal?"

"Absolutely," Kasem gave her a quick nod, still trying to shake off his anxiety, which had returned in full force. Should he wait for another night? He pondered for a second, then came up with an idea—she was right, the Canal would be quiet at this hour, and it offered a lovely setting for him to pop the question. The night wasn't ruined, this might even be better than proposing in a crowded restaurant.

They found an ice cream shop a couple of blocks away and then walked over to the Canal, cones in hand. As usual, Petra reached over with her spoon to sample his and savored the Stracciatella that he'd chosen, "Mmm…good choice."

"You always have to try my ice cream, hmm?"

They sat down on the stone bank, Petra slipping her shoes off and letting her feet hang over the Canal edge. "I have a secret," she whispered and leaned over to give him a kiss. "I really, really love you."

"I love you too."

Kasem waited until they'd both finished their ice creams, then walked over to a nearby trash can to throw out the napkins and spoons. When he returned to sit next to her, his heart was racing, *It's time.*

Before he could work up the courage, Petra met his gaze, "Did you have the chance to talk to Nico about that non-profit he's starting? It might be a good spot for you."

"No, not yet. I'll email him in a couple of days."

"Oh, okay."

Kasem sighed, clearly, Petra thought that he should have already taken action. "I'll get in touch with him tomorrow."

"Only if you want to—I just thought it might be good for you, a chance to start over."

Start over? Kasem inhaled sharply, *Is she referring to the Ahriman?* "Maybe," he stopped himself from saying more, from blurting out what he really wanted to say. Hadn't they been through this before? Besides, he couldn't change the past.

I thought you'd forgiven me.

"Sorry, I didn't mean to be pushy, I figured you wanted something to devote your energy to—"

"I know."

They sat in silence for a few moments. *She probably didn't mean it like that,* Kasem told himself. He and Petra had had numerous conversations about the role they had each played in how he became the Ahriman, and they had both worked to forgive themselves and each other. The past was the past. He looked out across the water and back at her, her café-au-lait skin and large hazel eyes as alluring as when they had first met. Whatever had happened between them before, this was the future that he wanted.

"Let's walk over to that bridge," he motioned toward one of the turquoise copper raised bridges that traversed the Canal. He helped her up, and they wandered toward the bridge, taking the steps up slowly.

When they reached the curved top, Kasem stopped to lean over and kiss her. "Petra, you're the most important part of my life, really the best and only thing I've got going for me. I couldn't do without you." He got down on one knee and reached into his jacket pocket to retrieve the ring box. The marquis-shaped diamond glinted as it caught the light from the nearby lantern when he opened the box. "I know we've had a tough road, with some crazy ups and downs. I thought I had lost you…" His voice quavered as he recalled the price that he had paid to ensure her freedom from General Majed. "Through all of it, I've always loved you, and we're so lucky to have this chance again. You're the light of my life. Petra Shirazi, my Lila, will you be my wife?"

Petra gaped at him, and he looked up at her, deep into the hazel eyes that he wanted to wake up next to every day as he slid the ring onto her finger. Her silence felt like an eternity, and for a second, he wondered if he had moved too fast, if he had read the moment wrong, until she answered in a soft voice, "Yes, yes I will. I love you too, Kasem."

* * * * * *

Chapter 4

Veronica walked up to the table in the Grand Central Station food court where Grant was sitting with his computer and sat down across from him uninvited. "Hi Grant, fancy meeting you here."

He looked up from the screen with a scowl and swung the top of his laptop shut with an excess of embellishment. "What do you want?"

"Not even a hello, how are you?"

"The Agency doesn't get much pointless courtesy from me these days, what can I say?" he shrugged.

"Considering that you hacked our servers? I think you're lucky to be off house arrest."

"There were mitigating circumstances... stuff that you don't know about. Besides, I'm still on a radius," he gestured toward his ankle on which he wore a tracking device since being released from house arrest two years earlier.

"I'm sure there were," Veronica said, not bothering to keep the skepticism out of her voice. She wasn't sure what those circumstances were, but as far as she was concerned, Grant had gotten away scot-free despite stealing intel off the Agency servers. Prior to that, he'd been a senior manager in IT with a promising career, but he must have been hiding his crazy well to go off the deep end like that. *I bet it had something to do with Petra...* She was pretty sure they were still dating when it happened. The details around that period were fuzzy, including the operation that Petra was involved with, despite numerous attempts on Veronica's part to dig up more information. All she'd been able to gather was that the op had something to do with the Ahriman and had required Petra to come out of retirement. She had heard rumors that Grant had hacked the servers to go after her, that he might even have helped her, but those were unsubstantiated. Veronica had heard enough rumors in her career as a spy to fill a hundred lifetimes, and while she recognized that they warranted further investigation, a huge portion of them never held water—one of the unfortunate realities of her business. Besides, even if he'd gotten into the records, he wouldn't have been able to decipher them.

Grant shot her a glare, "What do you want, Veronica? Chris already has me working overtime—if he told you that you could pile on more stuff, then we need to have a conversation. I'm not at his beck and call—"

"Keep your shirt on, dude. No extra work, I promise. Chris read me in on what he has you working on, so I just wanted to check in, take a few minutes to chat about it." She raised her arms above her head and stretched them out as wide as possible, a subtle intimidation tactic she used to establish herself as the dominant person within a conversation.

"I don't understand, I just spoke to him today," Grant looked perturbed. "What does he need now?"

"Nothing extra, but he asked me to make sure that you and I are on the same page."

"I don't get it—we still haven't found anything conclusive."

"Exactly," Veronica made a show of agreeing but kept up her superior tone. She had to keep Grant on the defensive so that he'd slip up and tell her what he was working on. "He didn't have a chance to take me through all the details, so I told him I'd talk to you directly, make sure we don't duplicate work."

"There isn't that much to tell—we've been trying to match the Ahriman's movements with what we know about Kasem, obviously, but we barely have anything on either of them. All we have is that they were in Iran at the same time, but that was hardly a secret since we already knew Kasem worked with the Ahriman."

WTF... Veronica steeled her reaction as her mind went haywire. That was what Chris had meant, he was investigating if Petra's boyfriend was the Ahriman. "Okay, you keep working on movement patterns, and I'll focus on known associates," she said and stood up. The faster that she got out of there, the less likely Grant would pick up on her deception.

Grant frowned, "Didn't Chris tell you I already looked into that? That's the first thing we tried, but everything about the Ahriman is a load of rumors. Nobody has any real intel, it's all smoke and mirrors."

"Hmm, he forgot to mention that, but I should still see if we can get anything from my contacts in the Middle East. I'll check in with you once I hear from them." She kicked herself for the comment about known associates, but hoped that he wouldn't say anything to Chris. She stepped away from the table, keeping her movements controlled to appear unfazed by their conversation.

* * * * * *

A few minutes later, Veronica was back at her safe house, still reeling from the conversation. *Petra is dating the Ahriman.* The possibility seemed incomprehensible, how on earth could that be true? *No way...*

Veronica triple-checked that both the front and back doors, along with all of the windows, were locked before she set a kettle on the stove to make some tea. Since Kevin's warning, she'd been taking extra precautions, even if she wasn't sure whether or not to believe him. Disbelief was the theme of the day, she stared at the kettle, willing the water to boil faster. If she was to suspend reality, Kevin had left the FSB, he loved her, and Petra was dating one of the world's most notorious terrorists. *Sounds about right,* she chuckled to herself.

Once the water was ready, she doled three tablespoons of her favorite jasmine green tea leaf blend into her French press, poured the water in, and settled down on the couch while she waited for it to brew. When it was ready, she pulled her feet up and sipped at it gingerly, savoring the earthiness that came from the brown rice mixed into the tea leaves. After the first few sips, she felt more level-headed and able to process both of her encounters from earlier in the day. The fact that Chris insisted on having someone accompany her on the op to find Kevin was infuriating enough, but having that person be Petra made Veronica want to scream. How could an ex-Agency operative almost ten years younger than her be the one to make sure that she had her head on straight? She sighed, wishing that Chris had at least nominated someone with as much experience as her. *Basically anyone else?* Veronica still hadn't made peace with Petra's decision to leave the Agency—Petra's choice amounted to a betrayal, albeit nowhere near as bad as what Kevin had done to her.

Veronica recalled one of the three therapy sessions Chris had mandated that she attend once the dust had settled on Kevin's duplicity. Although the therapist had wanted to focus on her feelings toward him, Veronica had redirected the conversation to Petra on more than one occasion, citing how upset she still was that her friend had left her in the cold. "Petra left right when we needed her most," Veronica had said.

The therapist had responded with, "Didn't she come back to help you on the op? To help you find the mole?"

"She did, but she didn't stick around. We still have to deal with this entire mess without her."

"Do you think you might be focusing your anger at Kevin, and perhaps at yourself, on Petra instead?"

Veronica had walked out of the session a few minutes later and refused to return, she couldn't believe that he would make such a ludicrous insinuation. When she thought about it now, four months later, she wondered if he might have had a point. She was, of course, angry at Kevin for what he had done, that was only natural given his betrayal of both her and the Agency, but she was also furious at herself. How had she been taken in like that? She blinked away tears as she recalled the mission in Moscow and the sacrifice that she had made to get away. Spy movies made it seem as if women used their bodies to get whatever they wanted on a regular basis, but in truth, sex was a last resort. If she hadn't slept with her Russian office mate, he almost certainly would have discovered who she was, and the intel that she had gathered would have been lost.

Deep down, Veronica recognized that she probably should have talked about that in therapy, especially the fact that Kevin had gotten her out of that situation. He had treated her injuries and cared for her, and he had supposedly helped her to safety.

And then he betrayed me, walked away as if it was nothing. When she had looked into his eyes a week earlier, she wondered if that was true. Yet the fact remained that he had lied to her and the entire Agency for years. Her hand shook, and she set the teacup down on the table before the hot liquid spilled over the sides.

You have a job to do. Veronica set aside her memories and zeroed in on her encounter with Chris—she could deal with her emotions later *after* she had Kevin locked up in a cell for the rest of his life.

The first option that she considered was going to Burundi right away, on her own, without Agency support. That would give her the highest chance of catching Kevin; the longer they waited, the more likely it was that he would move on. The downside there was that Chris was right—any whisper of her presence and he'd vanish. They couldn't lose this shot, who knew when they would have it again. She rubbed her chin, that risk ruled out her going in on her own, which left her with a need for Agency support. *Petra's support...* Even though she didn't like it, Chris had a point there, Petra had known Kevin for years, and they had already ruled out the few other operatives who knew him equally well.

Which puts me back at square zero, needing her help. Veronica contemplated her conversation with Grant. Petra may be off her rocker, but she couldn't possibly be that insane. The idea simply wouldn't compute, how on earth could Petra be dating the Ahriman? But why else would Chris investigate it? There must be some reason. With a deep breath, Veronica shut her eyes and considered the possibility. Deep in her gut, despite every reason not to believe it, she couldn't help but think they were onto something. She racked her brain to come up with any details on the Ahriman but came up blank. All she could recall about him from her operation in Russia was that Chris and Petra had brought Kasem in to impersonate the Ahriman. As far as she could remember, he and Petra had started dating after the op.

Maybe he had convinced her the Ahriman wasn't that bad? Veronica tapped her fingers against the microfiber armrest of her couch. Grant had said that all they have is smoke and mirrors. Chris might not be willing to use the intel yet, but she certainly was. She still wasn't sure if she believed it, only that it was her best shot. The mere threat of releasing Kasem's name as the Ahriman to global intelligence services would be enough to force Petra to work with her, and she knew exactly who could help her get started. First, she'd have to have another conversation with Grant—she had a hunch as to who could have helped him figure out what he had found on the Agency servers. She could work with smoke and mirrors—in fact, she excelled at it.

* * * * * *

Chapter 5

Munich, Germany

Carlos tipped his head back to relish his last sip of beer, then set the mug down with a flourish. He searched the beer hall for the waiter, hoping to signal for another one, but his waiter seemed more enraptured with a leggy blonde sitting two tables over. Surveying the rest of the beer garden, Carlos imagined how packed the area would be during Oktoberfest instead of the relative emptiness of the pre-lunch hour on a Thursday in April.

He waited a few more minutes before giving up on another beer; he left seven euros in exact change on the table and elected to wander the neighborhood streets. Since his wife Diane had been busy at her conference over the last couple of days, he'd gotten most of the standard tourist attractions out of the way on his own—she'd already been to Munich several times—and was now able to bask in the feel of the city. Such a contrast from when he'd visited for the Agency, he thought with a wistful smile. *Thank God those days are behind me.*

Turning the corner, he stumbled upon a hole-in-the-wall restaurant serving fries and bratwurst, and after ordering a plate, settled down on a bench in a park across the street. Even though it was far too early for such a heavy lunch, Carlos delighted in the quiet simplicity, especially with the unusually sunny and warm spring day. The fries were crisp and the meat was smoky and flavorful. When he stuffed the last bite into his mouth, he wiped his greasy fingers on a napkin and leaned his head back, a cool breeze fanning over his head. *I could eat three more of those,* he grinned, *but I shouldn't.* He stood and headed back in the direction of the boutique hotel where they were staying, a warm shower beckoning.

When Carlos emerged from the bathroom, he heard the sound of the suite door opening. Diane must have gotten out early. He wrapped a towel around his waist and walked out into the living room, hoping to entice her into the bedroom. He turned the corner from the hallway of their suite, using one hand to hold the towel in place, and almost lost his grip on it once he saw who was sitting on the couch with her feet up on the coffee table.

"Hi Carlos, how about you get dressed?"

"What the hell are you doing here, Veronica?" he asked through clenched teeth. *So much for a quiet day.*

* * * * * *

Chapter 6

Paris, France

Petra held up her left hand as she stared at the ceiling with her head propped up on two oversized pillows. The marquis shaped diamond sparkled in the sunlight streaming in from their east facing bedroom window. A lump formed in her throat. *Why am I not happy?*

She sat up, glad that she had the apartment to herself since Kasem had left for the gym early. Tilting her hand from side to side, she observed the ring catching the light as if the answers she sought would just emerge from its brilliance. She wiggled the ring off her finger and set it on the bedside table, a sense of relief flooding over her. *What's the matter with me?* She ran her fingers through her hair, ruminating on their relationship— Kasem was her partner, and she'd wanted him to propose. So why did she feel so empty?

She thought back to the night before, considering what Kasem had said. "Petra, you're the most important part of my life," that part made her smile and feel warm and comfortable. But then he'd said that she was the only thing he had. She exhaled, the pressure on her chest releasing.

The only thing.

No job, no friends of his own. Nothing else, except maybe the gym. In a way, it was a relief to figure out where the problem was, but that didn't give her any ideas on what to do about it. That couldn't be why he wanted to marry her, it couldn't be because he had nothing else in his life. That was way too much pressure.

Petra was still mulling over how to talk to Kasem about that when her alarm went off. She'd talk to him about it tonight, she decided as she rushed out for class. They'd already come so far, they could figure this out.

* * * * * *

Chapter 7

Munich, Germany

Carlos pulled a chair across the living room, cringing as it screeched over the laminate floor but grateful that it would cause Veronica the same discomfort. A million reactions screamed through his head, led by the repeated echo, *Why on earth is she here?* He wanted more than anything to take her duffle bag and fling it out of the window, followed by a strong nudge to shove her over the railing after it. A satisfying thought, even though they were only on the first floor and she'd be fine.

After setting the chair across the coffee table, he plodded over to their kitchenette to fill up a glass of water without offering her one; he wanted to delay the conversation as much as possible. He had learned that technique at the Agency, that holding up an important discussion could unsettle the other party, maybe even put them on the defensive, although he doubted that it was working. *More like unsettling me,* he sighed as he finally sat down. He drained the full contents of the glass, then placed it on the table before making eye contact. "Let's get this over with. What are you doing here, V?" he purposely used her nickname even though they had never been close—any illusions he could play with might serve to his advantage.

"I need you to help me find Petra."

"That's why you're here?" Carlos started to laugh, his chuckle turning into a full-fledged guffaw due to the tension in the room. At first, he played it up, but then he grasped his stomach, the more he tried to control the laughter, the harder it seemed to take hold. *Do they really think I'd help them?* The idea was so ludicrous that he wondered if he was being punked.

Veronica took her feet off of the coffee table with a stern expression, "Trust me, she'll want to talk to me."

"If you want to talk to Petra, just ask Chris. They're on decent terms these days, I'm pretty sure he knows how to get in touch with her."

Her expression flickered for a second before returning to the same somber façade, but it was enough of a tell for Carlos to realize that he'd stumbled onto something. "You can't go to Chris?" he raised his eyebrows. "Why not?" He instantly relaxed—he had all of the power in this situation.

After a brief pause, Veronica replied, "That's not important. I had a conversation with Grant yesterday—about stuff he thought Chris had read me in on—and he said something very interesting. You know how he ended up in house arrest, right? He hacked the Agency servers so that he could go to Petra's rescue—like some twisted knight in shining armor."

"What does that have to do with me?" Carlos crossed his arms, still portraying the same level of confidence despite a sinking feeling in his gut. He felt off-kilter, Veronica had taken back control.

"His story seems credible enough—and clearly, he deserved to be in house arrest for a couple of years, or worse—but it doesn't explain how he deciphered what he found. Agency files are stored in code set up by the lead operative. I checked his background, and other than some freelance work he's done since that whole debacle, he has absolutely no operational experience. So how do you think he figured out those files? He wouldn't have known Petra's operational history well enough to guess where she was—I think even I'd have trouble with it."

She knows... Carlos swallowed, determined not to divulge any extra information. If she knew something, she had to come right out and say it.

"I think someone must have helped him, someone who knows Petra really well. Maybe someone who was involved with recruiting her? An old mentor who'd be well-acquainted with the details in her personnel file?"

"What are you insinuating?" the words burst out before Carlos had a chance to stop himself.

"I would have thought that was obvious—whoever helped Grant broke the law and could be prosecuted. Maybe Chris decided to ignore that little detail. No one would have figured that Grant would lose his mind like that, but justice hasn't been served, has it?"

Carlos sighed, she had him, and they both knew it. "I'll help you find her, but there's no way she's going to help you. All I did was look at a few printouts, I had no idea where they came from." His confidence returned as he focused on that point, "Petra's not hiding from the Agency anymore, I doubt she'd mind you saying hello."

"I think she will, and so will you. I've got plenty to motivate you both."

"Right. Good luck with that." He picked up his empty water glass and walked back over to the kitchenette to refill it.

"I won't need it—but thank you."

A sense of dread washed over him, there was something in her tone. *What else does she have?*

"If she doesn't help me, I'll get you locked up, *and* I'll tell the world that her boyfriend's the Ahriman."

The now full glass of water slipped from Carlos' hand and fell back into the sink with a loud thump. Carlos fought to maintain a poker face to no avail, searching for words. Abandoning any attempt at diplomacy, he spouted, "Are you insane? You're going to tell the world that Kasem is the Ahriman? There is no way that's true!" Deep down, he wondered if she might be right—Kasem had indeed served in Iran, and both he and Petra had always been cagey about his past. *No way,* Carlos silenced his concerns.

"Grant seems to think so."

That little... "That's your source? Petra's lovesick puppy? You trust him? Come on, you know it can't be true."

"I'm almost inclined to agree with you, but it's too ludicrous for him to be making it up. That said, he's not sure, but it doesn't even matter."

Carlos gaped as her meaning dawned on him. "You're saying that you don't care. True or not, you're willing to ruin their lives—they'd be on the run forever."

"Now you're getting it."

"How could you do that? Petra's your friend." He still couldn't grasp what he was hearing.

Veronica's jaw set, "She acts like this is something you can just walk away from, both of you do. We have a duty, and right now, *my* duty is to catch Kevin. The Agency is floundering because of people like you. I don't care if you understand or not, all I care about is that you help me."

Carlos could see that he wouldn't be able to change her mind. As to her accusation, his gut said there might be something to it, but he chose to ignore it. Of course, Kasem looked suspicious of being the Ahriman—they'd even had him pretend to be the Ahriman; he recalled the op when he had first met Kasem two years earlier. *Petra wouldn't date the Ahriman, would she?* After another sigh, he nodded—he'd have to deal with his concerns later, but for now, he had a sinking feeling that Veronica wasn't bluffing. If she shared his role in what Grant had done, even though it had happened years earlier and was completely unintentional, there would be consequences that he was not ready to face. "What do you need?"

* * * * * *

Chapter 8

Paris, France

Carlos trudged up the four flights of stairs to Petra's walk-up apartment, sweating profusely. He doubled over and panted, unsure whether he was more out of breath because of the steep stairwell or still recovering from the discussion with Veronica earlier that day.

After agreeing to help her, things had moved quickly—the two of them went straight to the airport and boarded the next flight to Paris. Upon arrival, he'd convinced her to remain at her hotel, the conversation with Petra would go far better if he delivered the news, there was no doubt about that. Now that he'd reached her place, he hesitated, not wanting to knock on her door. She was his mentee, and he cared about her deeply, even thought of her as his little sister. *Now I have to bring her world crashing down.* He bit his lip and rapped on the door, delaying the misery would only make things worse.

When no one answered, Carlos knocked again before picking up his phone. He had hoped to deliver the news in person to lessen the blow, but clearly, Petra wasn't home. He sent her a text, "Hey kiddo, turns out I'm in Paris a couple of days early. When will you be home? I'm outside your place."

A moment later, Carlos' phone rang, "Hey Petra."

"Petra? Wow, I'm not sure when you last called me that. Is everything okay?"

"It's fine, I've just got something to tell you. Let's talk when you get home."

"You're scaring me, old man," she said, using the nickname in an obvious attempt to lighten the mood. "There's a key in the flowerpot on the window ledge by the door. I'll be home in fifteen."

* * * * * *

Carlos stretched out on the couch, fifteen minutes had never seemed so long. He glanced at his phone twice, only a couple of minutes had gone by, and he elected to shut his eyes. There was nothing he could do, so he might as well get some rest.

When he heard the door opening, he sat up in a hurry, rubbing his eyes.

"What's going on, Carlos?" Petra asked as she sat across from him. "Where's Diane?"

"I left her in Munich, told her an emergency came up, that I'd be home in a few weeks. She wasn't happy, I keep telling her I'm not a spy anymore and being proved wrong, but we'll deal with it. You and I though, we have a pretty serious problem."

"I gathered. What happened?"

"Veronica showed up in Munich."

Petra crossed her arms, "I'm guessing this was more than a social visit. What does she want?"

"She needs our help to catch Kevin," Carlos answered, still unable to broach the subject of the Ahriman. The nagging voice in the back of his mind refused to quiet, *What if Grant is right?* He considered lending credence to Grant's accusation but couldn't figure out why, logic told him it was baloney, yet he was unable to dismiss the possibility.

"You want to help her?" Petra frowned, "Kevin did turn on us too, but maybe it's best to let sleeping dogs lie? I'm not sure I want to reopen Pandora's box. If it's what you want though, I'm in—you know that, right?"

"There's more… she said that if I don't work with her, she'll turn me in for helping Grant find you in Kuwait." Carlos kicked himself for still being unable to share the worst part of his exchange with Veronica.

"Oh, God, I'm sorry. Of course, we'll help you."

Her use of the word *we* finally pushed him over the edge. "That's not all—if we don't, she'll tell the world who Kasem really is."

"You mean an Iranian agent?"

Carlos caught himself watching her reaction, he now realized why he'd subconsciously decided to approach the issue in such a roundabout fashion. *I needed to see her reaction. Crap,* Petra's facial expressions were too controlled, *something's off.* "She'll leak his name and face to the press, or even just to a few global intel agencies. Either way, she tells the world that he's the Ahriman."

The fear on Petra's face was gone in a second, a testament to her training. "That's crazy. You think she'd do it?"

"She would."

Petra leaned forward, "Kasem is a good man. You've said so yourself—tell me you don't believe her. Where did she even come up with that? I know he impersonated the Ahriman for us, but—"

"I don't know," Carlos snapped. *Dammit,* he resisted the urge to shake his fist at the universe. Based on the words she had used—she hadn't explicitly denied the accusation—combined with what he'd seen on her face, he knew in his bones that Veronica was right.

Kasem is the Ahriman. If he pressed Petra, if they had a real conversation about it, she would probably tell him the truth. His eyes wandered to the windowsill, where a picture of her and Kasem together sat. If he was indeed the Ahriman, there had to be redeeming factors, but he'd rather not know. It would be easier not to know, to deny the truth than be confronted with it. "Let's just get to Burundi and get this done. I've had enough of being under the Agency's thumb. I don't care whether or not it's true."

* * * * * *

Chapter 9

Paris, France

Petra waited for Kasem on a bench by the Seine and pulled her knees into her chest, putting all of her energy toward holding it together. She had originally planned to meet Kasem late in the afternoon after he completed his shift at the gym where he'd started working as a personal trainer—she had intended to bring up her concerns over what he had said when he proposed. *He said I was the only good thing in his life.* If Kasem had seemed more even keel emotionally, that would bother her less, but being his everything alongside the nightmares and continuing trauma was far too much. No couple could handle that kind of pressure. Now that Carlos had shown up with far more dire news however, she had no choice but to table that entire discussion; they had more pressing concerns to deal with given Veronica's threats.

She checked her watch and sighed, Kasem was running late, and her blood pressure was rising with each passing second. Wrapping her arms around her knees a little tighter, she wondered how her life had become so complicated, it was all a series of choices, small and large, that had led her to this place. They should have gotten out while they still could, broken ties and started over. Her mind lingered on the various opportunities that she and Kasem had had to get out of the spy game. Each time they had agreed to participate, to help the Agency, to help Carlos; they had placed the greater good above

44

their own welfare, but with each operation, they had increased the risk that someone would discover Kasem's true identity. *Now we have to pay for that.*

Her lower lip quivered, she had never been angrier about the position that her past as an operative had put her in. She recognized that Kasem had done awful things, terrible acts of violence, but she couldn't be more certain that he had paid the price and redeemed himself. Kasem had started down that path under the belief that he was ensuring her safety, paying the ransom for her release from General Majed's custody. That had all turned out to be a carefully executed ploy, and Kasem had been clawing his way toward redemption ever since. At first, Petra was unsure if she could forgive him, if she could put his past aside so that the two of them could move forward. On their last operation together in Madagascar, she had realized how much darkness she had inside her as well. She shuddered as she recalled how she had tortured a man who had killed one of their team members, how she had unleashed all of her anger on him and broken each of his fingers. She exhaled in an attempt to release the memory, and a tear rolled down her cheek.

As Petra wiped it away, she saw Kasem at the top of the ramp and waved at him. He smiled and approached her, but as soon as he drew close, he stopped with a frown. "What happened?"

She smiled through her watery eyes, "Carlos is here. Veronica found out, she found out that you're the Ahriman." Before he could respond, she continued, "They don't know for sure—my guess is that they can't prove it, but she's blackmailing us. If we don't help her to bring Kevin in, she's going to leak it to every intel agency in the world."

* * * * * *

Chapter 10

Paris, France

Kasem stayed on the bench by himself after Petra gave him the news. He watched her walk away as she returned to the apartment to speak to Carlos once again, reeling from the shock. He had allowed himself to believe that their lives were moving forward, especially now that he and Petra were engaged. Although he hadn't found a career for himself, their relationship seemed solid, and they were happy together. *None of that matters now...*

He could see his future stretching out before him—either an endless series of operations, taking orders from the Agency under the threat of capture and prosecution, or a life on the run. Part of him wanted to believe that life on the run wouldn't be that different—it was all he could do not to show Veronica and the Agency the finger and disappear into the night—but he knew it wasn't that simple. Releasing his name and profile as the Ahriman to intel agencies around the world would mean that Petra would never be able to see her parents again, that their life in Paris was burned. It meant that the only life they could hope for was starting over yet again, this time in some remote location, with no ties to their pasts. They might be able to figure out how to hide their bank accounts from the Agency, but no one would ever stop hunting him. They had been able to stay under the radar thus far without too much effort because no one had been seriously searching for them—a life on the run couldn't be more different. He couldn't put her through that, but where did it end? They couldn't be Agency slaves forever. He looked to his right where she'd been sitting and imagined her there once more, the ring sparkling on her finger and a smile on her face. *The way it was supposed to be.*

He leaned his head back, terrified of the return to their apartment—he couldn't imagine facing Carlos. He'd told Petra he didn't want to know. That could only mean one thing, Carlos had already figured it out, he was just choosing not to be told for sure. Kasem's throat trembled, over the last two years, he and Carlos had become real friends, and they had run through fire for each other. It didn't matter how many times he'd put himself on the line, all of the good he'd done. None of that mattered because of what the Ahriman had done.

Because of what I've done...

The realization left a bitter taste in his mouth, how long would he have to pay for the crimes he'd committed under General Majed's orders? Redemption, which had been within his grasp, perhaps even attained since Petra had finally agreed to marry him, was now lost once again. He might as well throw the ring into the Seine, they'd never be able to get married.

He wasn't sure how long he sat in silence, watching people stroll by, longing to trade lives with any of them. *As long as you aren't a spy, you have no choice but to be happy along the Seine.* Kasem took in the view, twilight had brought with it the spectacular lighting of the different buildings along the river, including the Notre Dame Cathedral, which was still under reconstruction. With Paris stretched out in front of him, the answer was clear—he wanted a life with Petra, a real one, not one that involved the two of them on the run forever. He was hesitant to capitulate to Veronica's demands. If they weren't careful, the Agency could string on demand after demand, but that was a risk that they had to take. He wanted to marry Petra out in the open, with her parents and friends, with Carlos as his best man.

He stood up with another sigh, he had to face the music sometime. The one thing that he clung to was Petra's emotional state—she was upset and scared, but she had not wavered on their relationship. They were partners, for better or worse. A year ago, he would have volunteered to go into hiding on his own, to leave her so that she could have a life unencumbered by his crimes, but today he could see that she didn't want that. Besides, it was something out of a cheap romance novel, the hero leaves his girl to somehow protect her, only to have both their hearts broken. New resolve washed over him, and he breathed in deeply; they were in this together, and all they could hope was that it would only be one more operation. At least this Agency op was a good one—Kevin deserved to pay for the attack on Washington D.C. that he'd almost executed successfully.

Kasem walked back toward the ramp, finally ready to return home. Carlos has a point. *Let's get to Burundi and get this over with.*

* * * * * *

Chapter 11

Paris, France

Petra walked back to her apartment, overwhelmed by a sense of drowning. *One more op, and we can put this behind us,* she rationalized on repeat. The one positive note was how Kasem had looked at her—she could tell that he'd expected her to have doubts, that he thought she might want to leave him now that his past as the Ahriman had caught up with them. Her feelings on the subject were a surprise even to herself—the surety that she felt about her life with him. She had no doubt that they should be partners, she just didn't want to be his crutch. *I have enough of my own emotional baggage.* Petra had always believed that Khalil Gibran's poem *On Marriage* was a better representation of life in a couple, how individuals had to flourish and support each other rather than simply leaning on each other—a belief that she'd seen in practice in her own parents' marriage. *The pillars of the temple stand apart,* she recited to herself from the poem. *Otherwise, the temple would fall.*

She drew in a deep breath, again reminding herself that that discussion would have to be delayed. For now, they had other things to focus on.

Petra unlocked the door to her apartment, antsy about how her interaction with Carlos would be. Under normal circumstances, she would have been able to talk to him about almost anything, she didn't have an older brother, but he was as close to that relationship as she could get. In part, she wanted to share the whole truth with him, to get his counsel. If anyone knew about the dark path being a spy could lead to, it was him—that was why he had left the Agency.

The living room was dark, but she could hear Carlos snoring, so she shut the door quietly and turned on a table lamp.

"Petra?" he sat up, squinting at her.

"Sorry, I didn't mean to wake you. Go back to sleep."

"It's fine, I must have dozed off." Carlos stretched his arms over his head and stood, "I'll go back to the hotel."

"Hotel? Oh, I didn't realize." Petra couldn't help but be taken aback, their situation must be even worse than she realized—Carlos was both cheap, or rather thrifty, *and* her close friend, under normal circumstances he would never volunteer to stay at a hotel.

"Veronica made a booking for me, I shouldn't waste it."

His tone told her he was lying, but Petra met his gaze and nodded, "Sure, I understand."

"Did you talk to Kasem?"

"I did."

"And?"

"What do you mean?" she raised her eyebrows.

"Are you in?"

"Of course—that was never really a question, not with the alternative anyway."

Carlos' jaw set, and he brushed past her, "There have to be some consequences."

His words felt like a jab to the heart. "That's it?" Petra's voice shook, "We've been friends for almost ten years, Carlos, and that's how you talk to me?" She wasn't sure if she was more hurt or angry.

"I've got to get out of here, kiddo before I say something that can't be unsaid."

"Whatever you've got to say, I can take it. Lay it on, *old man,*" she shot back, emphasizing the last two words, which were normally a sign of endearment, but were now more of an insult.

Carlos stopped in front of an armchair in the living room and looked back at her, "I don't know who you are anymore."

"There's more to this story than you know. He's a good man, he's not who you think he is," Petra sank into the couch. There was no point denying it, Carlos had clearly figured out that Veronica's intel was correct.

"Do you think there's some redeeming truth to this? You're dating; actually, more like a life partner, to the Ahriman," he paused briefly. "Try to deny it all you want, you can tell yourself that he's changed, or that he was under orders—but the truth is as simple as that. Don't worry, I won't tell Veronica I believe her. I don't need the whole world to know how much you've betrayed me, we can keep that between the two of us."

"How much I betrayed you? What has Kasem ever done but what we asked? In New York, I asked him to put himself on the line, and he was captured and tortured because of it. And last year, when *you* showed up in Kyoto because you needed our help to avenge Vik? He did the same thing again, almost got himself killed."

"So did I! Besides, I would never have trusted him if I'd known."

"Why?" Petra shot back, "Because the Agency didn't order you to cultivate him as an asset, to get him to steal intel for you? I don't know the details of every op you've ever done, but I can tell you he's a mile above some of the scumbags we both worked with. When I wasn't sure if I could forgive him for his past, you're the one who helped me. *You're* the one who said that everyone in this business has done terrible things and that I should trust him."

"I didn't have all the facts. I thought he was a normal operative, not one of the most notorious assassins and terrorists in the world."

"So, you won't even hear me out? Come on, Carlos, you know this business. You know that half of the malarkey about the Ahriman has to be fiction. There's no way one person could be responsible for all of that."

"I know it was bad enough that you kept it from me, that you want to keep it from the rest of the world." Carlos took a step toward her and picked up her left hand, "You didn't tell me that he'd proposed."

"I guess we had bigger things to talk about."

"Petra, I was always a huge supporter of your relationship with Kasem, I wanted you to have love. You deserve to be happy to have a partner. But if you think marrying the Ahriman will make you happy, you're delusional. I can't support you in this."

He turned and walked away, letting the door to her apartment slam behind him. Petra curled up into a ball and wept, finally allowing the tears to flow freely. She would pull it together the next day and find a way to make it through the op, but in the meantime, all she wanted to do was wallow. If even Carlos refused to hear her out, the future was even more bleak than she could have anticipated. A future of endless Agency blackmail stretched out in front of them, with no light at the end of the tunnel. The Agency would never stop, they would exploit their skills and connections in exchange for keeping Kasem out of prison. Until the end.

******

Chapter 12

Paris, France

Petra stirred when she heard Kasem crawl into bed beside her. "What time is it?"

"Just after midnight. Go back to sleep, I didn't mean to wake you."

"It's too late now," Petra moved in closer to nest her head against his shoulder.

"Where's Carlos?"

"Veronica booked him a hotel room." Her voice caught, and she considered whether or not to tell him about her earlier conversation with Carlos, how he had put two and two together about Kasem being the Ahriman.

"He figured it out, didn't he?"

Petra swallowed hard, obviously, her tone had given her away, "He did." She clung to a tendril of hope, "Don't worry, he'll see the real you again, he just needs some time."

Kasem stroked her hair, "I would love to redeem myself in his eyes—of all the people in your circle, his opinion of me always mattered the most. But somehow, I think it's a fool's errand. He's never going to see me the same way."

"I—" She searched for the right words, but optimism failed her—he was right no matter how much she wanted to disagree. "I'm sorry."

"It's not your fault. It's my past, and like it or not, I have to live with the consequences." He hesitated, "There's something that I wanted to talk to you about…"

"What is it?" Whatever it was, she could hear the uncertainty in his voice, and it made her sit up.

"After this op, I think we should run."

Petra's shoulders sank, some part of her had contemplated the same possibility, but she had rejected it. Did they really want that kind of life?

Before she could say anything, Kasem continued, "I know how much you would have to give up, and I'm so sorry, but I don't see another way. If we don't get out now, the Agency will never stop coming for us. I want to meet your parents and stand in front of them and all of our friends, but what I want more is to live my life with you. Whatever time we have left, there's always going to be someone who wants to blackmail us or lures you back in for the greater good—we have to end this now before it takes over the rest of our lives."

"But what if they release your identity?"

"I think we follow through on this op, and before they have a chance to threaten us again, we disappear."

Petra scanned the shadows of the room, dimly cast by the moonlight coming in through their picture window. "I'm so done with the Agency—every time something good happens in my life, they manage to take it away."

"It's not all bad," Kasem cupped her face in his hands. "Without the Agency, we wouldn't have met."

A laugh caught in her throat, "You're right." But he also wouldn't have been captured or kidnapped, and they wouldn't have almost died nigh on fifty times… Carlos wouldn't have lost all of his trust in her.

"You didn't tell me what you think," Kasem said after a few moments of silence.

"About running?" She stopped, unable to agree nor disagree. Finally, she took a deep breath, "I think you're right. I wish you weren't, but what else can we do?" She raised her hand to her mouth, "Do you still want to do this op?"

"I do—Carlos can't pay for my past, so we have to help him. We can't let him suffer for my mistakes, we owe him too much. But after this, no more."

Petra's resolve grew stronger as she agreed this time—there could be no more ops, no more blackmail, no more threats. *This ends now.*

* * * * * *

Chapter 13

Bujumbura, Burundi

Kevin Smith caught the reflection of the man tailing him in the side mirror of a parked car as he exited the decadent Roca Golf Hotel. He shrugged it off, not letting the tail faze him. He'd been under surveillance since he arrived in Bujumbura—or Buja as it was more affectionately called—several weeks earlier. Given his involvement with the Chinese, the Burundais secret forces kept a close eye on him, as were his employers. He had made sure to keep all of his overt dealings above board, he couldn't give away any of the clandestine work he was doing. If the Chinese thought that he'd betrayed them, even by mistake, they would have him executed, and, if by some chance he evaded them, the Burundais secret police would come for him as well.

Despite the more progressive current government, a small faction of the formerly formidable secret police had remained in force to keep watch on ongoing threats—President Markov had agreed to maintain an elite unit as a concession to the opposing political party. Essentially most of the force had been wound down, but the best agents had been retained to monitor foreign companies operating on the ground in Burundi. Kevin had to commend the agent's abilities—without his years of training, he probably would have missed the tail. The businessman he was playing as part of his cover would certainly not have been able to spot the agent.

Kevin waved to his driver, who was parked further down the street, and got into the car when it pulled up next to him.

"C'est bien passé?" his driver and handler Hong Li asked.

"Oui," Kevin answered and ran through a quick summary of the meeting's highlights, briefly mentioning the tail but dismissing it as unimportant. He had refused to wear a wire or any recording devices in case he was searched, and besides, the Chinese didn't need to know every detail of his discussions. *Not as long as I'm getting the job done.*

The rest of the drive uphill toward the Kiriri Garden hotel passed in silence, neither Kevin nor Hong Li had any interest in idle conversation. When they reached the vista point in front of the hotel, Kevin stepped out with a brief nod. He observed the clinical white walls of his one bedroom hotel room and sighed. At the kitchenette downstairs, he made himself a cup of tea, then settled down at the dining table with his computer to go over his notes. He'd been meticulous in writing down every detail on his followers—even the smallest detail could often be a lifesaver in his line of work. After adding in everything he'd observed that day, he scanned through the pages of notes, written in his personal code. He picked up a few similarities to previous pursuits and annotated those points, maintaining the code that he was confident even the best codebreakers would struggle with. Once he was satisfied with his review, he folded over his computer screen and stared out the window—these were the moments as a spy that he found most difficult. Although Kevin was most certainly an introvert, the long stretches of watching and waiting were the least glamorous and sadly most prevalent parts of the job. *When?* He pondered that question as he looked outside, it was only a matter of time, but the waiting had stretched out longer than he'd expected. *Don't worry,* he reassured himself, she'd be here soon enough.

* * * * * *

Chapter 14

Bujumbura, Burundi

Veronica shielded her eyes from the sun as the team stepped out of the car that had picked them up at the airport. She waited for everyone to get out, then stuck her head back inside to thank the driver and hand him a sizeable tip. As far as he was concerned, they were just a group of international aid workers from one of the donors that frequented the country— he didn't care to know any more detail than that.

After the car pulled out of the gate, their guide came out onto the patio to greet them.

"Bonjour, Kamal," Veronica said as he approached.

"Bonjour Madame, bonjour à tous," he replied.

They followed him into the house, and he gave them a quick tour, pointing out the four bedrooms, the kitchen, and the switch for the generator. "Until the new power plant facility opens up, we still have regular power cuts," he said in French with a shrug. "Most evenings, the power goes out around nine, but you can use the generator if you need to. Petrol is in short supply, make sure that the tank is kept at least half full so it doesn't cut out. I have two cars in the driveway for you, keys are over there by the door. If you have any questions, call me."

Veronica nodded and glanced at the rest of the group, wondering if they'd listened to any of what their host had said. She stepped out onto the patio with him and tested both cars to make sure that they started, then waved him off. When she returned to the living room, she frowned, Petra, Kasem, and Carlos had retreated into their two bedrooms. She rapped on each of the doors, "Team meeting in the living room, *now.*"

Taking a seat on the rocker in the living room, Veronica leaned back into the chair as the motion helped her to relax. The last two days had been even more tense than she could have predicted—Petra and Kasem spoke to her only when absolutely necessary, and Carlos refused to speak to anyone. He barely responded to direct questions and ignored anything that wasn't directly related to the op. His previously unflappable friendship with Petra had crumbled into something unrecognizable, they were no longer even cordial. Veronica's friendship with Petra had been compromised as well, but she'd been mentally prepared for that, so it didn't hit her as hard. The most unexpected consequence of their situation though, was that Kasem was the only one who deigned to speak more than two words to her. Even though he and Petra hardly spoke to each other—they were affectionate, but there was something off in their interaction. Veronica couldn't put her finger on it, but she wondered if they were keeping secrets; communication problems were usually the root of all evil when it came to couples. *Except if you're Kevin and me, then the biggest issue is that he was a Russian spy.*

She waited for the group to sit down, as Petra and Kasem clustered on the couch to her left, with Carlos taking the loveseat across the coffee table.

Veronica took a deep breath, a blip of nervousness made her stomach do a flip. *You've got this,* she told herself, she'd led almost a hundred ops, why would this one be any different? "Now that we're all here, I wanted to take us through the plan I drew up." She set her tablet on the coffee table and tapped onscreen so that it would project a map of Bujumbura into the air above it. "This is a topographical map of the city. This is where we are, in the highlands, away from the center of town," she pointed to a spot in the mountainous area of the city. "We don't have much intel on Kevin's dealings, so we'll have to gather most of it ourselves. The city's not very big, though, so we should be able to scope out a meetup point soon."

"Before we get to that, do we have a local source?" Carlos leaned forward with his elbow on his knee to scrutinize the map more closely, the most he'd spoken in the last couple of days. "We're going to stick out like sore thumbs around here."

"There's a small expat community, so we should be fine," Veronica answered. "I assume you all reviewed your covers already?"

"There wasn't much there," Petra frowned. "We're a non-descript NGO team to support infrastructure development, right? I mean, we're called Infra for Development."

"Exactly. The Agency used this NGO for a few other ops, so there's a working website and everything else that we need. Since we're focused on infrastructure and supposedly have aid money, we can access government officials and pretty much anyone we need to talk to. I have a local contact here who we've used as a source, but he only knows the cover story, nothing more. I did have him look into Kevin a bit—or rather the power plant deal that Kevin's working on for the Chinese—but so far, we don't have much. Kevin's met with a few officials, and they need different permits from the government. Officially he's an expert helping the Chinese lobby so that they get awarded the deal, but the government's been pretty hush-hush about the evaluation process." Veronica paused to take a sip from her water bottle, then continued, "Anyway that doesn't matter, we're not here to mess with the contract evaluation. I propose we reach out to him under the guise of the NGO and set up a meeting, then we grab him and get out of here. Simple, clean, and we can all cut ties as quickly as possible." She shut her mouth, regretting the last sentence—whatever the circumstances that had brought them here, a huge part of being on an op together was that they needed to have each other's backs. Even if what she had said was true, it wouldn't serve them to have that truth out in the open. *Oh well,* she shrugged to herself, *it was going to happen sooner or later.* She raised her eyebrows, "Any questions?"

"He's a former Agency source, doesn't he know about the NGO?" Kasem asked.

"Good question, but actually, no, he doesn't. I checked it against his file, and he wasn't on any ops that used this cover, so we should be in the clear." Veronica tapped her tablet again to highlight three different points on the map, "I picked out these three potential spots for the meeting. We should scope them out today and tomorrow and set the meeting for the following day. I'll update Chris on our plan and have him set up the contact."

"Looks like you've got it all figured out," Petra stood up with an obviously fake smile. "I'll check out the spots tomorrow, but now I'm going to take a nap." She shot Veronica a look daring her to disagree.

Veronica gave her old friend a tight nod. Petra disappeared down the hallway, and her bedroom door slammed moments later.

"I'm going to do the same," Carlos rose and left the room.

Once he was gone, Veronica met Kasem's gaze. She was surprised that he hadn't followed Petra, but she resisted the urge to point that out—she didn't need any more animosity from her team. Her arm-twisting tactics were beginning to backfire, she needed to win back favor if they were going to execute the mission successfully. *Making peace with Kasem would go a long way with Petra.* She caught his eye again and gave him a small smile, "Look, I know we haven't really spoken much, and you're not here willingly, but I wouldn't have asked if I didn't need all of you here. I wish it could have been under better circumstances." As she spoke, Veronica asked herself if any of what she was saying was true, wondering how much contrition she felt for turning their lives upside-down. A second later, the feeling passed as she recalled the moment Kevin had turned her gun back on her and escaped from her apartment just a couple of weeks earlier, *Never again.*

"It's fair to say that I wish the same," Kasem said in a soft voice. "I hope we catch Kevin, I know how important this is to the Agency... and to you."

Veronica tilted her head, trying to observe the contours of his face in more detail. If she hadn't suspected that he was the Ahriman, she probably would have believed him. His micro-expressions wreaked of pain and deep regret, not malice or deception. *He's an expert spy, he could make us believe anything,* she steered herself away from trusting what she saw. "Of course," she used a stern voice to convey that she wasn't buying his act.

"I'll go in and check on Petra and maybe review my cover profile. I'm sure I'll see you around the house," Kasem retreated toward the bedroom Petra had chosen.

* * * * * *

Chapter 15

Bujumbura, Burundi

Kasem sat down in bed and planted a kiss on Petra's cheek before setting up his laptop and opening the mission files that Veronica had shared. Something about the op didn't feel right, the question that kept nagging him was, *What is Kevin doing here?* Veronica had said he was supporting the Chinese to be awarded this power plant deal, but Kasem couldn't help think that there had to be more to the story. He rubbed his chin, for some reason, neither she nor the Agency cared to find out more. *Whatever he's doing here, it can't be good.*

He skimmed through the documents quickly, starting with an Agency overview report on Burundi, which provided a few details on the economy, the people, the history, and the government. After reading it from beginning to end for the fourth time, Kasem moved on to the update brief on the country's economy. The original report had been written five years earlier when the national situation had looked far more dire, but since then, a new progressive president had taken power, and he'd catapulted the economy forward. He'd focused on infrastructure development, including standing up to some of the Chinese developers who had done shoddy work all over the country. President Markov had also commissioned the development of three new solar plants along with a new hydropower facility in the north of the country. For the first time since the political crisis in 2015, Burundi seemed to be making forward strides.

Kasem sighed, the new solar farm project was massive, and he was apprehensive about the impact of Burundi placing itself on the international radar for a project like that. He'd seen and worked on infrastructure development projects in Iran before his days as the Ahriman and knew all too well how foreign governments could insert themselves into a country's politics to ensure their companies were awarded large contracts. The French had been doing it all over Africa since the end of colonialism. He grabbed his water bottle from the nightstand and kept reading, considering the ramifications of China's involvement in and around Africa—*Really all over the world, basically asset colonialism.* He skipped through the documents, searching for more information on the power plant deal, or at least on China's involvement in Burundi overall. As he reached the last file in the folder, his frown deepened; all of their intel lacked details on the power plant deal, or at best, briefly mentioned that China had funded some road construction works in Burundi without anything further. Shutting his computer screen, Kasem stepped out into the living room to ask Veronica about it.

When he found the living room empty, he ventured back toward the master bedroom that she had chosen. Kasem was about to knock when he heard hushed voices from inside the room.

"Veronica, I can't believe you went rogue like this. I didn't authorize this mission and you know it. I told you we had to wait to get Petra involved—besides, you can't possibly be objective about an op to catch Kevin," a deep voice said in a Scottish accent.

Kasem pressed his ear against the door, recognizing the voice as Chris'. *She didn't tell him?*

AHRIMAN: RECKONING FROM THE SHADOWS

"What's done is done, Chris. I couldn't let this chance pass us by."

Kasem chuckled at Chris' obvious indignance, Veronica didn't sound in the least bit remorseful.

Chris continued, "I made it quite clear that we can't be involved in an international incident in Burundi, especially if Kevin is doing legit work for the Chinese. We need to gather more intel on this power plant deal—"

"Who cares about the power plant deal? The government should award it how they see fit, and the Agency shouldn't be involved. Let's just get Kevin, and we'll get out of here."

"Veronica, you're turning into a loose cannon. How many times do I have to explain this to you? I could trust you to lead almost any op in the world, but not this one. You have to let Petra or Carlos take point. You're not objective, and you could compromise the whole thing. I want to get Kevin as much as you do, but this isn't the way."

"Take it or leave it. We may not be the ideal team, but this is what we've got. I'm leading this op whether you like it or not."

Chris' frustration rang through, "We'll discuss this insubordination later, but you're lucky I'm not sabotaging your mission. If this goes pear-shaped, so help me... I'll send you details on my local contact, he's an old friend who works with French intelligence. He's semi-retired now, been out of the game for a while, but if you're going to stand a chance, then you'll need his help. I'd have much preferred to deploy one of our agents out of Nairobi or another nearby station, but that'll take too long now. If he's willing, he's part of your team, and at the very least, he can help with scoping, planning, access to local services, etc. Use him to set up contact instead of that other guy you found. Do you understand?"

"I understand."

66

"Good. I also want you to steer clear of Chinese intelligence. No international incidents, okay?"

"All right, all right," she agreed.

Kasem heard movement inside and backed up to the living room, picking up another water bottle from the coffee table. When Veronica didn't emerge, he ventured back to her door and tapped on it lightly.

"Come in."

Kasem walked inside, "Hey, I'm sorry to disturb you. I was going over the files again—I wanted to ask if we had any more info on the power plant deal that Kevin's involved with. I wonder if it might be worth investigating—what if the Chinese are involved in something dirty?" He kept his tone level, wondering why Veronica seemed so against the idea, *It's a no-brainer. How can we not investigate what Kevin is doing here?* Kasem recalled when Kevin had held him captive in D.C. after they first found out that he had betrayed the Agency and suppressed a shudder.

Veronica gave him an exasperated look, "It doesn't matter what he's involved with, we're going to grab him before he can finish the job. All we need is to lure him in, capture him, and get out of here, then the rest of the deal can go through the way it's supposed to."

"Aren't you in the least bit curious? Based on the Agency brief, this could be the biggest investment Burundi's seen in two decades."

"Who cares? We're here to get Kevin, not interfere in an international power deal. Besides, we don't even know if he's involved—he might just be hiding out from the Russians since they have such a limited presence here."

"Sure," Kasem backpedaled. Even if Veronica thought that the power deal didn't matter or that Kevin might not be involved, his gut told him that she was wrong. *Kevin wouldn't be here for shits and giggles.*

Veronica sighed, "Sorry to cut you off at the knees there, we just can't get messed up in Burundi politics. We'll grab Kevin and let the chips fall where they may."

"Makes sense." Kasem headed for the hallway and paused on his way out, "I think Petra and I will order some dinner soon, let me know if you want to get in on that."

"Thanks, I will," Veronica replied in a softer tone.

******

As Kasem returned to his room, he was even more determined to get to the bottom of the issue. He hoped that he'd thrown Veronica off his tail by ending the discussion on a lighter note, but instinct told him that he'd need to tread carefully. If Veronica and Chris weren't working together, her promises could go up in smoke. He bit his lip, the primary reason that he and Petra had agreed to the op was to ensure that they would have a future together, a future without the Agency. They needed a hideaway, somewhere to go if it all hit the fan. Even without the risk that the Agency wouldn't hold up Veronica's bargain, what he'd heard was disturbing enough. If Veronica was this far into left field, the op was in deep trouble. *Great, just great.*

When he resettled in front of his computer screen, Kasem glanced at Petra, who was starting to wake from her nap. He contemplated both his suspicions on the power deal and the conversation that he'd overheard, wondering how much to share. There had been so much tension at different points between Petra and her former boss Chris—the two were once fast friends, but when he'd placed the Agency's needs above hers for the millionth time, it was the straw that broke the camel's back. After their last operation in Madagascar, their relationship had been on more solid ground; Chris had gone into the field off book to help them when they most needed it. She deserves to know that he didn't authorize Veronica's insanity, Kasem determined, putting aside his other suspicions. He needed to gather more intel anyway before he made making a case out of it. Regardless though, he needed to figure out an option for what they could do if everything with the Agency went sideways.

"Hey, babe," he whispered and gave her a kiss. "How are you doing?"

"If I don't wake up, then we won't be on an Agency op," she said with a small smile. She sat up against the headboard, her smile widening, "I love you."

"I love you too. I'm sorry this is happening," he hung his head. "I wish I could put a stop to it somehow."

"You aren't responsible for what the Agency's doing— you've more than paid your debt, but it's like you said, they're going to milk this forever. I've been thinking about your idea, and I think you're right—after this op, we run."

"It's okay if you change your mind," Kasem chose his words carefully, even though it had been his idea to disappear, he had already vacillated on the point several times. "Let's not talk about it again until we've got Kevin, okay? I want to marry you in front of your family, and if there's a way to not run, let's take it."

"Okay."

He detected something odd in her voice but chalked it up to the tension. Changing the subject, "I went by Veronica's room earlier to ask her a couple of questions, and I overheard her talking to Chris. There's something you should know—he never authorized Veronica to come after you."

"What? You mean she's doing this on her own? How?"

"I don't know—I just know he was pissed that she got us all out here." For a moment, he considered telling her about his concerns for their safety if the Agency didn't hold up Veronica's deal, but instead, he decided to save it for later.

"What *exactly* did he say?"

Kasem paused to recollect the conversation, "I think he said, I didn't authorize this mission, and I told you we had to wait to get Petra involved. Then he said Veronica couldn't be objective about an op to catch Kevin. It was actually kind of funny to listen to—he was pretty freakin' mad, went full on Sean Connery on her."

"Hmm," Petra chuckled, "so he knows about you being the Ahriman, but maybe not for sure. I don't even think Veronica knows for sure, she just used it to bring us to heel. That means Grant probably saw you sometime in New York or D.C., and they were trying to investigate." She ran her fingers through her hair, "I'm sorry about Grant, I was so scared this was going to happen, but the more time that passed, I thought we were in the clear."

"It's okay, babe. This stuff was bound to come out sooner or later. I'm surprised it took this long. At least you know Chris isn't the one who made the call to blackmail us."

"Especially since we left things on better terms last time," Petra nodded. "What did you want to ask Veronica?"

Kasem shrugged, "Maybe it's nothing, but I went through the intel files she gave us again, and there's hardly any info on what Kevin's doing here. He could be working legit, but Veronica doesn't care. I know we don't necessarily need to know, but it's fishy."

"Are you worried that the Chinese are trying to stack the deck?"

"Maybe, why else would you hire someone like Kevin? If that's true, then shouldn't we try to stop it?"

70

Petra squeezed his hand, "It does sound like an Agency op, but we said we wouldn't go any further down the rabbit hole. You're probably right, there's more to investigate, but part of me wants to keep my head down and get the hell out. Do what we came here to do and forget the rest."

"I understand."

"It's okay if you want to do a little more hunting." She gave him a nudge with her elbow, "I can see that look in your eye. Nothing super dangerous, okay?"

"I do plan to swim in the lake with the hippos. It's too stunning to miss out on, like you."

Petra wrapped her arms around his neck with a twinkle in her eyes. "We should do that together."

* * * * * *

Chapter 16

Bujumbura, Burundi

Petra rinsed off her dinner plate in the kitchen sink, welcoming the mindless task as she dissected the events of the last few days. Carlos had only said two words to her since they'd arrived, and the tension in their interactions had only increased since the blow-up in Paris. At first, she'd been distraught at the loss of one of her oldest friends, someone she considered family, but now her anger had risen to the surface. After all the years that they had known each other, how could Carlos treat her this way? He couldn't even give her the benefit of the doubt. *Haven't I earned that?* She had considered confronting him but had elected not to—she wasn't sure that she could lie to him if he asked her point blank if Kasem was the Ahriman. *He isn't the Ahriman anymore, but I can't pretend it's not part of his history—not to Carlos.* At the same time, she wondered if she could tell him the whole story: how and why Kasem had become the Ahriman, how much of the lore around the Ahriman General Majed had created and exploited for his own gains, etc. She had vacillated on that idea, but Carlos hadn't demonstrated enough trust to hear her out. Instead, he was behaving as if he couldn't remember any of the good Kasem had done, not even what he had done for Carlos in Madagascar. Petra wiped the last dish dry and came to a decision, *Let sleeping dogs lie, even if they're snarling.*

When she set the plate in the cabinet, her ring caught the kitchen light and glistened, and she let out another sigh. She still hadn't figured out when or if she should talk to Kasem about her concerns. She couldn't shake the fear that he only wanted to marry her because he had nothing else in his life, no matter how many times she had tried. Rationally, she knew that was baloney, they loved each other, and they were partners, but he still needed to find something to channel his energy. Even if he was going all out with personal training at the gym, there had to be something more. The other problem was that he wasn't currently in therapy now that the frequency of his nightmares had decreased to about once a month, instead of nearly every night as they had once been. *Still too many.* The night before they had left Paris, he had had another nightmare, one of the worst she'd seen. Given what had transpired with Carlos' arrival, she wasn't surprised, but the intensity had still been jarring. He had had another one since their arrival in Burundi, although less severe. *He needs to be back in therapy, and he needs something he can be excited about.* The longer she waited to speak to him, the heavier it felt, she'd only been suppressing the urge to engage in conversation for a few days, but it felt more like a few months.

Petra finished putting the dishes away and sped through the living room as fast as possible to avoid eye contact with Carlos, who was sitting with his feet up, watching something amusing on his tablet. Under normal circumstances, she would have called him out on his laugh—the "Carlos cackle" as she had teased him many a time. Much to Carlos' chagrin, his wife Diane had even picked up on it. *Oh well,* she made a beeline to her bedroom.

Shutting the door behind her, Petra smiled at Kasem, who was sitting on the lounge chair in the corner of their room with his feet propped up on a stool, engrossed in his laptop screen.

"How many times have you read it today?" she looked over his shoulder, noticing that he once again had Veronica's intel files open.

He gestured toward the screen as he tabbed over to a different window, "I was reading an article about China's involvement in Africa. You know, I remember them wanting to come into Iran, but it hadn't really started back then. Still, they built all of those highways and train tracks across Central Asia, and some of them cut right through Iran to the Gulf. They finance everything with this concessional debt to the governments, but most of them still wouldn't be able to pay it back. What happens when they call the debt? They're going to own all of those assets. It already happened with that port in Sri Lanka a few years ago. I know we're not here about the power deal, but it has to be relevant here."

"I think you're right," Petra wasn't sure what else she could say. She could see both sides—they were in Burundi to capture Kevin, so perhaps that was all that they should do? Still, she couldn't ignore what Kasem was saying and the potential greater good that might be at stake, even if she had just about had it with the greater good. "I don't know, babe—I'm sure you're right, there must be a reason why Kevin is here, but part of me just wants to do the bare minimum so we can get away from the Agency as fast as possible."

"Seems like we're having a role reversal. Look at me, talking to you about the greater good." He kissed her on the forehead as she sidled up next to him, "To be honest, I have wondered if this type of work is the only thing that I could do, but I don't want this to be our life. Still, we can't ignore something like this if it's staring us in the face. This has to still be who we are…"

His voice trailed off as Petra's mind raced, *This is my opening,* she realized, he had brought up his career frustration all on his own. She moved to the edge of the bed so that she could face him, but a wave of hesitation rushed over her. With a deep breath, she discarded the notion, "Kasem, there's something I wanted to talk to you about."

He met her gaze, then shut the screen on his laptop, "What's the matter?"

"I'm worried," she held up her left hand, "when you proposed, you said that I'm the only good thing in your life." Her throat went dry, "Did you mean that? I wish you could work on projects like you used to in Iran. I know how much that meant to you—"

"You are the best thing that's ever happened to me, that's all I meant."

Tears trickled down Petra's cheeks, she was touched by what he'd said, but she also knew that it wasn't true. "You would never have gone to prison if it hadn't been for me. Maybe you would still be doing the work that you loved."

"There's a lot of maybes, but we've been over this a thousand times. Petra, I promise you that I don't blame you, not anymore. I might have resentments that flare up sometimes, but that's why I've been going to therapy. I want to work through them, and I want us to be happy. We deserve that, don't we?"

"We do." She frowned, "But you stopped therapy a couple of months ago."

"I did, but judging from the past couple of days, I need to go back. I don't want to keep having these nightmares."

"I'm so glad you feel that way."

"Of course, I don't want my trauma to mar the rest of our lives. It's hard sometimes for me to admit that I need help, but I do." After a brief pause, he continued, "And you're right—I need to find something to focus my time on, something to make the day-to-day more than visits to the gym and the market. Maybe it could even be that volunteer work with Nico you suggested, I just haven't figured it out yet."

Petra bit her lip, that work would no longer be an option once they ran.

"I know that might not be possible anymore, but I'll find something else. Who knows, maybe I could run a café on the beach wherever we end up."

"That's very Bourne Identity of you," she chuckled. "I could see that, at least, I can see you walking around the beach shirtless."

Kasem burst out laughing and joined her on the bed, pulling her in close, "Would you take advantage of me? I'd like to see what you would do."

******

Chapter 17

Bujumbura, Burundi

Kasem wriggled out from under Petra's shoulder and pulled on his boxers and a t-shirt. He looked at her tenderly, she was still asleep but had turned over onto her other side now. He could no longer imagine life without her, not after all of the ups and downs they'd endured. The moment he'd walked out on her in Madagascar felt like a lifetime ago, although only a year had passed. *I don't want to run, but there's no other way.* He circled his left arm to restore circulation and wished for an easier way to get the Agency off their backs. They could attempt to make a deal, but he doubted they would honor it.

He resumed his position on the lounge chair, laptop in hand; he welcomed the distraction of the op rather than addressing the myriad of thoughts and emotions rushing through his head. As the screen lit up, but after re-reading one of the paragraphs for the fourth time, he set the computer aside. *I can't ignore these emotions.* He set up a guided meditation on his phone, letting the voice on the app take him through a breathing exercise. The meditation helped clear his mind, he could acknowledge specific thoughts as they came, then put them aside. A few minutes later, when he opened his eyes, his mind was clearer, but one realization left a bitter taste in his mouth. *Who I am will always be tied to the Ahriman,* he admitted to himself, *but Lila—Petra, she doesn't have to be.* She could be free of this, free to keep living her life in Paris.

Kasem shook his head, *This isn't Spiderman, 'with great power comes great responsibility.'* He inhaled deeply, glad that he had at least acknowledged the thought, pretending it didn't exist made it all the more powerful. Petra had made her choice, if she had wanted a life separate from him, she could have had it at any time. Relief rushed over him. *She chose me, knowing who I was.*

Petra grunted at him in a groggy voice, "Come to bed. The laptop will still be there tomorrow, I promise."

Feeling lighter, Kasem shut the computer down once again to join her in bed. *She's right, this deal will still be here tomorrow.*

* * * * * *

Chapter 18

Bujumbura, Burundi

Kasem rose early the next day and shook Petra awake. "Let's get a real coffee, and we can scope out the café at the same time."

"Sure." She yawned and crawled out of bed, "Every time I deal with jetlag, it gets worse and worse." She stretched her arms overhead, leaning her torso from side to side, then bent over and touched the floor.

"Much as I like the view, you should get dressed," he grinned, eyeing her curves and long legs. "It never gets old."

Petra chuckled as she disappeared out into the hallway. When she returned from the bathroom ten minutes later, she looked fresh with her black hair combed out. She pulled on a pair of jeans and a t-shirt, then nodded toward the bedroom door, "Are you ready? Get your shoes on." She slid on a pair of black flats next to her, suitcase, "Let's go."

On the way out, Kasem grabbed the keys to one of the SUVs parked in their driveway. Petra held her hand out, "I'm driving."

Kasem tossed them to her with a shrug, heading for the passenger side. When he opened the door, he saw the steering wheel on the right side and jumped in, "Too bad you went to the wrong side—it's a British style car."

"Fine," she grumbled as she handed back the keys.

The ten-minute drive to the café passed in silence as Kasem mulled over the intel he'd read, still contemplating what Kevin was involved with. They parked just down the street and ventured in on foot, each ordering a coffee and croissant—Café Gourmand was famous for its baked goods. Kasem carried their tray upstairs to the rooftop, where they sat at a table in the corner, far from the stairwell and relatively isolated. It was early in the morning, so both the café interior and rooftop were almost empty, but he suspected that that wouldn't last for long.

After draining his coffee, Kasem looked around, considering how they could grab Kevin at this location. "Did Veronica mention where he usually likes to sit? We'll have to run surveillance for at least a week."

"I don't think so—since we're setting up a meet, I'm sure we could do it however we want."

"The meet could be here on the rooftop—early to mid-afternoon when the sun's too hot for most people to come upstairs. Maybe that one?" he motioned toward the table directly opposite the stairwell.

Petra frowned, "The problem isn't how or where to meet him, it's how to get him out afterward. If we knock him out, everyone will notice, and if we try to subdue and lead him out at gunpoint, we risk a fight." She rubbed her chin, "What about a window from the bathrooms?"

"That won't work either, it's a crowded street."

"Right." She drummed her fingers against the table, "What if we have Veronica's contact do the meet?" She considered further, and a smile spread across her face, "I've got it—it's simple, we drug him."

"But how do we get out of here then?"

"In an ambulance—no one will think anything of it."

"Her contact would have to be really connected to make that work. We'd need a local ambulance, uniforms, the whole shebang. Do you think Veronica can pull that off?"

"She's Agency, isn't she? She'd better be able to pull it off."
Petra wolfed down the last bite of her croissant, "I think we
better go tell her."

"You go ahead, I want to walk around a little, then I'll take
one of those taxis on the street back. There's a gym nearby as
well, so I'll check that out too."

"You sure? Let me know if you want me to pick you up. V
said team meeting at noon, so don't get lost, okay?"

"Sure."

Once Petra headed off into the stairwell, Kasem moved to
the edge of the patio and finished munching on his pastry. The
rooftop offered a good view of the surrounding area—most
buildings in Buja were only two stories, so he had a decent
vantage point. He oriented himself, tracing the road they'd use
to get there and identifying the street that would lead him into
downtown so that he could get a better feel for the city. *And
perhaps the contacts Kevin was meeting with.* He hadn't told
Petra, but he had his eye on *Arena* in particular, the restaurant
and bar which was frequented by one of Kevin's contacts.
Veronica's file hadn't provided much detail, only that Kevin
had been seen there, meeting with the Deputy Head of the
Agence d'Electricite, which regulated new power developments.
Under normal circumstances, it would be too early to visit—the
restaurant only opened in the late afternoon, but Kasem had
noticed that there was a gym on the same property. He could
kill three birds with one stone, knock out his workout, get a feel
for the city, and start setting up a contact or two to help with
his to-do list.

* * * * * *

Chapter 19

Bujumbura, Burundi

Kasem set down the seventy-pound dumbbells he'd been holding and ran his hand over his brow. The gym was well-ventilated with numerous windows and two large fans, but he hadn't considered how difficult it would be to get through his leg day workout without air conditioning. *Not to mention jetlag,* he grabbed the large water bottle he'd purchased and savored the last few drops. He spoke briefly to the trainer-in-residence, opting not to do a training session, but instead bonding with him over their shared passion for the gym in between his sets of squats and deadlifts. If he hadn't been on an op, they could even be friends. Once he felt that they had bonded enough, Kasem asked him for advice, first on the workout before he moved on to another part of his agenda.

By the time he started on his last set of deadlifts, he and Joseph, the trainer, were best buds, but Kasem was glad when another client showed up to occupy his attention. Kasem finished off his deadlifts, now focusing on the workout, although a few subliminal details related to the operation continued to percolate in the back of his mind. Afterward, he climbed up to the lofted stretching area. As he'd hoped, it was empty, and while he stretched his quads and hamstrings, he was able to survey the layout of both the gym and the overall bar and restaurant area. The restaurant entrance was off the street, leading to the bar, with a small pool and a lawn. At the very back of the property, behind all of that, were the gym and men and women's shower stalls. Kasem traced the layout in his head, then redirected his focus to the plan he and Petra had started to formulate at the café.

He was almost done stretching when something caught his eye. The gym had a specialty coach who'd been taking two young women through an improvised CrossFit routine, but a third person had just joined the group. The curly hair and stature of the man looked familiar. Kasem pegged him as the man that Kevin had met with, Gilbert Ngkirunge, the deputy from the regulatory agency.

He added in a few extra stretches—he wasn't going to miss the chance to follow Kevin's contact. He checked his watch, glad that he still had plenty of time before Veronica's team meeting. *Back in high school,* he thought as he recalled his coach's curfews from when he had traveled with his high school track team.

To further prolong the workout, Kasem added several bodyweight exercises, followed by an ab set. As he finished his workout with a set of two-minute center and side walking planks, he was relieved to see Gilbert's workout wrap up. Kasem ventured back downstairs, where he purchased another water bottle, listening to Gilbert converse with the coach as he guzzled the water. The two were discussing Gilbert's workouts, nothing out of the ordinary for a gym.

A few moments later, Kasem watched Gilbert head out and decided to follow, he still had time before the team meeting.

He kept his distance as Gilbert exited onto the street and turned left. At the next crossing, Gilbert took another left and walked into Oasis, a pizza restaurant that Kasem had noticed earlier.

Just an early lunch, Kasem thought with a shrug. He was about to hail one of the taxis parked across the street—he couldn't risk Gilbert spotting him if he went inside—when a black car pulled up in front of the restaurant. A middle-aged man got out and waved off his driver, then walked into Oasis.

Is that...? Kasem asked himself, remembering the documents that he'd read on Burundi's history. *It can't be...* he moved quickly, hoping to catch a better glimpse. Kasem paused outside the entrance, pretending to evaluate the menu and praying that Gilbert wouldn't see him. From a quick glance, the middle-aged man looked like Pierre Nziza, former head of Burundi's secret police. *Please don't be him,* Kasem pleaded the universe, he would much rather be wrong. The report on Burundi's history had provided only a high-level summary of who had been in charge of a number of the atrocities committed during the country's civil war and the political crises that had followed, but Nziza's role had been clear. He was one of the primary architects of it all, a war criminal. Kasem strained his eyes as the middle-aged man sat down across from Gilbert, his viewpoint now obscured.

A waiter approached, and Kasem asked whether there were any pizzas without tomato sauce, citing an allergy. *Don't be Nziza,* he repeated to himself.

The waiter agreed to check and disappeared into the kitchen, buying Kasem a little more time. He shifted to the side, thankful that Gilbert's table was at the edge of the restaurant patio. *Turn around, oldie, turn around, and I'll know you're not him.*

Several moments later, the older man stood, and Kasem's heart sank. *It's him...* Kevin's contact was lunching with the former Head of the Secret Police. His stomach somersaulted as he made a quick excuse to the waiter and headed back to the house. *We're in so much trouble.*

******

Chapter 20

Bujumbura, Burundi

Petra glanced at her watch, looking forward to berating Kasem for being late to the team meeting. She looked over at Veronica, who was seated in the neighboring armchair, tapping her foot against the ceramic floor. *He's only fifteen minutes late,* Petra wanted to protest. *Besides that incessant tapping isn't making it any better.*

Petra counted out Veronica's foot taps and, when she reached twenty, retreated to the bathroom to steal a few seconds of silence. Splashing some water on her face she looked in the mirror, squashing the nervousness in the pit of her stomach. For the third time, she checked her phone for a reply to any of her messages, but came up blank once again. While Kasem had claimed that he was only planning to take in the downtown area, she knew him well enough to know that he wanted to do some investigating. Under normal circumstances, that wouldn't concern her, but given how little they knew about Buja, she couldn't help but worry. *I should have stayed with him,* she chastised herself.

After another deep breath, Petra ventured back into the living room, grateful that Veronica had now stopped the tapping. "Where's Carlos?" she asked, noting his absence from the living room.

Veronica looked up from her tablet, "He went back to his room, said he'd come out when Kasem got here. Any word on lover boy?"

"I'm sure he's on his way back." Petra's jaw set at the nickname she'd used to refer to Kasem—it could have been said with endearment, the way Carlos would have, but in this case, it was more of a jab.

"Right."

Petra's phone buzzed, and she read the incoming text in relief. She glanced at Veronica with a forced smile, "He's on his way, sends his apologies."

"Okay."

Petra looked at her old friend more closely, examining her micro-expressions. It was hard to tell, but it seemed like she was barely holding it together. Still, Petra was unsure how much she cared; once upon a time, they'd been close friends, but that felt like ancient history. After a long sigh, Petra leaned forward, "Are you okay, V?"

For a second, it seemed as if no bad blood had passed between them, they were just old friends sitting together. "I'm fine," she answered, looking away. "I just need your boyfriend to get here on time."

"Right," Petra recognized the defensiveness of Veronica's posture. Leaning back into the couch, Petra wondered how she would feel if their roles were reversed. According to what Kasem had overheard, Veronica had been in love with Kevin, and that was why Chris didn't want her on the op. "Are you sure? This can't be easy, going after Kevin."

"I'll be fine."

A wave of compassion enveloped her, and Petra reached out for her friend's hand, "You're not fine. I can't imagine how hard this is." *Actually, I can,* she remembered the moment she first realized that Kasem had become the Ahriman when she had run into him in Kuwait a few years earlier.

Veronica's lower lip quivered, and she snatched her hand away, "I'm fine."

"Why are you doing this to yourself?" the question burst out before Petra had the chance to stop herself.

"What are you talking about?"

"Why are you here, Veronica? Any of us could lead this op. You don't need to be here to catch Kevin, let the Agency take care of it."

"Have you lost your mind? Of course, I need to be here, who else is going to catch him?"

"Don't you want something more from your life? The Agency's taken everything from you, even someone that you love. Don't get me wrong, he betrayed you and all of us, but I know you loved him. So why put yourself through this? You should be on a beach somewhere, drinking cocktails and flirting with cute bartenders—"

"Would you be able to do that if you were me?"

"I, I don't know," Petra was taken aback by her friend's challenge. Her mind ran through all of the times that she'd run from the Agency, only to end up right back on another op. Yet she kept saying that she didn't want this life. Kasem was right, when this was all over, they had to run and leave it behind. She had agreed to it, but she wasn't sure that she'd understood or accepted how important it was until now. The acknowledgement was painful, but she'd never been more certain of that choice.

This has to be the last time. "Maybe you're right, maybe I wouldn't be able to—but I still don't get it. I cut ties with the Agency as soon as they upended my life, or at least I tried to. You've been to hell and back for them, we both know you shouldn't be in the field anymore, yet here you are."

"My shoulder's better," Veronica protested, in reference to the injury that had forced her to leave the field eight years earlier before she'd been redeployed in Russia.

"I'm not a doctor, but I saw you wince when you pulled your suitcase out of the van yesterday."

"Maybe I won't be doing handstands, but I'll be fine on the op. We can't let him get away again, Petra."

"What do you mean?"

"Isn't it obvious? I want to catch Kevin."

"You said we can't let him get away *again.*" Petra frowned, Veronica's language couldn't be a coincidence, at some point, she had let him go. Her voice softened as she continued, "I'm sure it wasn't all a lie, V. No one can fake that—he did love you."

"You can't possibly know that."

"Maybe not, but I do."

"Why are we even talking about this? At least when I found out who he was, I didn't run away from the world, turn my back on everyone who cared about me. You're engaged to *the Ahriman*—do you realize how messed up that is?"

Petra's throat constricted, but she forced herself to speak, "Your intel is wrong. Kasem is a good man, and I'm lucky to have him." *Even if he was the Ahriman.* The words made her feel stronger, on more solid ground. "He put himself on the line for two Agency ops, only for you to turn on him based on faulty intel. It's pretty clear why it was right for me to leave."

Petra stood up to head toward her bedroom. "You might not want a life outside of the Agency, a life that means something to *you*, rather than some twisted notion of the greater good, but that's not me. That will *never* be me. You talk about me walking away as if I chose specifically to hurt you. That betrayal is *yours,* Veronica. You showed up at my house and threatened to end everything I care about. I never turned my back on my friends, and when the Agency asked me to serve, I followed through. When Carlos needed help last year, Kasem and I both went through hell to help him. When you needed help to get out of Russia, I did the same. But you—*you* did this to me—it's not even the Agency, so you don't get an opinion on my life. I have someone who would walk through fire for me if I asked him to, and I would do the same for him. Is that really the man you're accusing him of being?"

Petra was about to walk away when the living room door flew open, and Kasem appeared. "I'm sorry I'm late, you won't believe it when I tell you why." He glanced between Petra and Veronica. "Where's Carlos? What did I miss?"

* * * * * *

Chapter 21

Bujumbura, Burundi

Kasem could feel the tension in the air as soon as he stopped to take a breath and sat down. Petra and Veronica refused to look at each other while all of them waited for Carlos to emerge. He was especially apprehensive considering what he had to tell them. Even knowing that Kevin had almost gone through with a terrorist attack on Washington D.C., Kasem was struggling with the realization that Kevin would be willing to work with the old Secret Police. Working with someone who committed genocide seemed too low, even for him.

A disgruntled Carlos appeared, and Veronica pursed her lips, "Now that we're all *finally* here, let's get this meeting started—"

"I'm sorry—just wait 'til you hear what I have to tell you, you'll understand," Kasem interrupted.

"We'll get to that," Veronica waved him away. "I spent some time reviewing different meeting points we could use to grab Kevin. I had my contact set up the meet for two p.m. next Monday, we just have to confirm the location."

"Why would you do that without talking to us first?" Carlos frowned.

Veronica looked flustered, "We don't have time to waste. The city becomes way more crowded in the evening—this is a party town, after all—and we can't risk getting caught in traffic. I want to make this as seamless as possible."

"You made all those decisions since you know so much about this town?" Carlos retorted.

Yikes, this team is a mess. Kasem's gaze flitted between the two on opposite ends of the coffee table and then back to Petra, who was sitting on his left. He tried to catch her eye, wishing that he could vent his frustration.

"I'm not an expert, but Carlos, neither are you," Veronica shot back. "I put this team together, so I'm leading the op. Anything you have to say, you can say at the end when I'm done. Kapeesh?"

Kasem shifted to give Petra a nudge, she seemed lost in her own world, and he wanted her to intervene. The bickering was pointless, they had to get past it and focus on the op. She finally glanced at him and shook her head.

"Of course, Veronica, my apologies, I pledge my humble loyalty," Carlos bent over with an exaggerated hand gesture. "Please go ahead, tell us your miraculous plan."

"I was going to say that Chris set us up with a retired French intel agent here who he knows. He's the one who suggested next week—"

"Why didn't you start with that?" Carlos looked like he was about to have a fit. "And where is he? He's the most important part of this team, we can't have a discussion on where or how to grab Kevin without the only person who knows anything about this place."

Veronica glared at him in silence, then stood up with a grimace. "Carlos, I was also going to tell you that he'll be here shortly, I just wanted us to have an opinion going into that conversation."

"Fine."

She continued without waiting for any further response, "There's two cafes that could work for a daytime grab, Café Buja and Café Gourmand. Café Buja is a little quieter, with more of a yard area, but Café Gourmand is more central. I believe we should go with Café Gourmand, but I'm open to discussion."

"I'd lean toward Café Gourmand as well," Petra agreed. "It's closer to here, and since there's more foot traffic, we're less likely to be noticed."

Kasem breathed a sigh of relief, glad that his fiancé had provided constructive input and, as a result, reduced the tension in the room. He was no fan of Veronica, but since they had decided to participate in the op, he wanted to survive it. "A team that can't work together loses everything," one of his trainers, Lieutenant Afshar, used to say. A wave of regret overpowered him as Kasem recalled how he had killed Afshar in a rage. Afshar had been trying to help him, but Kasem had killed him before he could explain.

"Exactly," Veronica nodded. "The question is, where, specifically, should we grab him? We could get to him in his car, but we won't know exactly when they arrive, or we could convince him to follow my contact out of the café somehow…"

"We should drug him," Petra suggested. "Drug him and pick him up in an ambulance—simple and clean, I'm sure we've all executed similar ops."

"Normally, I'd be all for that," Carlos said, "but I'm not sure any of us can pass for Burundais. This is a small place, and we stick out like sore thumbs. Why not just have Kevin meet the contact here, at the house?"

"It's too risky, I don't think he'd go for that. I like the idea of drugging him," Veronica agreed. "Carlos, you're right about the ambulance—I'm not sure how functional that infrastructure is here, so I'd rather fly under the radar. Let's roofie him and get him out of the café before he completely passes out."

Petra stood up, "All right, let's do it. Veronica, do you trust this guy to do the meet, to be the one who drugs him?"

"I'd rather he didn't."

"Here's what I propose," Petra continued, "Kevin's only met Kasem once, and he doesn't look the same, his hair's grown out now, and so has his beard. With glasses, I think we can get Kevin to the table long enough to drug him and get out. I already scoped out the café, so I can take position beforehand to grab him. We should keep it under surveillance for the week, see if there are any patterns, but it's a café so I'm not expecting much. Veronica, I think you being out there is too high risk—Kasem and I get him out of there, while Carlos does surveillance from the street, and then we all meet you back here."

Veronica crossed her arms, "I can't sit this one out, but I'll do street-side surveillance. I won't go inside."

From the look on her face, Kasem wanted to add, *You better.* He was willing to wager that she couldn't be in the same room as Kevin without decking him. "There's more," he said, finally speaking up. There would never be a good time to relay what he had seen. "I know we said we weren't interested in what Kevin's involved in, but I have to raise it again. Veronica, in your file, you had surveillance pictures of him meeting with the Deputy Head of the Agence d'Electricité, the energy regulator."

"So what? We know he's supporting the Chinese on their bid, and none of the Agency intel shows anything shady. I already told you, we can't get involved, Chris was really clear that we don't turn this into an international incident."

"I know, and I wasn't planning on going there. I went to the gym, and the deputy regulator—Gilbert Ngkirunge—was there, so I followed him to lunch—"

"Get to the point," Veronica snapped.

"He sat down with Pierre Nziza," Kasem finished.

Petra turned toward him, aghast. "Nziza? Are you sure?"

"That can't be—he's in Europe in exile, it had to be somebody else," Veronica shook her head. "We would know if he was here."

"I'm telling you, it was him," Kasem repeated.

"That means Kevin's involved with a genocidal maniac..." the color drained from Veronica's face.

"Okay, you're getting ahead of yourselves." Carlos knocked his hand sharply on the coffee table, "We have no clue what Kevin's involved with, it could be *bad,* or it could be *really bad,* and it could even be legit. We might as well grab him before we start jumping to conclusions. Once he's here, we'll ask him. Petra, as long as Frenchie agrees it's a good one, we'll go with your plan—you and I will head to the café early, have lunch there, get you situated before I head back to the car. Kasem, you arrive a little earlier than the meet, say, quarter to two. After he gets there, we pick him up, bring him here, question him, and have the Agency extract us the day after. Simple, easy—and besides, if we capture Kevin, whatever he's involved with gets stopped in its tracks."

Kasem locked eyes with Carlos. In his gut, he was sure that Carlos was only placating the situation. A year earlier, they'd gone after an illicit arms dealer, there was no way Carlos would let a war criminal go free.

But then that arms dealer killed his friend. Kasem grimaced as a feeling of disbelief struck him. This was an Agency op, and regardless of Carlos' sentiments in either direction, they would be subject to Agency orders.

Would the Agency let Nziza go free?

* * * * * *

Chapter 22

Bujumbura, Burundi

Petra stifled the overwhelming urge to laugh as she stared at their newest team member. In her years with the Agency, she'd worked with many different sorts and flavors of operatives from all over the world, none of whom ever completely fit the stereotypes associated with where they were from. To be fair, neither did the man seated across from her; in fact, he fit two clear stereotypes, neither of which she would have ever expected to encounter in real life. First, there was his physical appearance, the man looked like a dead-on clone of the actor Idris Elba. The thought that had occurred to her when he'd walked into the house was, *Are we in a Bond movie now?* He was tall and well-built, with a swagger to his step and a deep husky voice when he spoke with the group. He was dressed in a collared shirt, a blazer, and jeans, giving off an image of being both very stylish and comfortable at the same time. Their initial exchange had been in French, the only deviation from what Petra would have associated with a meeting with a hypothetical James Bond. Unsurprisingly, he oozed charm at every turn, flirting in turn with both Veronica and Petra.

When Veronica mentioned that not all of their group was fluent in French, however, the entire image transformed. Gaston switched to English, and while the huskiness in his voice remained, he had the most stereotypical French accent Petra had ever encountered despite years of living in Paris. She had always said that French people didn't actually sound like what English speakers made them out to be, their words when speaking English weren't simply an array of extended letter z's and r's. Yet, here, in front of her, was the perfect counterexample. If she were to close her eyes for a moment, the image that would appear alongside Gaston's voice was the cartoon Pepé Le Pew, a French skunk who was a Looney Tunes character she had watched with her parents during her childhood. Gaston's voice and physical appearance could not have clashed more, combining the suave appearance with the overeager intonation of the skunk's romance-starved demeanor.

Petra forced herself back to reality, she had to focus on the op instead of bursting into peals of laughter. A bittersweet pang hit her as she thought of the exchange she and Carlos would have normally had following such an odd encounter. She was sure that she and Kasem would be able to laugh about it, but that was a far cry from the hooting that would have resulted from Carlos' take on the Monsieur Gaston Lareve seated across the coffee table.

After switching to English, Veronica was now in the process of describing the plan they had come up with, she explained the different options they had considered and how they thought Café Gourmand was their best option. Gaston listened intently, asking the occasional question, but for the most part, remaining silent. When Veronica had finished, he nodded gravely, "For a group who has just arrived, and never worked in Burundi before, your understanding of the place is very impressive."

Petra suppressed a smile at the extended r's, still contemplating the fact that most French people did not sound like that, in contrast with all the American stereotypes.

"That said, I have to disagree on a couple of pieces—first, you said that one of you will meet him upstairs on the roof." Gaston turned toward Kasem, "I believe that's you, yes?" He didn't wait for a response, "You are here as a group with an NGO, and it would be very unusual for a traveling group here to send only one person to such a meeting. So, I will accompany you. Then, your idea to simply drug him and drag him out, well it's not a bad one, but an ambulance would be a much better option. I have the access you need to get this, I will make a few calls."

"Are you sure?" Veronica asked.

"But, of course," Gaston replied with a smile. "Now that we've settled that, there's the matter of what happens between now and this meeting. We'll make the appropriate arrangements, etcetera. I don't think you need to surveil the café, but you should all visit it a few times, most foreigners would, along with several of our nicer restaurants."

Petra frowned, "Won't that risk running into Kevin?"

"A little bit, that's true. But you must understand your covers here, and what most groups of expats get up to when they visit Buja. There's quite a community here, and they hold rather elaborate soirées. If you think about the country's troublesome history, the Burundais have dealt with this by really letting loose. You wouldn't be a credible NGO team if you didn't go to one of these parties or enjoy some of the local—" he paused for obvious emphasis, "the local hedonism."

Veronica looked like she was about to object, but before she could, Carlos stood with a wide grin and said, "All right, Frenchie, you've convinced us. Show us the way to these *soirées* you speak of."

* * * * * *

Chapter 23

Bujumbura, Burundi

Kasem parallel parked on the street behind Gaston and turned toward Petra, "Here goes nothing," he said with a grimace.

"I know how you feel," she agreed. "He's got a point, we do have to play the part of the visiting expat, but I can't say that I'm completely comfortable with this."

"Frenchie did say that the Chinese expat community doesn't really mix with this group, so, all things considered, we probably won't run into Kevin here."

She raised her eyebrows, "I didn't realize that you'd also adopted that nickname for him."

"Are you kidding? It's perfect."

"Indeed, trust Carlos to come up with something that apt."

"Yeah," Kasem sighed and reached out to squeeze her hand, he could see how much the absence of her closest friend was affecting Petra.

She caught his gaze, gave him a quick nod, and looked away. A moment later, Kasem saw Veronica, Carlos and Gaston descend from where they had parked a few paces away, and he and Petra followed them toward a gated property across the street.

Loud music was playing from inside, he recognized an old pop hit from a few years earlier, Taylor Swift's "Shake It Off." From outside the property walls, Kasem could see what looked like the second story of an old Spanish villa. There were lights on inside that cast a pale glow on the cream color of the house, in contrast with the darker crimped roof. The image reminded him of many of the houses he'd seen when visiting parts of Los Angeles as a teenager. Although the wall blocked most of his view of the house, he could tell that the property was massive, far larger than the grounds of the place that they were staying.

Voicing his thoughts, he heard Carlos ask Veronica as they neared the other group, "How come you didn't dig up a team house like one of these? We could have lured Kevin out by having a party like this."

Kasem broke into a grin, but Veronica didn't bother to respond. They waited while Gaston greeted the security guard at the gate, and then followed him inside. Once they were inside the walls, the music was even louder. They headed to the front door, walking through the foyer into a vast living room. Most of the activity was in the garden outside French doors which had been left open. Several people were dancing on the patio, with others splashing in the swimming pool beyond it. He glanced at Petra, "I know the briefings said that some of the expats live large, but I never realized it was quite like this."

"I think a lot of the embassy staff in Iran had something similar too."

"Maybe, but I guess you never invited me to their parties."

The grim expression on her face vanished, "I guess not. Maybe you weren't charming enough."

He gave her the most indignant look he could muster without bursting into laughter. "That's one of the first things you said about me."

"I know," she stepped closer and planted a kiss on his cheek. "Maybe *I* was the charming one." She grabbed his hand, pulling him out toward the patio. "Let's go for a swim. We're here, we might as well have some fun."

******

Chapter 24

Bujumbura, Burundi

Kasem looked across the table at Gaston, who was leaning back in his chair with both arms outstretched, basking in the sunlight on the Café Gourmand rooftop. In contrast, Kasem's stomach did a nervous flip. This was the moment of truth for them, when they would hopefully catch Kevin and end his and Petra's relationship with the Agency.

Or we don't, and I end up in a hole in the ground.

"You know what your problem is?" Gaston reached forward and grabbed his cup of café au lait, then tilted his head back with a flourish to sip on it.

"I'm sure you're going to tell me," Kasem answered, amused.

"You and your team, you don't know how to enjoy life. If you're going to do these kinds of operations, you must let loose when you can. What is that American saying, be sure to smell the flowers along the way?"

"You mean stop and smell the roses?"

"Why just the roses? You should smell all the flowers."

"Sure." Kasem broke into a grin and teased, "But what do you do in the winter? If there aren't any flowers around?"

"Oh, come on. When there are no flowers, you should stop and have a coffee, or maybe a drink," Gaston gestured toward his now empty cup.

"We certainly went to some parties with you this last week, had a few drinks."

"I know, but you were just playing a part. You have to relax, relieve some of that pent up stress." Gaston reached out and pinched Kasem's forearm, "Look at this, your muscle is like a rock, too much stress."

"I know how to relax," Kasem couldn't stop a note of indignation entering his voice now that Gaston had turned the tables on him.

"You, relax? I didn't even see you enjoy the food when we went out for dinner. You could not savor the freshest fish from the lake, and you talk about being able to let go. You had the same expression on your face when you were doing pull ups in the garden! I know exercise is important, but you cannot tell me it's as enjoyable as eating a barramundi with lemon butter sauce. You and your whole team, you soak up all the fun in the room, just a regular group of fun police."

"You don't know what this op means to me," Kasem said in a quiet voice. "Catching Kevin, it means—it means everything."

"My boy, you are a spy. The stakes will always be everything. What were they yesterday? Everything. Or with your last mission? Everything. And tomorrow? Everything. You can count on that. Convenient, isn't it?"

"I suppose."

"You can take it as a given, that the stakes are everything. But what you cannot take for granted is a bottle of Chateau Neuf du Pape, or a plate of really good Chevre. Or the party where you have both."

Kasem bowed his head in an exaggerated manner, "All right, I guess I could lighten up a little bit."

"But of course, now we are getting somewhere."

"So glad to have your approval." Kasem checked his watch and his pulse quickened, the entertainment of the conversation draining away since they were drawing close to the meet. "In the meantime, let's focus on those really high stakes, okay?"

"I believe we must."

* * * * * *

Chapter 25

Bujumbura, Burundi

Veronica guzzled half of her water bottle as she kept watch on the entrance to Café Gourmand from her car. She'd parked on the opposite side of the street and shifted to the back seat, grateful for the tinted windows which offered some cover. The café was on a busy street, and the site of someone asleep in a parked car was unlikely to faze anyone—drivers often slept in their cars while waiting for their charges. While there were few female drivers in Buja, a quick passerby was unlikely to notice her, especially with the dark scarf she had used to cover up her more noticeable blond hair.

She tapped her earpiece to check in with Carlos, "Are you in position?"

"Same as when you asked me five minutes ago," he replied in a disgruntled voice.

"Sorry, my nerves are running high."

"That's painfully obvious."

Veronica peered out of the window, perhaps she should have listened to Petra and stayed at the house. *You could be compromising this op,* she ruminated on what Carlos had said after the team meeting. How could he expect her to sit this one out? How could any of them? She pushed back a strand of hair that had come loose from her scarf and noted where Carlos had parked for the third time. After much deliberation, she had finally agreed to let him have the primary vantage point on the café's entrance—it was too much of a risk for her to be closer.

She could still see the café from where she was parked, but the angle was far from ideal, and they couldn't risk using binoculars; that would be noticeable, even on a crowded street with tinted windows.

Turning to the other side of the street, Veronica glanced at the two-story shops on her right. In a better-planned op, she would be up there on the roof—no risk of sighting from the street and all of the view. But this was far from an ideal op. None of them, besides Gaston, had any experience in Burundi, and she and Petra were the only French speakers in the rest of the group. Personal ties within the team were strained, and none of them had worked with Gaston before, so trust was limited all around. Plus, in the heat of the moment, she had to admit that Chris was right: she wasn't being objective, and she couldn't be. She squinted toward the entrance to Café Gourmand, her phone's clock said that it was 1:40, which meant that Kevin would be arriving soon.

They were right, I shouldn't be here. Veronica considered what that acknowledgment meant, should she return to the house? What if they didn't catch Kevin because of her?

She made a game-time decision and moved over into the driver seat. The shawl covering her hair fell to the side as she started the engine. Shifting into drive, she was about to pull out when another car sped past her on the street, and she froze. She'd only gotten a glimpse in her peripheral vision, but she'd never been more certain of whom she had seen. Tapping her earpiece again, she said, "He's here, he just went by me on the street. Guys, I think he made me."

* * * * * *

Chapter 26

Bujumbura, Burundi

Carlos cursed under his breath as he heard Veronica's update, why hadn't she stayed home? He watched a white Honda CR-V speeding down the street and clung to the hope that it might still stop in front of Café Gourmand. *Don't let this plan fall apart,* he pleaded with the universe, all he wanted was to go home to his wife.

He let out another series of expletives as the car sped by the café and turned a hard right onto the street in front of him. "He's gone, I'm following," Carlos shouted into his earpiece as he revved the engine.

"He won't be able to get far," Petra said, "not while he's still downtown, and he won't risk attracting attention with a car chase. We're following, don't let him lose you."

Although her words were reassuring, Carlos had known her long enough to recognize the anxiety in her voice. *I should have explored, figured out the city, instead of partying with Frenchie,* he scolded himself—he'd been too angry with the group to do much else. The only mission homework he had done was to study the map, but it would have to be enough.

Traffic on the Avenue de la R.D. Congo was at a standstill, and Carlos joined the rest of the drivers on the street in hitting his horn hard. At least Petra was right, Kevin wasn't going to get far. He squinted and caught sight of Kevin's SUV, three cars ahead of him, also stuck in the traffic, then saw it turn into what looked like an empty parking lot on the side of the road.

"He's stopping at a lot across the street from Arena," Carlos radioed to the team. He racked his brain, if he pursued Kevin on foot, then he increased his chances of being made. *But he already made Veronica. F-that,* he determined.

Carlos waited until Kevin's car was behind the gate he was turning past, then pulled over to park illegally on the side of the road.

Turning off the engine, he slid to the passenger side, then dropped out to the side of the road. As his feet hit the ground, he crouched down to keep out of sight, kicking up a cloud of sand.

He pulled the brim of his hat low to shield his face and sauntered toward the lot where Kevin had stopped. Before he reached the lot, Carlos spotted Kevin heading across the street and pretended to be on his phone, hoping he wouldn't be recognized. A moment later, Kevin disappeared into Arena's outdoor hallway leading to the restaurant patio.

"He's gone into Arena," Carlos informed the rest of the team over his com. "Is there another way out besides the main entrance?"

"No, that's the only way in and out," Kasem answered.

"Are you sure?"

"There might be a service entrance, but I didn't see one when I was in there."

"There is a service entrance, but it is only accessible to the staff," Gaston's nasally voice clarified. "We will be there shortly, I can follow him inside."

Rubbing his chin, Carlos contemplated what to do. Why would Kevin have gone into a fixed location when he knew he had been seen? If there was no other way out, he'd be a sitting duck. "I'm heading in after him, what's your E.T.A.?"

"We'll be there in about five minutes," Petra replied.

"See you soon."

"Carlos, there's no good spot to grab him in there. We'd have to follow the same plan—Gaston and I could get in there and try to spike his drink," Kasem said.

"I'll stay out of sight—we'll proceed with the plan once you get here. He must be trying a double cross, there's no way he'd go in there otherwise, but we can't afford to lose him." Carlos crossed the street and nodded at the bouncer in front of the hallway. Since it was only mid-afternoon, he wasn't sure what the bouncer's purpose was. *Guess he doesn't care, so long as he's getting paid.* He moved down the hallway and stopped to fiddle with his shoelace near the corner which led into the bar. Carlos scanned the room and spotted Kevin on the far side of the restaurant, then turned left toward the bathrooms instead of heading inside—with so few people in the restaurant, he couldn't risk it. *Let's hope Petra's right that he won't make Kasem or Gaston immediately.*

"We're here," his com crackled with Petra's voice.

Carlos glanced around to confirm he was alone, "I'm in the bathroom." He rubbed the back of his neck, "He's at a table by himself on the other side of the bar. Kasem, our best bet is for you to walk straight up to him and use the tranq needle. Without a pre-scheduled meet, surprise is our only chance. You and Frenchie are too noticeable to approach him for a conversation."

"I've got this," Kasem said. "I'm heading in now."

* * * * * *

Chapter 27

Bujumbura, Burundi

Veronica paced back and forth in the living room on tenterhooks. She clung to the hope that they still had a chance to capture Kevin, that she hadn't ruined everything. She had let her emotions run the show, casualties be damned, all because of her guilt at letting Kevin get away when he had shown up at her apartment weeks earlier. She resisted the urge to kick at the wall, Kevin had betrayed all of them, how could any of them be objective about his capture?

She chewed on her nails without thinking, then looked at her hand in disgust, she had kicked the habit years ago. Forcing herself to sit, Veronica picked up her tablet and attempted to get through a game of Tetris, the focus required to play would distract her—she no longer had control of the op anyway, so what else could she do? She cursed under her breath as she failed to turn the descending blocks quickly enough, her mind was far too occupied by whatever was happening at Arena.

Veronica shut her eyes, if Kevin had made her, why wouldn't he go into hiding? He would know that she had backup. So then why run to a restaurant or bar? Carlos was right, it had to be some sort of scheme, but they couldn't just let him get away. Her stomach churned, they were in for a trap, she just didn't know what yet, and it was all her fault.

* * * * * *

Chapter 28

Bujumbura, Burundi

Kasem was in the hallway across the restaurant when Veronica's voice burst through his com. "Abort, it's a trap, abort. It has to be—he would know I have backup, which means he knows we're coming."

He almost froze mid-step but managed to keep going. As far as he could tell, Kevin was facing the other way, so was unlikely to have spotted him. Gaston was on the other side of the patio, also moving toward Kevin, but Kasem was several paces closer. The metallic needle of the tranq dart felt cold in his pocket as he moved forward.

"This is our only shot. Kasem and Gaston are already out there. It's too late," Petra said, echoing his thoughts.

Now or never, he was just a few steps away. Kasem maneuvered around the last table ahead of him, and his jaw dropped as Kevin turned to face him.

"Hi Kasem," Kevin said with a wave. "Why don't you join me?"

******

Chapter 29

Bujumbura, Burundi

Petra watched Kasem and Gaston sit across from Kevin; she scrunched her eyes shut and reopened them to be sure that she wasn't dreaming. *This can't be real,* she thought as Kasem waved toward the narrow hallway in front of the bathrooms where she and Carlos were standing, pretending to share a cigarette.

"Does your fiancé work for the FSB now?" Carlos growled as they made their way toward the table.

"Go to hell," Petra glared, hoping that her old friend wasn't serious. He had to be joking, he couldn't possibly think that after Kasem risked everything to neutralize the FSB threat in DC. *How quickly they forget.* The saddest part was that under normal circumstances, she would never have associated Carlos with any of the Agency's traits, they'd both been through too much together for that. Her frown deepened as they approached Kevin's table, the loss of her mentor's trust and friendship was an open sore. She suspected spending time with Kevin would only make it worse.

"Hi Petra, Carlos," Kevin gestured toward the remaining two empty seats at the table. "Good to see you both."

"The feeling's not mutual," Carlos grumbled. "I'd much rather see you in cuffs."

"That's understandable." Kevin shrugged, then waved for the waitress. "Let's order, I find it's always better to discuss uncomfortable subjects on a full stomach."

Petra felt dazed, the situation was surreal, they were sitting across the table from Kevin at a restaurant in Burundi. *Am I dreaming?* she wondered yet again. Her gaze moved between the four men at the table, three of whom had betrayed her trust at different points in time. She let out a long exhale, while she and Carlos were on shaky ground, she had no doubt that he would come through for her if the need arose. Kasem had clawed his way back from the atrocities he had committed as the Ahriman, and despite their past, their relationship was stable and solid. He, and their lives together, were her future. When she looked at Kevin, though, all she could feel was hurt. They, too, had been friends since training, and if he hadn't betrayed them two years earlier, she would have trusted him with her life.

Say what you will about the Agency, those friendships are strong. She glanced at Kevin and Carlos again, two former colleagues whose lives had taken them in completely different directions.

The waitress appeared, and they ordered drinks, Petra still grappling with the strange reality. Although she was tempted to order a double gin and tonic, she selected sparkling water, as did Kasem, while Carlos and Kevin both ordered beers and Gaston settled on a glass of white wine.

"Might as well take the edge off," Carlos said with a shrug. "We're going to need it."

When the waitress reappeared with their drinks, Kevin ordered a burger with fries. "Nothing for all of you?"

Petra shook her head but was surprised when both Kasem and Carlos decided to follow his lead and Gaston chose a chicken kebab dish. For a moment, she considered doing the same but decided against it. Kevin was right—the food would indeed temper the mood. *I'd rather be angry.*

The waitress was about to leave when Kevin added a plate of *ndagala* to the order, a tiny fish from Lake Tanganika just a few miles away. Petra crossed her arms, recalling that the dish was a local specialty. If it wasn't for the company, she would have certainly wanted to try it. Tapping her fingers on the table, "Enough stalling. What do you want, Kevin?"

"Before we get to that, how's Veronica? I'm surprised that she isn't with you."

"She's fine, let's just get to it," Petra gritted her teeth.

"All right," Kevin hesitated, "I need your help."

Petra's eyes widened, this day was getting stranger by the minute, unable to believe what she was hearing. *He wants us to help him?*

While she worked to regain composure, Carlos spoke up, "Assuming this isn't a crock of bull, why would we do that?"

"I'm trying to stop this government from collapsing."

* * * * * *

Chapter 30

Bujumbura, Burundi

Kasem glanced at Kevin in the passenger seat repeatedly as he drove back to the house, struggling to grasp their current reality. The discussion over lunch had been brief—once Kevin had convinced them there might be some validity to his request, they had decided to postpone further detail until they were in a more secure setting. As a popular restaurant, Arena was far too public to get into any details, and shockingly Kevin had agreed to join them back to the house, even to ride with one of them. Petra was driving his car back with Gaston, and Carlos had nominated Kasem to take custody of Kevin.

"You have the least history with him," Petra whispered as they were leaving the restaurant, "you can be the most objective."

Reflecting on that, Kasem wasn't sure that he agreed—didn't his past as the Ahriman make him more likely to buy Kevin's story? The elevator pitch summary that Kevin had given sounded plausible: the Burundi government was leaning toward awarding the new energy contract to the Indian joint venture, but in order to make sure the government awarded it to them, the Chinese were setting up a military coup. *Wouldn't be the first time,* Kasem thought, wishing that wasn't the case. He remembered his parents' stories about the Shah of Iran and shuddered, then shoved them aside.

"I'm surprised you don't have more to say," Kasem glanced to his left, wondering if he could get Kevin to open up. Maybe

Petra was right—he barely knew Kevin, and even with his doubts about his ability to be objective, he could offer a different perspective to the team. At the very least, he might be able to get Kevin to open up since he didn't have all of the personal baggage that came with the rest of the team. If this conversation was only about being objective, Gaston would have been an even better candidate to spend time with Kevin alone. Any of them would also be more objective than Veronica, who was awaiting them at the house. In fact, they might have to stop her from killing him.

"What do you want to hear? I could tell you I regret what I did, but it wouldn't do much good."

Kasem frowned, Kevin sounded halfway sincere. "Why? If you do regret it, tell me why."

"I was wrong. The Agency made me pull some questionable ops, and after it happened enough times, I thought it would be better if I traded in for something better, but I was wrong."

"What happened?"

"What always happens," Kevin shrugged. "The people you work for ask you to do something wrong, and it doesn't sit right. After it happens enough times, you look for something else, someone that will stop that from happening. You must know what I mean, why else would you have become an Agency asset?"

Why indeed? Because the woman I loved tricked me into it.
"Right," Kasem nodded, "but why the FSB? You didn't actually think they were doing the right thing?"

"Not at first, I thought they were the bad guys like we were taught at the Agency. Eventually, it got more complicated—I had to burn an asset, and one of their operatives approached me, gave me a way out. The asset didn't get burned, but I owed him one. One turned into two, turned into ten…"

"Why are you telling me this?" Kasem's brow furrowed.

"Not much point in keeping quiet anymore. I've had my doubts, but they always stood by me, at least out in the open. But when they went after Veronica, they tried to keep me in the dark. I couldn't let that stand…"

Kevin's voice trailed off, and Kasem found himself at a loss. What would he do if someone were coming after Petra? He had already given up everything for her once—he'd handed himself over to General Majed and done his bidding, all to save her from capture. Kasem turned right into the gateway to the house, already open since Petra's car was just ahead, and exhaled in relief, glad that someone else would take over the questioning. *Objective, my ass.*

* * * * * *

Chapter 31

Bujumbura, Burundi

Veronica heard the cars pulling into the driveway and glanced out the window from the living room. Her pulse was racing, she had heard everything over the com, Petra had left it active while the team was at the table with Kevin.

He wants us to help him? She held on to those words although they were incomprehensible, she hated herself for hoping he could be telling the truth. Her stomach did a flip as she tried to get a handle on her emotions—some combination of anger, hate, relief, regret, sadness. And love, no matter how much she wanted to extinguish it. They had no future, she had no doubt about that, but she still cared about him. That was why she had let him go. *Because I still care,* she admitted to herself for the first time. Whatever happened next, he would remain in custody. She exhaled in relief, her weakness in letting him go before had now been rectified. Kevin would have to pay for what he had done.

The door flew open, and Veronica stood. Carlos, Gaston and Petra came in first, followed by Kasem and Kevin. As soon as he stepped inside, she moved forward, oblivious to the rest of the group. Approaching within a few inches of his face, she locked eyes, her hands shaking—at five foot ten, she matched his height, and he looked different, the same as he had that night in her apartment, sincere, caring, even contrite.

"I'm so sorry, V," he whispered.

The use of her nickname in front of the team, evidence of how close they'd been, shattered the image of someone sincere. Her composure snapped, and she dealt a slap with her right hand. The sting that shot through her palm was so satisfying she followed it by another blow, this time with her left, before taking a step back.

"I guess I deserved that," Kevin said, recomposing himself.

Veronica reacted before she had time to process, and this time her left fist landed on his cheekbone, the full strength of her shoulder behind it. He reeled backward and his hand flew to his face as Petra pulled her to the side. *Finally,* Veronica sighed, vindicated for letting him go a few weeks earlier.

She nodded at Petra and retreated to the dining table on the other side of the room, "Don't bother, I know what you're going to say. One of you can lead the questioning."

Petra seemed surprised, but she exchanged a glance with Carlos and dragged one of the other dining chairs to the middle of the room. "Have a seat, Kevin. Let's get started."

* * * * * *

Chapter 32

Bujumbura, Burundi

Petra waited for Carlos to secure Kevin before she began, glad that she hadn't faced any resistance from the rest of the group for taking charge.

"Is this really necessary?" Kevin flexed his arms, the only motion possible with his now-restrained wrists. "I came here willingly."

"Do you want another beat down? Because I can arrange it—" Carlos glared.

"You would do the same if the roles were reversed," Petra interrupted. "Although we do appreciate you coming in. What do you want, Kevin? You said you need our help."

"Haven't you seen what I've been working on? The Chinese are stacking the deck on this power deal, and they're doing it with a coup. Frankly, I'm surprised the Franco-American consortium isn't doing the same, but either way, we can't let them get away with this. Every bit of progress would go up in flames."

"Slow down," Petra frowned. "Start at the beginning, tell us what happened."

"Fine," Kevin sighed. "I left the FSB a month ago when they wanted to come after Veronica—"

"Back it up, buddy," Carlos made a circular gesture with his hand.

Kevin sighed, and his gaze wandered to the dining table where Veronica was seated, "After I left all of you in D.C., I went back to Moscow. Since my cover was blown, the FSB had me settle into normal day-to-day surveillance, identifying foreign assets on the ground, that kind of thing. It was all pretty mundane for a while. Then I got word that Rasskazov wanted revenge for how the op ended in such a cock-up—he didn't know how to get to any of you, but he had had his goons secretly tracking Veronica for months." He looked at her again, "You'd managed to evade them for a while, but then they found you, they had the location of your safe house, with surveillance confirming it. I couldn't let them come after you— they would have killed you. So, I ran, first to warn you, then away."

Petra crossed her arms. "Why here?"

"I wanted to pick somewhere the FSB didn't have its claws super deep, so I figured somewhere in Africa would be a good bet. I worked in Burundi on one of my first ops."

"No, you didn't," Veronica shook her head. "I've read your file."

"The Agency ran it off-book—I was in Nairobi most of the time anyway, but I met with contacts here and in Rwanda. We were working on securing assets in the opposition party after the political crisis in 2015."

"When exactly was the posting?" Petra sat down in the living room armchair and racked her brain—at the time, she and Kevin would have been just completing training. She remembered returning from Paris—where she had first met Kasem—and how Kevin had held her up when she almost collapsed with exhaustion. Could he have returned from an op around the same time?

"My first trip was in the last couple of months before I finished training, back in 2016, then again right after graduation for about six months."

Petra nodded, so far, the timeline seemed plausible. "Go on."

"Before I got here, I reached out to one of my old assets. I thought he was still in Kenya, but he moved back a year ago since the crisis had stabilized. He said he was working as a consultant, and he could process a visa under the table if I wanted to join him." Kevin shrugged, "It was as good an offer as any, and I knew the Russian presence here is limited. I figured I could lay low for a while until my next move. I didn't realize at that point he was working for the Chinese."

Petra leaned forward, "Who's the asset?"

"I can't tell you that."

"You asked for our help, not the other way around." She examined his micro-expressions—he was too well-trained to give much away, but she could sense that this asset was important to him.

"He's a friend, works in the government now."

Petra's eyes narrowed, Kasem had said that Kevin had met with the deputy at the electricity regulator, who'd then met with the former head of the Secret Police. "The deputy, Gilbert Ngkirunge?"

Kevin looked surprised that she'd figured it out so quickly, but he nodded. "I confronted him—asked him why he was working for the Chinese, and why he hadn't told me, but all he said was that everyone works for someone—he was just hoping to make a little extra money on the side."

"When did the Chinese approach you directly?" Carlos' eyes narrowed as he spoke, and Petra could sense his disgust at Kevin's flippant attitude toward shifting allegiances.

"Not long after that. At first, they threatened me, but then when they realized who I was, we came to an arrangement."

"An arrangement?" Carlos' voice dripped with repulsion.

"Look, I needed a paycheck, and I need protection. I didn't have a whole lot of options," Kevin said with a shrug. "I had no idea what they were involved in, I thought it was just glorified surveillance, at most a protection detail or some B-level corporate espionage. That's all the Chinese do in Africa anyway—make things easier for Chinese companies to come here and build and rebuild stuff. I wasn't expecting it to be riveting work... but I also wasn't expecting this—"

"Tell me more about Gilbert," Petra interrupted but kept her tone level—she and Carlos had fallen into a good cop, bad cop pattern that she might as well take advantage of to see if Kevin would divulge more details. "Why was he meeting with the Secret Police? We had him under surveillance. I still can't believe Nziza is here. He should be on trial in the Hague."

"I'll get to that. At first, that's all it was—I was basically a bodyguard for a couple of executives, managed security for their movements."

"I thought you said you were working for the M.S.S.?" Carlos interjected.

"With the Chinese, all the corporations work with the M.S.S.—at least tangentially, or so I thought. Anyway, after a couple of weeks, Gilbert reached out to me—he was working on permitting for the big power deal, was funneling information on how to expedite the process, when he found out his boss was on the take too. He didn't think it was a big deal until he realized that Nziza was involved. That's when he asked for my help."

Petra froze as the meaning behind his words started to sink in, if the Chinese had brought back the Head of the Secret Police, that could only mean one thing. A shiver ran down her spine as she looked back at Kevin, "Are you saying that in order to get the power deal, the Chinese government is willing to reinstall a war criminal?"

"Not the Chinese government, the company Omicron. I'm sure they have government support, but I want to believe it doesn't run that high."

"So, you're a corporate spy?" Kasem looked up from across the coffee table. He exchanged a glance with Petra, and she gave him a nod, he'd spent more time studying the power plant contract, so it made sense for him to take over.

"I'm surprised you didn't know that," Kevin raised his eyebrows. "Yes, Omicron signs my checks. Isn't that how you figured out that I was here?"

"We did, but the Agency noted it as a probable cover. It's poetic—you didn't like working for the government because of their morals, but now you're a corporate slave," Kasem added.

Petra frowned, she could tell from Kasem's posture that, despite the demeaning language, he was considering trusting Kevin. She even found herself starting to concede that there might be something there. Kevin had come in willingly and could easily have gotten away after he spotted Veronica. He also wasn't the only one who thought something was off about this power deal. Kasem, too, had expressed reservations.

Echoing her thoughts, Kasem asked, "Why should we trust you, Kevin? This could all be a ploy to stay out of Agency custody."

"I saw Veronica in the car this morning, but I let you catch up to me anyway. I could have run, but I didn't. We need to stop this coup—we can't let a war criminal be back in the president's chair. No one has managed to unify the ethnic groups here since before the civil war, if Markov's government collapses, it'll be worse than the genocide in the nineties." Kevin looked around the room, pleading, "This is a wonderful country, but one that's been under the heel of so many abysmal powers. Whenever I came here, the people, the mountains, the lake, all of it spoke to me, but it was never stable—they never seemed to get it together politically. But now they have, and things are *good,* not perfect, *but good.* I can't be involved in taking these people back to the dark ages, that's not what I signed up for. We can't let Markov's government fall."

He continued to scan the room, but his eyes skirted Veronica, and Petra shifted—no matter how hesitant she was to trust him, his words rang true. She had done little exploration since arriving, but the city was most certainly beautiful, and the people very friendly. The parties they had attended were chock full of hedonism, with good food and drink. At the surface, they hadn't offered anything particular, but the attitude had begun to speak to her, the openness of everyone that she had met, how they were happy and ebullient despite the tumultuous history. Her impression was that this perspective had been with the population far longer than the recent more stable government, but she'd only been there for a week.

Making a mental note to ask Gaston more about that later, Petra approached Kasem, placing her hand on his shoulder before moving forward to crouch in front of Kevin's chair and look straight into his eyes. As she did, she knew it in her bones, whatever else he had lied about, he wasn't lying about this—he really did love Burundi. That much was real.

Taking a step back, Petra glanced at Kasem, and she could see that he felt the same way. In fact, he was even closer to it, he had to remember this kind of mess from Iran, where a stable government fell because of corporate interests. Her throat constricted, she had grown up hearing the stories of the Iranian Revolution—of her grandparents' escape, first to Iraq, and then to Kuwait, but what had hammered it home had come much later. She'd had to study the revolution more objectively in preparation for the op years earlier, and that had led her to Kasem. Since then, the pictures of the dead, the atrocities committed by the Shah and the revolution itself, all of it remained imprinted on her brain.

Petra looked at Carlos, who shrugged. *No way to know, kiddo,* she could imagine him saying under normal circumstances. She hesitated, other than Veronica, she was closest to Kevin, but they had all been duped by him before. Could she trust her gut? She walked over to the window, taking in the vivid greenery, the sun shimmering on the leaves in the garden. If he was right, something was wrong here, and they couldn't let it stand.

She turned around and nodded at Kasem, signaling him to take over. They had discussed it briefly before starting the interrogation, she and Carlos could play good and bad cop, but they were known entities for Kevin. Kasem was an unknown, and as such, had license to behave like a loose cannon if need be.

He marched forward and grabbed Kevin by the shoulders, then leaned over close to Kevin's ear. "This better not be a smokescreen at the expense of the people here. God help you if it is, I'll make sure—we'll make sure—you pay." His tone was icy, and the intent clear. "But if the Chinese are trying to turn this into another Iran, I won't let that happen. Nziza will never become the shah of Burundi."

* * * * * *

Chapter 33

Bujumbura, Burundi

Kasem wanted so badly to shake his fist at the screen as the team argued with Chris over videoconference. *How can you let this happen?* he wanted to shout at the video link. He and Petra had managed to steal a few minutes earlier, and she had reassured him that the Agency would intervene.

"They would never let a progressive government in Burundi fall in favor of a war criminal," she had said unconvincingly. The situation seemed all too familiar to him, reflecting so many similarities to the Iranian government before American and British intelligence had orchestrated a coup and installed the Shah. Thinking about it made him sick to his stomach, he felt as if the stories that his parents had told him about Iran during that time were replaying in front of him. That he was powerless to stop it. Petra understood—her father's side of the family had also been through the Iranian Revolution—but she seemed less affected, more certain in the Agency's purpose.

But why? They haven't given you any reason to trust them.

"If there was ever a time to stand up for the greater good, this is it," she'd added.

With a sigh, Kasem glanced between her and Veronica, then back at the screen. He hadn't shared his most serious concern, acknowledging it aloud would make it real in a way that he wasn't willing to grapple with, at least not yet. Since he had started digging into the power plant deal, he had done some research into the three different bids that were in play—the Chinese one, which was the cheapest and easiest to finance given the backing of the Chinese government and Central Bank, the American and French joint venture, which was the most expensive, but arguably made use of the most cutting-edge technology, and the Indian-British joint venture. In his mind, the last one was the clear winner—while their technology wasn't as cutting edge as the American offer, it was up to the mark and came with a much lower price tag. The price tag was only slightly above that of the Chinese offer, but Kasem had no doubt that the quality of the equipment far exceeded the Chinese bid. China had great technology of its own, the pictures of massive solar farms on their territory didn't lie, but they didn't sell it to Africa.

Kasem had seen the business model time and again when he was working on infrastructure projects in Iran—the Chinese brought cheap and easy money, but they also sold an inferior product, especially when it came to their dealings in Africa. It was in their interest for a bridge to break down every few years since they would be brought under contract again to rebuild it.

"For the last time," Chris repeated, "I'm going to run this up the chain. Until we get an answer, all of you are to stand down."

"You can't be serious," Petra said. "Kevin is here, in our custody, and we have concrete time-sensitive intel. But you're still saying we should wait for you and a group of bureaucrats to give us the go-ahead? We're honor-bound to do something. We can't just let another African government fall because of colonialism. The Agency has to mean something; that has to still be who we are."

Kasem looked over at her, her words echoed his thoughts, but cynicism colored his perspective. How many times had Western governments taken a backseat when action didn't serve their interests? They had watched the genocide in Rwanda and Burundi take place in the nineties and done little, if anything, to stop it. Western values were merely words when acting in their favor brought no accompanying windfall or global power gains. For Iran, values had been a smokescreen—British and American intelligence had removed a democratically elected and progressive government in favor of a dictator who would serve their interests. How many people had died as a result? How many people had died here, in Burundi, because of their inaction? If the rumors were to be believed, the French had stood by and watched the genocide happen, ignoring it entirely. Values were cheap when all they entailed were words. Most people weren't willing to stand up for the consequences. American lives, French lives, they were all just people, but governments didn't see it that way, and lives from developing countries were so often seen as expendable.

I'd like to see an Iranian or a Burundais life worth as much as an American or a European one. Acting for good was always overshadowed by money and power, often with dire consequences for locals.

Much as the words threatened to burst out of him, Kasem didn't dare speak his thoughts, he wasn't sure if he could stay in control. His grandparents had died during the Iranian revolution, and he already knew that Chris was going to say his hands were tied unless he got the go-ahead. Instead, Kasem focused on Kevin, still bound in his chair—monitoring him helped to occupy his mind. The Agency would have to let them do something. He refused to consider what he would do if they were ordered not to intervene. Besides, why would it be in their interest to let the deal go to the Chinese?

* * * * * *

Chapter 34

Bujumbura, Burundi

Petra gulped the contents of her water bottle and sank into the couch. She stretched out her arms, glancing at the ceiling. Her brain felt foggy, she hadn't felt this exhausted in quite some time. Probably not since the last time she'd had to deal with the Agency.

She stared at the white trim along the ceiling joint and let her mind wander. Kasem had already gone to bed, but she was hesitant to join him—their conversation about their marriage and partnership weighed on her, and she wasn't sure she was ready to rehash it. He'd seemed to understand—after all, her concerns about being the only positive piece of his life were valid. They hadn't had an argument, but the discussion had been heavy, there was too much at stake for it to be light or easy. Petra was also dreading how Kasem would react to the events of the day once they were in private. She'd seen the expression on his face and worried that anything she said would sound like it was in defense of the Agency.

Petra nestled into the couch cushions, the exhaustion of the day made her wonder if she would rather limit any additional heavy discussions and remain on the couch.

She'd just dozed off when she heard a door slam, and her eyes flew open. Sitting up, she saw someone moving out of the storage room where they had locked up Kevin. Petra reached for the table lamp and squinted, then recognized Veronica once her eyes adjusted.

They looked at each other in silence, Petra debating what to say. They both knew Veronica wasn't supposed to see him without anyone else present, but that was also a rule designed to be broken. "Are you all right?" Petra asked finally.

"I don't know."

Petra swallowed, since the start of the op, Veronica's tone toward her had been cutting, so different from their former friendship, but the woman speaking to her now sounded far more like that memory. Those three words conveyed so much of Veronica's distress. "Do you want to talk about it?"

"What's the point?"

Petra hesitated, then decided to barrel ahead. "What did he say?"

"Same old stuff... he said that he did love me, that he couldn't put my life at risk, and that's why he left the FSB."

"What did you want him to say?"

"Why can't it be simple?" Veronica shook her head. "If it was all a lie, I could just be angry and march him straight to a cell. But if what he said is true, then what? If he's telling the truth about the coup here, then what? Are we supposed to forgive him? Am I supposed to pretend none of this happened?" She curled into the fetal position on the armchair next to the couch. "What would you do?"

"I don't know."

The silence in the room was deafening, and Petra fidgeted, considering how to excuse herself.

"Do you think we should trust him?" Veronica asked.

"I wish we didn't have to—but we can't let the government here fall."

"Like you care? Besides, that isn't our job—I'm not getting into the middle of it unless Chris gives the order."

Petra controlled her reaction, it was pointless to engage until Chris made a decision. "I guess we'll see."

"I don't get it, Petra. Are you even the same person I met eight years ago?"

"What do you mean?"

"When I met you, you were so committed to the Agency, to everything we stood for. Now you're the moral authority—your values, your plan, the list goes on. There's no way the person I knew then would compromise her integrity to be with a man who has so much blood on his hands."

Once again, Petra found herself at a loss for words, she could scarcely believe what she was hearing. As what Veronica had said sunk in, her nostrils flared. "You self-righteous, sanctimonious piece of crap," she said. "When I think about what I hate most about the Agency, it's not the danger or the uncertainty of that life, it's people like you. *You* are the worst the Agency has to offer, someone who treats every single other person like an expendable chess piece. I don't give a shit what you think of my relationship, look at your own damned life. When you needed help in Moscow, who got you out? That was Kasem, and that was *me*. You've spent what, five minutes with him in the last five years? Maybe twenty minutes with me? Get your head out of your ass—you may think I'm engaged to the Ahriman, but at least we know he's here to help us. You're the one that lived with the guy who betrayed all of us, the one that we don't know we can trust. I haven't wanted this life in years, and there's nothing wrong with that, but I still showed up for you. Get off your high horse and stop living in denial." Petra continued to glare at Veronica as she rose and circled the coffee table to head toward the hallway.

"I, I didn't—" Veronica started to say, but Petra ignored her.

As Petra reached the hallway, she noticed Carlos emerging from his room. "That goes double for you, asshole," she snarled, opening her door. "You two better get off your damned soapboxes," then slammed the door behind her.

* * * * * *

Chapter 35

Bujumbura, Burundi

Petra awoke the next morning with her jaw clenched as she recalled what Veronica had said the night before. Much as she wanted to surrender to her anger, cooler heads would have to prevail this morning. She took a deep breath and counted to ten, then repeated the sequence three more times. When she opened her eyes, she ran through Kevin's story, considering whether they should trust him. She reflected on the question for a few more moments before affirming her decision. The stakes were too high not to intercede.

Petra emerged and ventured into the hallway with her back rigid. She stopped in the bathroom to freshen up and ran into Kasem on her way out, coated in sweat from a run. "How was it?"

"Great, but the sun's up now. It's going to be a hot day."

You have no idea. Petra nodded as he moved past her into the bathroom. Gritting her teeth, she braved the living room where she found Carlos and Veronica drinking coffee in silence.

"There's plenty more if you'd like some," Carlos motioned to the coffee pot on the table.

She detected a hint of his old fun tone but dismissed it, "Thanks." Petra grabbed a mug and poured herself a cup, her gaze moving between the two of them as she settled into the remaining armchair.

A few minutes later, Kasem joined them, and Veronica looked up, "We've all had a little bit of time to reflect on what

Kevin told us yesterday. Before we get to that, I wanted to say thank you for being here—I know it was a big ask."

Petra raised her eyebrows and exchanged a glance with Kasem. *How is he so calm?* she noted the lack of anger in his expression. She was still livid, now even more so because apparently, she had to be angry for both of them, and not just for herself.

"I spoke to Chris earlier, and he's still waiting for a go-ahead from the higher-ups. That said, I wanted to hear what you think. I'll start—obviously, Kevin's betrayed all of us, so I'm not sure we can trust him, but at the same time, I'm not sure we can afford not to. Part of me wants to walk away from this—why do I even care what happens here? Yesterday you reminded me what the Agency's supposed to stand for, though—" She looked over at Petra, "I don't know what the Agency leadership will decide, but the progress Burundi's made over the last five years has to mean something. We can't let that disappear because some bureaucrat doesn't want to get their hands dirty. So, I'm in, but only if we do this as a team."

Petra blinked, *I guess she was listening last night.*

"Carlos?" Veronica turned to him, and he nodded before moving her gaze toward Kasem. "I know I haven't been the most inclusive, but you're an important part of this team. I know Petra's in, so I'm assuming you are too, but I want to hear it from you."

Kasem's eyes widened, and it took him a second to respond, "I appreciate that, and yeah, I'm in."

* * * * * *

Chapter 36

Bujumbura, Burundi

Kevin grunted as he heard movement outside of the storeroom where he was being held. For better or worse, the soundproofing in his "cell" left much to be desired. On the bright side, that meant that he could listen in on most of the team discussions. Bits of the conversations in the living room would end up muffled, but he could usually get the gist of what the team was speaking about. He had been on high alert as much as possible, napping on the camping gear laid out for him in the corner in between any interesting discussions he wanted to listen in on. In accordance with his plan, most of the conversations he had overheard focused on the situation in Burundi rather than him. He clung to the hope that they would help him, whatever had happened between them in the past, stopping the coup was of paramount importance.

When Kevin had been posted in Nairobi years earlier during training, he'd visited Burundi several times. With each trip, he had fallen more in love with the setting, and more importantly, the people. Really, the attitude, the way in which the population could look into the face of adversity—war, genocide, colonial oppression. Instead of crying out, the people here chose to smile and laugh, dance, and party. They chose to be open and friendly, even to outsiders, despite a history of outsiders being the cause of great strife. He had seen other African countries face similar situations and handle it in completely different ways. In Rwanda, the country that had faced the most similar situation and history, the population coped by quietly going to work, channeling their trauma into their employment. As a result, Rwanda's economy had grown faster than Burundi's, but the relaxed attitude he found on the hillside here in Bujumbura could not be replicated.

Since his return to Burundi several weeks earlier, he felt an even deeper affinity for the place. For the first time in a couple of years, he could roam the streets freely, with little worry about the FSB's pursuit. Eventually they would find him, as the Agency had, but in the meantime, he could enjoy his life. He had visited all of the cafés around the city, drinking the exquisite local coffee. He'd spent time at the lake, swimming and sunbathing, along with eating the decadent mix of foods which combined quality local ingredients with French preparation techniques. Fresh fried plantain chips were his snack of choice, especially when he was lazing on a deck chair by the beach. Most of his activities, besides those for his assignment with Chinese intelligence, had initially been permeated by a need to relax, to let loose and enjoy the temporary respite and freedom from both the Agency's and the FSB's pursuit. Those moments had particularly underscored why he'd fallen in love with the place to begin with.

It's the spirit, he had identified on one of his early visits; a spirit that meant Burundais would spend their Saturday mornings on a massive collective run, playing music and dancing along the way, rather than brooding on their tumultuous history. Or perhaps, as would be most beneficial to their economy, rather than working. His background as an economist—which had set him up well for many undercover assignments as an economic advisor—frowned upon this type of coping mechanism, far better to focus on activities that generated employment or income. Regardless, the Burundais spirit was both captivating and contagious. It almost grew on the trees like the wild fruit, ripe and ready to be picked. It had survived the boot of colonialism and years of civil war. All he could pray for was that it would survive the upcoming coup attempt.

Kevin drew in a deep breath and tried to relax, hopefully he could get a few minutes of shut eye in before they summoned him into the living room for an umpteenth round of questioning. They seemed to think that if they asked him the same things again and again his answers might change, although he couldn't blame them for that—it was how the Agency had trained them to break through a target's cover story. The process was exhausting, and much as he wanted to eavesdrop some more, the ordeal was beginning to wear him out.

His eyes grazed the contents of the storeroom; for the most part, they had emptied it when they had decided to keep him there. *When they decided to store me here,* he thought with a half grin. On one side there was an entrance to the kitchen which was bolted shut from the other side. At the opposite end of the room was the doorway to the old servant's bathrooms, an old colonial feature to the house. That bathroom was dingy, and he was sure in far worse condition than the facilities in the main part of the house, but it did the job. That door was kept locked as well, but a couple times a day they had allowed him access to relieve himself. He suspected, as likely they did, that he could find his way out of this "prison" if he really tried—probably another test of the validity of his story. If he attempted an escape, he would show them that what he had told them was a fabrication, regardless of whether he was successful. As a result, he had no intention of trying any such thing. He needed their help, and he wasn't going to squander this opportunity. Besides, he could imagine the look on Veronica's face if he did anything to indicate that his story was a lie. Despite her hard exterior, it would crush her, and that was the last thing he wanted. *It would also lead to my immediate imprisonment,* he looked around again. The storeroom was hardly comfortable, but it was far superior to an Agency black site.

Drawing himself back from his thoughts, Kevin practiced some more deep breathing before closing his eyes. Whatever happened next, he would need to be as rested as possible to deal with it.

* * * * * *

After another day of rest and listening in on the discussion in the living room, Kevin had hoped in vain for a better gauge on the team's reactions, but there had been minimal further discussion. They all seemed too frustrated with each other to have a constructive conversation. Grumpy, he tossed and turned; the team's disfunction and continuing lack of direction or leadership was far too disheartening to endure.

He wasn't sure how long he'd been asleep when he heard the door, grogginess clouded his awareness. The light from the tiny window several feet above had faded, but the open doorway brought in a flood of fluorescent lighting from the kitchen. It took several seconds for his eyes to adjust, but when they did, he was surprised to see Kasem standing in front of him.

Kevin waited a few seconds for Kasem to speak, then asked, "What do you want?"

Kasem hesitated, "I want to make my own judgement. Hard to do that when you're in the room with all of them. They'd rather chew each other out than listen to what you have to say."

Kevin stared at him, surprised by the candor, "I see."

138

"Tell me why you want us to stop the coup, and how you ended up here. You told me you were supposed to burn an asset, but I want to hear the whole story, every detail. From the beginning."

* * * * * *

Chapter 37

Bujumbura, Burundi

Veronica's jaw fell as she stared at Chris's sheepish expression through the video link on her tablet.

"I'm sorry, but my hands are tied. The Agency won't authorize backup, and they want you to stand down. Bring Kevin in, and after he's debriefed, we'll revisit the idea of intervening in Burundi."

"You can't be serious," Petra interrupted. "If we wait that long, it'll be too late. Kevin said that the Chinese op is already in motion. If we wait until you've managed to get a full confession out of him in New York, we won't stand a chance of stopping it. Whatever's going down here will have already happened."

Chris frowned, "What about Istanbul station? Alex could debrief him."

"This is pointless, we already did a full debrief," Veronica shook her head. "If we're going to stop the coup, we have to move now. We barely have any idea what they're planning and how, and they'll be moving forward within a month. In that time, we have to get the intel that we need, develop a plan, and execute it."

"And we need military backup," Petra added. "We have no idea how much of the current secret police is on Nziza's side."

"I can't authorize that..." Chris sighed, "Look, unofficially, I agree with you. We shouldn't let Burundi's government fall, but my bosses don't agree. They don't want us mixed up in another regime change that could bite us in the ass later."

Veronica scanned the room, considering their options. They could try on their own, a five-man team including Gaston would probably be sufficient for most covert ops, but not with the military or Secret Police involved. Her gaze flickered to the room where they had locked up Kevin. *Six, if we decide to use him.* The mere thought left a bitter taste in her mouth, but she wasn't sure they had much of a choice.

"Look, I'll take another pass. Until then, see what else you can get from Kevin and sit tight." Chris disconnected, and the video projection of his image disappeared.

Veronica surveyed the room, searching for the right words, "What do you want to do?"

"We already told you," Petra said, her voice still resolute, although Veronica detected a twinge of disappointment and fear underneath. "We can't sit idle and let this happen."

"If the Chinese have access to the entire Secret Police, the four of us will be severely outmatched. We'd need military backup," Veronica rubbed her chin.

"We can't do nothing," Petra exclaimed. "The Agency, the greater good, all of that has to mean something."

"It won't mean much if we die doing the right thing, Petra," Kasem whispered, touching her forearm.

"This argument is pointless," Carlos stood up. "All of us, we already said we're in. But if we're going to move on this, we need a plan. Get Kevin back in here—we need to get started."

* * * * * *

Chapter 38

Bujumbura, Burundi

Petra had her pistol ready as Carlos brought Kevin into the living room. The fingers in her right hand were stiff from over-gripping, but despite several deep breaths, she couldn't ease the pain in her joints. *I'm too old for this shit,* she remembered Carlos saying on their last op together in Madagascar. He'd always been good at defusing the tension in a group before an operation. She missed their camaraderie—the lack of banter made her feel like she and Kasem were separated from the rest of the team by a brick wall.

"You said there's a plot against the president, but we need to know more. Where, when?" Carlos took a step back from the chair after securing Kevin, "Time to get talking, buddy."

"I already told you, I don't know, just sometime in the next month. If you let me go, I can find out."

"Let you go? Are you insane?" Veronica blurted from the far corner of the room.

Petra shot her a glance, they had agreed that she would stay out of the interrogation but be able to watch in silence, then turned back toward Kevin. "You know that's never going to happen. If you don't know when, what else do you know?"

Kevin locked eyes with her, "Like I said before, the M.S.S. is working with Nziza, that's how he managed to get back in the country. He still has a stronghold on the generals who used to serve him, even if they're officially loyal to the President."

"Are you saying they would fall in line? If Nziza got to the President?" Carlos asked.

"Minus the two that the president appointed last year, yes, I think so. Nziza's been back-channeling with the rest of them in secret, and with the M.S.S.' help, he's sent some strategic gifts, made some headway."

Petra cursed under her breath, if Nziza had control of the military, then the situation was even worse than she had thought. "Who else is involved?"

Kevin raised his eyebrows, "Who else do you need? The former head of the Secret Police, a chunk of the military, along with Chinese intelligence, all working together? It's pretty self-explanatory. They've already infiltrated the president's guard, just waiting for their moment to pull the trigger."

Petra nodded as an idea occurred to her. "The whole plan—it revolves around Nziza, right?"

"Of course—he's the one who could command the generals," Kevin answered.

"If we take him out, the whole plan falls apart?" Carlos looked over at Petra as he asked the question, and she noticed a thaw in his demeanor.

"Yes," Kevin agreed.

Petra's eyes narrowed, "What's your play here, Kevin? You brought us in, you must have a plan to stop it."

"I already told you, get the Agency to send a military team, bolster Markov's defenses. The M.S.S. pulls the op because it's too high risk—"

"You don't expect us to buy that bull?" Veronica glared at him. "I know how you operate, and more importantly, we know that you know the Agency's M.O. Besides, even if we set an entire squadron at the presidential palace, we can't guarantee that the M.S.S. won't move anyway—"

"She's right, Kevin," Petra interrupted to stop Veronica from losing it. The cartoon version of this scene would have smoke coming out of her ears. "Your plan, let's hear it again."

"I didn't think you'd trust me with that. But yes, I'll admit, I did have an idea." Kevin paused, "You don't have to stop the entire coup attempt—you were on to something before, all you have to do is neutralize Nziza."

"So how do we do that?" Petra's eyes seared into him.

"Get to him before the coup starts—I have intel on where he's been hiding."

"Show us." Kasem tapped on his tablet to project a map of Bujumbura above the coffee table.

"He's not in the city most of the time—it would be too risky. The M.S.S. has been moving him between three different safe houses in the outskirts. The last one they had him at was over at Blue Bay, but it looks like he's been moving between there and the Club du Lac."

"Blue Bay and Club du Lac?" Carlos rolled his eyes. "Great, all you've got to do to stay at the fanciest resorts in the country is become a mass murderer." He moved the onscreen map to focus on the coastline south of the city along Lake Tanganika.

Petra holstered her pistol and stared at the projection as it shifted to the Blue Bay resort, which consisted of several beach houses set up along the coastline. "Do you know which house?"

"The Chinese have the entire place booked out, but they've been keeping him on the southern end of the resort, furthest from the main road that goes along the beach." Kevin squirmed, "I can show you—on the map. I also have their security protocols and guard formations."

Petra pointed toward the two beach huts located on the southernmost cove of the resort, "You mean down here?"

"Exactly. He was in the second one."

"What guarantee do we have that Nziza will be there? You said he's been moving around, switching between the two places," Carlos crossed his arms.

Kevin shrugged, "The truth is we don't. My bet is that as it gets closer to D-Day, the M.S.S. won't let him move around anymore."

"But we don't know when D-Day is." Kasem looked at him pointedly.

"That's true, we don't."

"So, we have to keep both places under surveillance, figure out an access plan that could work for either one." Kasem glanced at Carlos and Petra, seeking their input.

"Agreed," Carlos said with a nod and moved the map to focus on the resort area north of the city where Club du Lac was located.

Petra peered at the map, then asked, "Do they have the run of Club du Lac too?"

"I don't think so, it's much bigger, more crowded, and loads of locals frequent it on the weekends," Kevin answered. "It would be too big of a deal to close it to the public."

Kasem nodded, "So we keep watch on both, then figure out how to make our move."

"Exactly. Nziza is the center of their plan, so with him out of the way, the coup falls apart," Petra's expression brightened.

"I have some ideas," Kevin said. "We could—"

"We'll lead the planning from here," Carlos tapped on the map to zoom it out. "Best guess, water access for Blue Bay, but not the Club. That one we can walk right into without anyone noticing us, just a group going to the beach." His eyes landed on Petra, "Or maybe a single girl at the pool, depending on his proclivities."

Petra's eyes narrowed, with Veronica out of the picture, Carlos was certainly best placed to lead the op and plan out their approach. That said, she no longer trusted him, at least not like before, but at first assessment, his plan made sense. "Let's go see both places before we figure out the approach, but you're right, that could probably work."

"Of course," Carlos agreed, sounding a tad taken aback. "If it's Blue Bay, it'll be just like Mada—in and out by boat."

Because that went so well. "Sure," Petra said, recognizing his attempt to inject some levity into the conversation, just like the old Carlos. Still, she couldn't help but think how close they had all come to dying on the island in Madagascar. Definitely a great plan to emulate.

******

Chapter 39

Blue Bay, Burundi

Carlos' stomach grumbled as he drove past the entrance to the Blue Bay resort. He reached for the now empty bag of peanuts he had brought with him to snack on and tossed it onto the backseat in disgust. He turned his focus back to the resort, the brush line and fencing to his right hid most of the view of the beach and the resort cottages, but he caught glimpses in the various gaps as he continued forward. Once he spotted the corner of the fence, he confirmed on the map that he was passing the southern end of the resort. He took the next right turn and parked, then emerged from the car at a small bluff viewpoint. In front of him, the Lake Tanganika stretched out as if it were the ocean. To his left, the coastline was mostly empty, just an expanse of green dotted with a few brown settlements. Beyond the road behind him, another cliff face overlooked the resort where Kasem had taken position to maintain surveillance on the main stretch of the Blue Bay resort. That vantage point, however, did not capture the very southern end, so they had had to find a work around—hence Carlos' current position.

He walked to the edge of the bluff and glanced to his right, the cliff descended directly into a cove, with one of the resort cottages about one hundred yards in. Taking it all in, he had to admit that he would prefer approaching Nziza here rather than at the Club du Lac. From a practical standpoint, this location was more secluded, and it would be easier to use darkness to their advantage on a water approach. More importantly though, he found himself compelled to spend as much time in this spot as possible—most locations and views of the lake that he had seen in and around Buja were nothing short of spectacular, but this one blew them all out of the water.

What he would give to watch the sunset out here with his wife Diane in his arms. Things between them had been fine on the surface, but the tension underneath was building. So far, he had told her little as to why he had abandoned her in Munich, just that something urgent had come up. They had always prided themselves on a "no secrets" policy within their marriage; she knew all about his recent operations in New York and Madagascar. This time though he found himself at a loss, he didn't know how to tell her what had forced him to come to Burundi. All he had said was that he had crossed a line several years ago, and that the Agency was using it against him. He hadn't even said anything about Petra or Kasem.

Or the Ahriman, the biggest secret he had ever stumbled upon. One that he had struggled to speak aloud, one that had prevented him from making more than short phone calls to his wife. He drew in a long breath and reached for his phone, something about the expanse in front of him emboldened him.

A hazy picture of her face appeared on his screen. "Carlos, hi," she said with a smile. "I was wondering if you would call today."

"I'm sorry I've been so out of touch."

Her expression tightened, then returned to normal. "I know you're doing it for the right reasons, and that you'll tell me when you're ready."

"I can't tell you everything, at least not yet, but there's something I had to do." He glanced at the ground before returning his gaze to the phone, "I found out something,

something about Petra's boyfriend, something terrible that he did."

"What? What did he do?"

"I'd rather not get into it…"

"Okay," she nodded. "Does Petra know? Have you talked to her about it?"

"She knows, or at least I think she does, but she says there's more to the story."

Diane frowned, "So you haven't talked to her about it?"

"Not really." Carlos sighed, this is what he had known would happen, that his wife would want to give Petra the benefit of the doubt.

"Don't you think that's a little closed-minded?"

"You don't understand—how can she know and still be with him?"

"Why not? You've all done terrible things, haven't you? In service of the greater good? You said yourself that's what this time was about, how the—" she stopped, knowing better than to mention the Agency by name over a standard phone line. "How they were using that against you. Besides, didn't he help you out last year?"

"It's not the same."

"Of course, it's not, silly," she broke into a grin. "But you and Petra have been friends for I don't even know how many years. You've always said that she's like your little sister. Doesn't that buy her the chance to tell you the whole story?"

"Maybe."

"This isn't about what Kasem did or didn't do, or even what Petra's done. You're hurt because she didn't tell you herself, because she didn't trust you with this."

"Don't be absurd—I just can't support her marrying someone with that kind of a past."

Diane ignored his protest and spoke in a soft all-knowing voice. "I bet she's hurt too, you know, that you can't trust her enough to know the difference between someone who's truly bad and someone who has done bad things. I imagine someone who hasn't done anything bad is hard to find in your line of work."

He shot her a glare, her words resonated more than he cared to admit. She was probably right, but he still wasn't ready to deal with it. He wasn't ready to hear Petra out, not yet at least.

"Just think about it," she continued quietly.

"All right, I will." He tapped onscreen to rotate the camera to display the view of the lake, edged by the greenery to his left. "Have a look at this view, isn't it amazing?"

They stuck to small talk for a few more minutes, then Carlos hung up, the echo of Diane's words running through his mind. He mulled them over as he set up a small tent near the edge of the bluff, out of sight of the road. Thankfully, there were enough makeshift settlements for an odd tent not to attract much attention, as long as it wasn't obvious that the tent was from a fancy American camping store. Rather than risk being spotted if they made the drive the city regularly, Carlos had volunteered to spend a few days out here alone to surveil the property at Blue Bay and plan out their approach. When he was done setting up, he stood back and took it in, the tent framed by the blue of the lake.

The campsite was one of the most beautiful he had ever seen. The colors in every direction were spectacular, and the cliff face was so dramatic. He rolled out his sleeping pad and stretched out on his belly, grabbing his binoculars. He swept them over the lake to begin with, then redirected toward the Blue Bay resort.

Could be worse. He'd certainly never had such a glamorous surveillance post before. He opened his cooler and hovered his head over the ice. Despite the stunning location, it would be a hot campsite during the day. Shrugging it off, he took a large bite out of a sandwich he had picked up that morning from Café Gourmand. The bread had gotten a little soggy, but it still tasted decent. He munched on it, continuing to ponder what Diane had said while keeping an eye on the Blue Bay property. At the very least, the alone time would do him good, one of the reasons he had volunteered. He needed space and distance to process everything that had occurred over the last few weeks.

******

Chapter 40

Bujumbura, Burundi

Kasem entered the warehouse, ignoring the sound of sobbing children that reverberated in the air. They were locked within a large storage unit with mesh walls to his right, but he kept his gaze fixed ahead, moving to the third unit on the opposite side of the building. A child's hand reached out and tugged at his sleeve, "Will you let us out? My sister needs to go to the bathroom," a high-pitched voice said in Farsi.

He brushed the child off brusquely, but a few steps on, he shuddered. What was he doing here? A moment later, he squelched the sentiment. He had agreed to General Majed's demands for a reason, Lila's life hung in the balance. Nothing, and no one else mattered. He had a job to do.

When he reached the cell on the other side of the warehouse, he turned to face Commander Derderian. The normally formidable man looked like a shadow of himself, his eyes sunken and his face gaunt. "Please, let my family go, they've done nothing. Whatever you want, I will give it to you, just please—my family."

Kasem felt his throat constrict, but his earlier sentiment remained top of mind: he was here on orders, orders that he would follow no matter what. "Come with me," he said in a gruff voice, unlocking the storage unit. Derderian's wrists were secured together, but regardless, he wouldn't try to escape, not with his family being held hostage.

Something we have in common, *Kasem couldn't help but think. He grabbed Derderian's arm and led him outside without another word.*

The first signs of dawn were visible when they stepped out of the warehouse, tendrils of light appearing against the sky, which turned a lighter shade of gray from when Kasem had gone inside. He shoved Derderian onto his knees on the parking lot, tuning out the stream of pleas that continued to emerge from Derderian's mouth.

They waited a couple of minutes before an SUV approached and General Majed emerged from the backseat. "Derderian, you scum," *he cursed.* "You thought you could get the better of me, but here we are, the tables have turned."

A note of boldness appeared on Derderian's face, then vanished. "You have my family, you know I'll do as you wish," *he said in a resigned voice.* "Let them go, and I'll stop the investigation. You can go on with whatever you're planning, I won't get in the way. Please."

"Well, that's the catch isn't it, you think you figured it out, right? Do you know what I'm planning?"

Derderian looked up at the General, "You planned the attack at Suez. And when the fallout comes, you're going to position yourself to take over the government."

"Quite a conspiracy theory, isn't it?" *General Majed snickered, looking at the troops that were clustered behind him.* "You think anyone would believe you?"

"I have proof, but I'll hand it over. Just let my family go free." *Derderian's voice had leveled now, he was no longer begging, he was negotiating.*

"Perhaps we will, but the price is your life. Are you willing to pay it?"

Derderian's face turned ashen, but he straightened up and looked General Majed in the eyes. "If that is your price, then yes, I will pay."

"Good." The General nodded at one of the men standing beside him, who approached Kasem holding an old Nokia cell phone.

"The code is one, two, three, four, five," the man said.

Kasem took the phone and a lump formed in his throat, he had an inkling of what the code meant, what it had to be. I can't do it, *he said to himself,* I can't.

The General's eyes narrowed as he glared at Kasem, "You heard him, enter the code."

Kasem thought about protesting. He wanted to say something, he had to. He scanned the scene, his gaze moving from General Majed to the soldiers to Derderian, and finally, to the warehouse. There was only one reason to enter such a code. He looked back at Derderian as understanding dawned on him as well.

"No, please," Derderian cried out. "Please, they've done nothing to you. I'll hand over everything."

"Even if you die, do you think I can let your insubordination go unpunished? Even now, when you just tried to negotiate with me, you piece of Armenian filth," General Majed retorted. He turned toward Kasem, "Now do it. Enter the code."

Kasem's thumb hovered over the one button, the battle inside him raging. Lila's life or the family inside the warehouse? What choice did he have?

"Remember what you have to lose," the General added in a cold voice.

Biting his lip, Kasem pressed the first key, then the second, then the third, squeezing his eyes shut along the way. He heard the explosion before he could open them, three loud clangs, followed by a massive bang and the heat that filled the air as the warehouse burst into flames. Only then did he open his eyes to stare at the destruction he had just wrought. What had he become?

******

Kasem bolted upright, panting, his face bathed in sweat. He looked around frantically, where was he and what had just happened? As his breathing slowed, a tremor shot down his legs, then ran back up through his torso. The room was dark, and he didn't recognize it. Hadn't he just been outside of the warehouse?

Within a few seconds, his recall returned—he was at the team house in Burundi, he had already lived, and survived, the warped memory from the dream. *That wasn't how it happened,* he realized slowly, but the dream's depiction had been close enough. He had indeed followed the order to blow up the warehouse, to send that entire family to their deaths. His stomach did a flip and he stumbled out of bed, barely making it to the bathroom to retch over the toilet. He heaved several times, then splashed water on his face and crawled his way back to bed. After a couple sips of water, the nausea started to abate.

He dabbed his forehead with a tissue and listened for any sound. The nights in Burundi tended to be extremely quiet since the house was far out of the party area in the center of town. At the moment, it was even quieter than normal. The house was unusually empty with Carlos still at his campsite and Petra and Veronica spending a few days at the Club du Lac to do surveillance. Someone had had to stay behind to watch Kevin, and Kasem had volunteered—he had the least associated baggage. While Petra still seemed to think he could be objective about Kevin, Kasem had his doubts. That said, he would probably be more objective than anyone else on the team, although that wasn't saying much. Not with this team, anyway.

He also had to admit to some continued curiosity, Kevin's actions intrigued him, and he even felt a degree of empathy for him, not that he would ever admit it out loud.

Kasem glanced at the clock at his bedside, then decided to give up on sleep, as it was nearly six. He returned to the bathroom and after a long hot shower felt moderately human once again, then went to the storeroom to check on Kevin. Since he hadn't tried to escape, they had unlocked the entrance to the old servant's bathroom, allowing him to use those facilities as needed. *Way better than having to keep watch while he did his business,* Kasem thought with a grimace.

"Morning," Kevin said as Kasem opened the door.

"Morning." After a few seconds of silence, Kasem added, "I'm going to make some coffee."

Instead of grunting as he normally did, Kevin said, "Any chance I could get in on that?"

Kasem frowned, then shrugged, "Sure, why not?" He shut the door and walked the few paces into the kitchen where he went about making coffee. The awkwardness between him and Kevin didn't faze him, this had become something of a routine for them in the last few days, now that it was just the two of them at the house. It was, however, the first time Kevin had responded to him since their conversation a week earlier about why he wanted to help the Burundais government. Kasem had only been able to process that conversation in pieces, but he had to admit that with each day that he spent in Buja, he understood the sentiment more. There was something about the place that drew you in, that made you fall in love with it despite the problems. Perhaps even because of them.

Kasem put the percolator on the stove and waited for the water to heat up. Despite a modicum of boredom, he was mostly enjoying the quiet since he'd been left alone at the house. He'd gone out on errands, and to do short rounds of surveillance, but he had mostly stayed home, studying various maps of the city and surrounding areas.

The most excitement he had had in the three days since Petra and Veronica had left for the Club du Lac was Gaston coming over with a bottle of gin the afternoon before. While Kevin had remained in the storeroom, Gaston and Kasem had sat out in the garden drinking gin and tonics for the better part of two hours as they watched the sunset. The bonding experience had been both enjoyable and useful on several counts—in addition to helping with the operation, Gaston had been able to help Kasem with a few personal favors, ones that he hoped he wouldn't need, but were necessary safeguards given the current circumstances. Now that he had some insurance in place if everything went to hell, Kasem found himself more relaxed. *At least in the daytime,* he sighed, staring at the percolator. The water inside was just starting to bubble, so he turned off the heat and poured the contents into two small cups.

Cups in hand, Kasem returned to the storeroom where he handed one of them over. "It's black, I didn't know how you take it," he said as he backed up to stand a few feet away. Kevin had been more or less compliant, and had shown no desire to escape, but he wasn't going to take any chances.

"That's fine." Kevin held the cup and took a long sip, "Burundi coffee is the best, I don't think I've had better anywhere in the world."

"It is excellent." Kasem nodded, grateful that Kevin had taken it upon himself to initiate some sort of conversation.

"Where'd you get the beans from? Café Gourmand? Or the supermarket?"

"Café Buja, actually."

"Good choice," Kevin said, "I'm impressed, most people don't discover the coffee there on their first trip."

"I guess."

"How's it going with the surveillance?" Kevin asked. "I'd wager that's why you're here by yourself."

Kasem raised his eyebrows, but there wasn't much point in trying to deceive Kevin when it came to preparing for the op. "I'm here often enough," Kasem replied instead.

"Don't worry, I have no plans to escape. If I'd wanted to evade you, I wouldn't have approached you at Arena."

"Right."

"Have you thought about what I said the other day? About Burundi, and why I want to help the people here?"

"I have," Kasem kept his response short, not wanting to give away how much time he had indeed spent thinking about that conversation. *And not just what it means for the op and Burundi.* He'd also considered what he would have done if faced with the same circumstances.

"You understand, don't you? Why we have to do this? Why you can't let this government fall?"

"Maybe."

"Come on, you have to get it. The people here, they don't deserve what's about to happen."

Kasem frowned, feeling a thread of irritation. "Of course, they don't. The question is about you, whether we can trust what you've told us." He quickly added, "Besides, you already know we're looking into it."

"Yes, but the Agency won't stand with you—"

"What are you talking about?" Kasem interrupted, an alarm bell going off in his head. How did Kevin know that Chris hadn't authorized the op?

"It doesn't take a rocket scientist—if the Agency had authorized this, you'd have way more people here, maybe you would have already alerted the government, moved Markov to a

158

safe house. I don't know how it would be, not exactly anyway, but I know you keeping watch on me by yourself isn't it."

"Fair."

"Besides you're not exactly a stranger to people not trusting you."

Kasem only barely tempered his reaction. "What are you talking about?"

"I mean, you were Iranian intelligence. Before starting with the Agency and getting swept away by Madame Paris?"

"Oh, yeah," Kasem's shoulders relaxed, Kevin hadn't picked up on the investigation into his past as the Ahriman, just that he had been with Iranian intel.

"I bet the Agency was super trusting of that, even if they needed your help in New York, and who knows how many other times."

"I guess." Kasem's guard went up, was Kevin fishing for more information? How much did he already know?

"I guess? Come on, they didn't just welcome you into the organization, it's not like you turned yourself in. They trusted you because they had to, the same reason you're trusting me now."

"I wouldn't call it trust."

"Fine, but you're looking into what I told you because the stakes are too high not to."

"True, but what are you getting at?" Kasem frowned, trying to figure out how they had ended up on this line of discussion.

"My point is that everyone deserves a second shot. You got yours, and I want mine. I want my chance at redemption, same as you had."

"Our situation isn't the same."

"Of course, it's not, but it's similar enough."

"I still don't understand what you're getting at." Kasem ran through Kevin's possible intentions, but came up blank.

"I want you to tell Veronica that I've changed."

Stifling a guffaw, Kasem gave him a slow nod. "I hate to break it to you, buddy, but fat lot of good that would do you. I'm not exactly in her good books."

"Really?" Kevin looked surprised, "I knew she and Petra were having some issues, but I didn't realize it extended to you too."

"There's a whole truck load of baggage there." Kasem wondered if he'd said too much, if this conversation was going to bite him in the ass later. "Anyway, I'd better get a move on my day. See you later."

"Later."

Kasem turned and headed back into the kitchen, processing the discussion that they'd just had. He had no doubt that Kevin's desire to get back into Veronica's good graces was genuine. Since their conversation a few days earlier, he'd felt more solid about the direction the operation had taken, that there was a legitimate need for them to intervene to stop the military coup. He'd remained skeptical as to the full extent of Kevin's motivations, after all, it couldn't be entirely about his love of the country or the people here. The mission was legit, but perhaps Kevin was planning to use it to get the Agency's protection from the FSB. Bad as the Agency was, they weren't the FSB… Now he wasn't so sure, he had started to experience some of the Burundais spirit that Kevin had alluded to. The night before on the patio with Gaston had been particularly special, with Gaston telling stories about the people he had encountered since moving to Buja ten years earlier.

As he continued to ponder the situation, Kasem stepped out into the backyard, breathing in, and savoring, the scent of the flowers and trees. Sunlight bathed the ground, with the different shades of green shimmering in the light. The heat had yet to pick up, so the garden was particularly pleasant.

He thought I was already redeemed, Kasem ran through Kevin's words in contrast with his dream. He'd been responsible for so many deaths, Commander Derderian and the lives of his family among them, but he had done a lot of good since then. *That's what Petra would say, anyway.* Was Kevin right? Did he deserve another chance like the one that Kasem had had? They both had blood on their hands, they had both betrayed people they loved. Kevin had done it for his asset, while he'd done it for Petra. Was there any difference?

He shut his eyes, enjoying the warmth without the intensity that would come later in the day. The sensation took him back to a garden party he had attended in Tehran, one that his boss had hosted so many years earlier. He could feel it, he could see how Kevin might have fallen in love with such a place, with the spirit that he had spoken of. Kasem opened his eyes, in his bones, he knew that at least that part of Kevin's story was true. There was more to it though, that much he was sure of, more that Kevin hadn't revealed. Whatever it was, he still had to find out.

* * * * * *

Chapter 41

Bujumbura, Burundi

Kevin had dozing off on his cot when the storeroom door swung open again, a stream of bright light landing on his face. He grunted and sat up, looking over at Kasem who was standing there, holding two bottles of water. "Is it tomorrow already?" Kevin asked. "Or did you get lonely in your room?"

Handing over the bottle of water, Kasem dragged the chair from the center of the room—where Kevin kept it because it allowed a tiny view of the sky and greenery through the small corner window. After positioning the chair next to the bed, Kasem plonked down and handed over one of the water bottles. "The day we talked, when you told me everything, there was something missing."

"I don't think so," Kevin frowned.

"There was—you told me how you got posted in Nairobi, how you spent time here, even fell in love with the place, the spirit. You told me about your asset. Then you told me about how you made your way back here, and how you had to get the Agency involved when you realized Nziza was involved."

"Exactly. You asked for the whole story, and I told you."

Kasem shook his head, "No, that's not it. You told me all about the op, what I want to know about is why. There's a hole in the story—you came back here for refuge, and then you ended up getting the Agency involved. Sure, I think you want to make up with Veronica, maybe you even think that's possible, but that isn't it."

"I already told you, I found out that they were plotting a coup. I had to do something, and it's not like I could just call up the FSB—they aren't a huge fan of mine at the moment, in case you missed that. So, I got myself leaked into Agency intel and you guys found your way here. Only took you long enough—"

"Yeah, whatever, you did such a good job at luring us in. That's not what you said before though. Kevin, you said that you found out Nziza was involved, then you figured out the MSS was helping put him back in power. Now tell me why— why does Nziza scare you so much? I saw the look on your face when you told the story before, first to the team, then with more detail to me. Both times you skipped that part." Kasem crossed his arms, "You know something about him."

Kevin looked up at the ceiling. Kasem was right, he had indeed stumbled upon the gap in his story—a piece of the puzzle he wished that he didn't remember.

"I looked at all your Agency files," Kasem said. "There's no mention of Burundi, is this part of why?"

The wave of guilt that washed over him made Kevin cringe. He didn't want to admit to this part of the story, it was far easier to pretend that it had never happened. He opened his mouth to answer, at this point, the longer he waited the more Kasem would figure out on his own. Despite his best efforts, he found himself unable to form the words, all he could see were the images of the memorial.

"Tell me what happened, Kevin."

"You have to understand, I didn't know what I was getting myself into, I was just trying to make a name for myself at the Agency—"

"Just tell me."

Kevin swallowed, then started at the beginning.

* * * * * *

Chapter 42

Bujumbura, Burundi

Kasem waited, urging himself not to pre-empt the story that Kevin was about to recount. An ominous cloud had drifted over him, but he ignored it. He had to listen and focus on what Kevin actually said, rather than making up his own version of what had occurred. Still, the weight in the pit of his stomach remained.

"When I was posted in Nairobi, I was assigned to cover Burundi as well, took over handling what they called a minor asset. You know who he is, Gilbert, now works with the electricity regulator. Anyway a few months in, we got intel that a former Burundais leader was trying to be recruited, that he would provide key intel in exchange for protection and some funds to return," Kevin said quietly.

"Go on."

"I didn't know much about him, and I didn't understand the history here, or in the region at all. I knew the basics, I guess, the Civil War in the 90s, how the conflict engulfed both Burundi and Rwanda, even though technically it wasn't considered genocide here."

Kasem nodded, he too had read the Agency's historical accounts, accounts which had probably sanitized most of the destruction and despair of the war. That was how the Agency would depict Iran's history, why would Burundi be any different?

"At that point, we didn't even know who the leader was, all we had through a contact was that it was somebody who was powerful before and during the war. I ran it up the flagpole—"

"This was before you got involved with the FSB?" Kasem asked.

"It was. Anyway, I ran the info I had up the flagpole and the Agency assigned me to investigate further. That's when I found out that the leader seeking sanctuary was Nziza. I did some reading on him, saw that he was definitely a bad guy, but I didn't really get it. I didn't put together how much of what happened here that he was responsible for."

"Did you ever meet with him?"

"Not directly, he always used an intermediary," Kevin shook his head. "I don't know where he was hiding at the time—I have my suspicions, but they're still unconfirmed."

"How many meetings did you have?"

"Three over about four or five months. Nziza wanted Agency money and there was a lot of negotiation involved. In the meantime, he slipped us intel on the government at the time. Burundi went into political crisis in 2015, and by a couple of years later when we were having these meetings, things were starting to stabilize, at least on the surface. Underneath, though, the reality was that the president had expelled most of his political opponents, they were hiding out in Rwanda or other parts of the region. That's what was going on in the background when I came here the first time, right before Petra and I finished training together."

What a bunch of sanctimonious hypocrites. Kasem felt his emotions starting to bubble—how could the Agency have considered getting in bed with that monster? How could this be the first time they were learning about that atrocity? He tamped the questions down, he had to hear the whole story before he exploded.

Kevin took a sip from his water and continued, "The Agency was still trying to decide what they were going to do, the ramifications of turning someone like Nziza and getting him back into power. They were worried about all the bad history around situations like that—the Americans with Mubarak in Egypt, the French with Ben Ali in Tunisia, all of the West with Ghaddafi." He paused, looking pointedly at Kasem, "The Shah of Iran."

"Right."

"So, they asked me to go to Kigali to investigate someone in the opposition party, one of the people Nziza was trying to sell out. As an aside, I think he'd sell out the whole lot, not just the opposition, any and all of the democratically elected officials if it meant he could get back into power."

"Of course." Kasem gave him a tight nod, still maintaining an iron hold over his emotions. The fact that the Agency had been involved in something like this, and so recently, made him want to be sick.

"I don't know what I expected from my trip to Rwanda." Kevin's voice grew hollow, "Everything was so orderly, so regimented, completely different from here. I did surveillance on my target for about a week, then the Agency told me to approach him. We set it up and had a couple of conversations, I was posing as a Western aid worker and tourist, someone who didn't know anything about the history of the region. Someone who would seem interested, but actually didn't care at all. It was an easy role to play, because that part was true, I didn't care, I just wanted to get the job done and make my name at the Agency. He must have been able to tell, I'm sure he'd encountered that type before. Until he took me to the Kigali Genocide Memorial…"

Kasem's posture shifted, noting the grief in Kevin's tone and demeanor. He'd heard that the Rwandans had set up several memorial sites to commemorate the genocide, and now that he thought about it, was surprised that the Burundais had not done so. Technically the conflict in Burundi wasn't considered a genocide, but regardless, 300 thousand people had died. "Keep going," he said softly.

"I don't know how much you know about the conflict here versus what happened in Rwanda."

"Just what I've read in the Agency briefs."

"I was the same way," Kevin said, "but the memorial, that changed everything. There were these walls with all the names, and all these bones—so many skulls." He shuddered, "The worst was the pictures of children who died. I remember this one plaque to commemorate a baby. *Theirry Ishimwe,* I'll never forget that name. Age, nine months, characteristics, a small and weak baby. Cause of death, machete in his mother's arms."

Finishing the water bottle, he gave Kasem a helpless look. Kasem handed over his own still sealed water bottle and waited, with a feeling of numbness.

After several gulps, Kevin spoke again, "Vincent, my contact in Rwanda, he was a former judge in the Burundais high court who fled during the 2015 conflict. He took me to a coffee shop afterward, and we sat there in silence for a while. Finally, I asked him why he'd taken me there, why he'd subjected me to that, especially when it wasn't even about the Burundais Civil War. That's when he explained—it's true that in Burundi it wasn't genocide. The Rwandan Civil War was four years, and at the end, a million people died in a hundred days, while the world looked away. In Burundi, the conflict lasted longer, protracted over a decade. The ethnic groups are the same, but in Burundi, the Tutsi were in power, and the Hutus were the rebels. And then it was just coups and slaughter. He said there wasn't a memorial in Burundi, but that there should be. The military, the rebels, they were all scum.

They broke into people's homes, threatened their families, children as young as seven. They called the militia *les Gardiens de la Paix*."

Kevin spat out the name in English, "The Guardians of Peace. Nziza was one of their lieutenants, he was the one who championed recruitment of children, said it would make sure that the kids were strong, that they had to be involved in the future of their country. After the war ended, he went on to become the head of the secret police, taking care of anyone who opposed the government until he fell out of favor because he didn't stop the coup attempt in 2015. When I left Kigali, I told the Agency we shouldn't touch him with a ten-foot pole, that he was a war criminal even if the international community never identified him as that. I went as far as saying that the Agency would do better by assassinating him, that if we wanted to recruit an asset, it should be Vincent."

"And then?"

"The Agency said they would stop working with Nziza, and then they reassigned me, had me focus on work in Kenya instead, just maintain occasional contact with Gilbert."

"What happened to Vincent?"

Kevin stared at the ground, "He tried to go back to Burundi a year later, wanted to get back to working with the opposition political party."

"Tried?"

"He made it across the border, and initially he seemed to be doing okay. But then, he died. Car accident near the capital in Gitega, at least that's the official story."

"I see." Kasem exhaled, they both knew that the secret police must have been involved with Vincent's death. "Did the Agency help Nziza after that?"

"I don't know."

******

Chapter 43

Bujumbura, Burundi

Petra stared at Kasem, grappling with what he had just told her. "I—I don't understand. That can't be true, how can that be true? The Agency tried to recruit Nziza? And Kevin was the lead operative until he bowed out?"

"I know, babe. I didn't want to believe it either."

"There has to be some way to vet this. We can't just take it at face value, this is Kevin we're talking about—"

"I already told you, there's no official Agency reports on the op. Everything was off book. The only thing I could check out was that Kevin was indeed in Kigali on the dates that he said."

"What about the museum?" Petra asked, "Could we verify that he actually went?"

"I don't know, they don't issue tickets by name, and he would probably have paid for his ticket in cash. There might be security footage, if we could get our hands on it."

"The exhibits he mentioned, could he have found out about them online?" she persisted.

"I suppose, with enough research. I was able to crosscheck the type of exhibits that exist with everything that he said. There might be pictures or videos on social media that have everything else."

"But you think he's telling the truth."

"I do."

She sat down on their bed, still struggling with everything he had recounted. "I guess it's just a lot," she said after several moments of silence. "You've had a few days to process this, since he told you, even to look into whether it could be true. This is the first time I'm hearing about it, even the first part. Why didn't you tell me about your earlier conversation with him?"

"You already said it, I needed time to process. I wanted to be sure before I told you that I—that I could empathize with his situation."

"You are nothing like him," she shook her head firmly. "You may have gone down a dark path for a while, but you turned it around. You've helped so many people, look at what you did for us in Mada last year. Or what you did in DC? We never would have stopped the FSB without you—"

"The Ahriman did much worse than Kevin ever did for the FSB."

"No!" Petra refused to acknowledge the truth of what he was saying. If the question was should they trust Kevin now, on this operation, she was inclined to believe that they didn't have a choice. Yet she refused to look at him as her old friend after his betrayal, after the breach of trust. "No," she repeated once again. "As soon as you realized that people you cared about were in the crossfire, you stopped it. You didn't go through with the op in Kuwait."

"True, but he left the FSB for Veronica. He could have killed any one of us in DC, but he didn't."

"He would have taken out half of downtown if the FSB's bomb had gone off."

"I know," Kasem said in a soft voice. "That's the part I don't have a gauge on, I don't know if I believe him when he says that he never intended the bomb to go off. If that's true, I don't know why he broke cover. The rest of it though, I think he's telling the truth. I think he was posted in Nairobi, that he worked here, and that he fell in love with this place. You should have heard him talking to me about it. There was so much heart in what he said—"

"It could have been an act."

"You're right, it could all be an act, but every time there's one more piece to add that becomes less likely. He told us about the coup attempt, he talked to me about how he ended up at the FSB."

She nodded, she needed more time to come to her own opinion, but Kasem's was clear enough.

"Petra, he loves this place, he couldn't have been making that up. Or the stuff about the memorial. Those were real emotions, on his face, in his voice. Al Pacino couldn't have pulled it off."

"But maybe Ryan Gosling." She gave him a small smile, he had taken it very personally months ago when one of her girlfriends at a dinner in Paris had mentioned how hot Gosling was and she'd agreed.

"Besides, don't you see what he means? The spirit that Kevin was talking about here, that vibrancy in the people. I've seen it," Kasem continued.

"Have you fallen in love with Burundi too?"

"I don't know," he chuckled. "But I do think it's special."

"It is."

"That's enough from me, how was it at the lake? Anything you want to talk about?"

"It was fine, nothing as emotional as back here apparently. I'll save it for the team debrief when Carlos gets back tomorrow."

He shifted his back toward the headboard, and she leaned over to rest her head on his shoulder. "I missed you," she gave him a long soft kiss.

"I thought you were tired."
She pulled him in closer, "Tired, but not *too* tired."

* * * * * *

Chapter 44

Bujumbura, Burundi

Carlos waited while Petra finished debriefing the group on the intel that she and Veronica had gathered after spending a long weekend at the Club du Lac resort where Nziza had spent much of the last few months. He had provided his update on the Blue Bay resort earlier that morning, and from an operational standpoint was content. They had gathered far more reasonable intelligence than he would have expected, especially given how much they had to rely on Gaston for any and all local knowledge. *Still better than Kevin,* he thought with a shrug.

"The best approach for Blue Bay is by boat over the water at night, but for Club du Lac it's out in the open, at the swimming pool?" Gaston asked as Petra stopped speaking.

"Exactly," she agreed. Her eyes drifted toward Kasem before returning to Gaston, "I would join him at the pool, wait until he approaches me, and get him to invite me back to his room. That's where we would make our move—"

"You're certain you are his type?" Gaston interrupted.

"I'm sure," Petra said with what looked like a slightly annoyed smile.

Carlos changed the subject, "You said that you saw him, did you approach?"

"No, just a quick glance, but I can definitely catch his eye again."

"Good," Carlos agreed. "We have two reasonable approach strategies depending on where we have to take action, now we just have to figure out which one to bet on. Any idea how long he's staying at Club du Lac this time?"

"I asked around at the hotel—the staff think he's some big shot businessman from Kenya—pretty cliché if you ask me," Veronica answered. "The concierge said the security detail would probably be around for a whole week this time."

Carlos considered this point in conjunction with the surveillance at Blue Bay. He had witnessed what looked like a few training exercises for the ten men who appeared to be living there. Nothing that would attract too much attention, wind sprints and other types of runs up and down the beach, use of one of the cottages as a staging ground of some type. "If the concierge said they would be there a week, and the MSS is using Blue Bay for training right now, our best window is probably Club du Lac. What do you think, Petra? Could we get this set up before he leaves?"

She ran her fingers through her hair, "It's Sunday, so an approach during the work week would probably be better. Less tourists on the beach to have to get around for the approach. The problem is whether we can be ready on the other side. If he takes me back to his room, he'll dismiss his entourage for some privacy, but then what? We still have to access the room without alerting any of the perimeter guards and get him out and to the safe house." She turned to Gaston, "Can your contact at the club have him moved to a different room? One that we set up?"

"I think so, but it will be tight. We have to make sure no one will get suspicious."

"We could arrange for a leak from the room upstairs, or I guess from the roof since he's in the presidential suite," Kasem suggested. "I doubt Nziza would have any objection to changing rooms under those circumstances." He tapped on Petra's tablet to project a three-dimensional map of the hotel over the coffee table, "The presidential suite is here, and they have this side of the top floor. On the other side is the royal suite, where they could move him while they repair the leak."

"Good idea," Carlos nodded, "that could work. Even better though, let's take his room out of commission, do the meet while his stuff is being moved."

"You mean invite him to my room instead?" Petra returned his nod. "You're right, he wouldn't be able to have his entourage if I tell him it makes me uncomfortable."

"Exactly," Carlos agreed. "Let's initiate tomorrow—get access to the roof in the morning."

Gaston looked flustered, "But for the hotel to move him, you cannot just make it look like a leak. The leak has to be real, how do we make sure it's isolated to the one room."

"Also, a good point," Petra said. "Why can't we just be part of the repair crew? We'll still need access to the royal suite for staging, and we have to make the leak look real. Can your contact sell it? Comp a generous meal or something while the repairs are underway? It's good timing for me too—he'll basically be prisoner on the beach, and I can strike up a conversation."

For a moment, Gaston appeared deep in thought, but then he flashed a wide smile, "Okay, chérie, on y va. Let's do it."

* * * * * *

Chapter 45

Bujumbura, Burundi

Carlos grinned at the image of Chris, once again projected upward from Veronica's tablet on the coffee table. "Now that Kevin's escaped and is hiding out at Club du Lac Resort, it's imperative that we go get him," he concluded. He had no doubt Chris knew what was really going on—Kevin was safely in the next room, but they had devised a strategy to circumvent the Agency's orders—and thankfully, Chris had decided to go along with it anyway.

"I take full responsibility for what happened," Veronica added, "but we can get him back before anyone's the wiser."

"I'll get you some backup, give me a minute," Chris nodded.

Give us some rope, and we'll hang ourselves, Carlos repressed a grimace. He looked around the room, his gaze stopping on Kasem for a moment before he turned his head. The pit of his stomach was heavy, and he felt an urge to reach for a cigarette, to inhale the intoxicating poison despite having kicked the habit years earlier. When Veronica had first told him about Kasem, he was furious—furious that Petra had kept something so tremendous from him, furious that she could be with such a monster. After the time they'd spent together in Burundi, he was no longer so sure of how he felt. He and Petra had barely said two words to each other outside of operation planning, and he'd mostly given Kasem the cold shoulder. While Petra was clearly angry, Carlos couldn't help but notice that Kasem had handled the situation with grace. Instead of confronting anyone on the team, Kasem had showed up and done his part without complaining. Carlos focused on the projection once again, but Chris had yet to return. Maybe Petra was right, perhaps there was more to the story, more to Kasem. He sighed, recalling that she had never denied that he was the Ahriman. But there still had to be more—why else would she want to marry him?

"All right, I got you some discretionary funds. Veronica, get in touch with Gaston to get outfitted with whatever you need. For everything else, Carlos, you're in charge." Chris paused, "Be careful—there's a lot you don't know about Burundi."

Carlos stifled a laugh at the confirmation that Chris knew exactly what was going on. He just couldn't officially authorize the team to use Kevin as an asset. *Stupid bureaucracy.* "Thanks, Chris," he answered. "We'll be in touch."

"I'll be away from the office, so use my personal line. I'll make sure it's secure." Chris paused for a second, "And Carlos, whatever you do, don't give him a gun."

"Will do," Carlos grinned and disconnected. He and Chris were definitely on the same page when it came to trusting Kevin.

Back down the rabbit hole—away we go.

* * * * * *

Chapter 46

Bujumbura, Burundi

Petra fidgeted as she looked around the room. An unofficial spy tradition was to let loose a little the night before a major operation. Under normal circumstances, this was a tradition that she had no objection to, in fact, she might even have enjoyed it. In this crowd though, she felt as if she couldn't let her guard down, not even a little bit.

Gaston had initially suggested that they all go for a night on the town—Buja did, of course, offer vibrant night life, but she'd politely declined. They had already filled the required quota of parties for a team of expats visiting the country for the first time, and she wanted to get some rest. She'd hoped that he and the rest of the team would go, leaving her and Kasem behind. Instead, Carlos had completely flip-flopped, pushing the group to have their own party at the house. Gaston had been the only one to object, but finally conceded.

Shortly after they'd reached an agreement, Gaston had disappeared, returning just a few moments earlier, hands laden with an assortment of food and drink. An Auchentoshan-12 single malt, a Bombay Sapphire gin, and a Nero D'Avola red wine, along with several different mixers and a giant bag of cheese and charcuterie.

"What can I serve you?" Gaston asked brightly. "I brought these from my personal collection. It's not easy to find all of this here in Burundi."

"Thanks, buddy," Carlos shook his hand vigorously. "We can all help ourselves to food, but why don't you get us started on the drinks. I'll have some of that whiskey. Kasem, you too, right?"

"Er, yeah, sure."

Petra watched in silence as Gaston handed over generous pours of the Auchentoshen to both of them. Veronica requested a glass of the gin, and then he finally turned to her. "What about you, chérie? Will you join us with some whiskey?"

"I'm all right, actually. I'll stick to water."

"Come now, that's no way to enjoy the evening. Tell me, what would you like? I can see if we can get something else for you." Gaston gave her an imploring look. "S'il te plait, chérie."

"D'accord," she agreed with a small smile. He was the only one on the team besides Kasem that she felt comfortable with. His demeanor had no pretenses, and no baggage. "I'll have some of the wine, but I must say—Italian wine? Where is your French pride?"

"I have no problem saying that Italians know how to drink wine. Nero D'Avola is excellent."

"But you must be holding out on us, then. You said this is from your private collection? You can't tell me you don't have any French wine there," she teased.

"I know," he said, shaking his head in horror. "I ran out of my collection last month. I have to fix it when I go home in a few weeks. I will open a bottle of specialty Bourgogne for you then, from a vineyard near my home. You will have some?"

Petra chuckled, "Of course." It wasn't as if she could refuse Pepé Le Pew or Idris Elba.

Gaston handed her a glass and looked out at the room, raising his glass as if he was about to make a toast. He stopped with a frown, "We are missing someone. I don't know exactly what your history is, but you can put him back in the storeroom after. The whole team has to be here to toast. It's bad luck otherwise."

Before anyone else could respond, Veronica stood up. "No, Gaston. I understand where you're coming from, and tomorrow, he'll move around with us like a full part of the team, but you're right. You don't know the history. I will not have him moving freely around this house."

"Very well," Gaston looked taken aback but nodded. "I wanted to thank all of you for welcoming me into your team. I know there has been tension in this room, but where there is history, there will always be tension. I know any one of you would stand up for the other if the time came. I am proud to count myself among you. Donc, à votre santé. Tomorrow, we will stop a dictator."

Petra clinked glasses with the rest of the team one by one. When she met Carlos' gaze, Gaston's words sunk in further. There was indeed tension. The words resonated even more when she touched her glass to Veronica's.

Maintaining a fake smile, Petra settled back onto the couch to sip the wine. He was right that they would come through for each other if the need arose, or at least, she believed that they would. Still, she had to hope nothing would test that belief. There were far too many agendas in the room for her liking.

* * * * * *

After finishing her glass, Petra retreated to the garden, saying that she wanted to get some air. She poured herself a refill and exchanged a glance with Kasem. She could tell that he was wondering if she wanted him to join her, but she shook her head. He seemed far more relaxed, and one of them might as well enjoy the party.

182

If you could call it that.

She stretched out on the bench in the garden and looked up at the sky, the expanse of stars stretching out above her. The stars in Burundi still took her breath away. The last time she'd seen a night sky like that was on a family vacation when she was twelve, in Wadi Rum in the Jordanian desert. The temperature had cooled, and she welcomed the slight briskness in the air, quite the contrast to the warm days.

Petra heard the patio door open behind her and turned to see Gaston standing a few feet away. "May I join you?" he asked in French.

"Bien sur." She pivoted her feet to make room for him on the other side of the bench.

"Have you enjoyed your time here?"

"A little," she said with a shrug.

"I don't mean with the team, I mean here, in Burundi. I hope you've been able to enjoy it a little bit. It's a beautiful place."

"It is."

"Come now, you must feel it more than that, if you're out here, looking at the stars."

"I do." She sighed and nodded, "It's just complicated, but you're right. It's a wonderful place."

"Take comfort in that. However complicated it is, we are doing the right thing. The people here deserve more than what has happened to them. Than what governments like mine have done to them."

"They do, I know."

"My family, originally, is from Togo, but I was raised in France. Buja is home now, just as much as Dijon though. In Togo, too, we have a troubled history, but things are changing now. Things are getting better. Here too, but not if we don't stop Nziza. It's time the West stood for the values that we

183

preach, time we weren't the cause of the problem. Take comfort in that."

"I will."

"Tchin-tchin," he said as he clinked her glass once again. "I'm going to head home, but I'll see you tomorrow. Good night, chérie."

"Good night."

Petra inhaled deeply, once again alone with the night sky. She would indeed take comfort in their actions here. Despite what had brought her and Kasem here, along with her discomfort with the team and the limited time and preparation for the op, they had made the best of a bad situation. They couldn't let Burundi's government collapse. They couldn't let a war criminal take power. The Agency had done many questionable things, but this op was a good mission. She didn't believe in the greater good above all else, but she'd never been able to shy away when it confronted her like this.

Not when she could do something about it.

After tomorrow, there would be no more missions for her and Kasem, but now, in this moment, they had to do what was right. They had to stop Nziza.

That has to still be who we are.

* * * * * *

Chapter 47

New York, United States

Chris kept his gaze straight ahead, hoping not to give away his disbelief. *I must be dreaming.* He considered pinching himself to wake up, but he knew that the situation was very much real. He steadied his voice and requested clarification, "I'm not sure I follow, Sir. What exactly would you like my team to do?"

Edward Simmons looked at him with raised eyebrows, "I believe I've made myself quite clear. We'd like your team to intervene, to stop the coup attempt."

That hadn't been all Edward had said, and they both knew it. Chris contemplated his reply, despite the urge to utter a stream of expletives. Had Edward authorized this before, he could have sent the team in with backup, with resources.

Before Chris could speak up, Edward continued, "For the president's safety, they can take him into protective custody. Once they've neutralized the Chinese threat and the M.S.S. personnel are out of the picture, it should be fairly easy for them to persuade the president to award the power deal to Solaire Plus, the French-American joint venture."

"But sir, all of our intel indicates that the best deal for the Burundais people is the third bidder—the Indian JV. Have the terms changed?"

I'm going to make you say it. If Edward wanted his team to engage in corporate espionage, he was going to have to be explicit. *It's a bloody corporate coup.*

"Of course not, I just want your team to explain to President Markov that it's in his best interest to award the deal to the Americans."

"This could get the Agency in a lot of trouble if it ever got out," Chris said quietly. He'd seen this movie before, what Edward was talking about meant a puppet government set up by Western intelligence. He recalled the file on Nziza that he'd pulled after Kasem reported the sighting and suppressed a shudder. Even the sanitized version the Agency had left little to the imagination. Yet, if the Chinese were to succeed, the alternative was even worse.

"So, make sure it doesn't get out—we're not executing regime change, we're simply ensuring that the president makes a decision in his country's best interest. It's really quite simple."

"But, Sir, they don't have the manpower to stop a coup— we'd need a full military unit for that to work."

"Oh, don't be so dramatic. You'll figure out a way—you always have before. We can't authorize that kind of backup without a full Agency intervention, and we simply can't allow that in this case."

Chris had never found Edward's posh British accent to be quite as patronizing as at that moment, but he managed to hold his tongue.

A corporate coup, with no backup. Just dandy. "I understand, Sir. I'll inform them shortly, make sure the team understands your orders before they move on the resort."

"Good, but I'd prefer you didn't call them, this kind of news is always better explained in person. You never know how they might react, especially right before the start of an operation. Join them—you said they're moving at nightfall, correct? You won't get there in time, but I can have you on my private plane, so you arrive tomorrow morning. Once they have Nziza in custody, you can tell the president yourself." Edward rubbed his chin. "We have to make sure that it all goes swimmingly, after all. I'm sure the team could use your support."

* * * * * *

Chapter 48

Bujumbura, Burundi

Petra applied a layer of lip gloss and surveyed her reflection. She looked the part, back in the light disguise she'd put together a week earlier—as much as she could hope to, anyway. A pair of blue contact lenses and wig of auburn hair had altered her appearance enough that she felt like the character she would be playing. The brilliant red bikini framed her curves well, and with the limited Wednesday afternoon rush at the beach, she stood a good chance of attracting Nziza's attention. She removed a hair tie and brushed out the wig, letting it fall onto her shoulders in a series of soft waves.

Her stomach did an involuntary flip and she sighed, sitting down at the head of the bed. She pulled her feet up and turned on the TV and scanned a few channels before settling on a mindless French soap opera. The characters droned on in the background as she waited for confirmation from the rest of the team.

She and Veronica had arrived at the hotel the evening before, just two local tourists returning for more time at the beach. The night had been restless and neither of them had been able to sleep much. At around four that morning, Gaston's friend in the concierge office at Club du Lac, Boulel, had taken him and Carlos to the rooftop above the presidential suite. Meanwhile Kasem spent two hours depositing bugs and cameras all around the royal suite. Rather than watch Kevin during that time, she and Veronica had been stuck on guard duty until the suite was ready and Kasem could take over once again.

For the first time in the last day, Petra was alone. Veronica, Kasem and Kevin were on the beach now, waiting for the rest of the plan to unfold. If they had timed it right, the device that Carlos had rigged into the pipes above the presidential suite had already been dripping for the last hour, since around eleven in the morning. The water would leak through the food coloring in the device, turning it an ugly grayish brown, and then seep through the ceiling of the presidential suite. As soon as the drip was visible, she had no doubt that Nziza's staff would call it in and he would be promptly moved to the royal suite. Or rather his staff would move his affairs while he went to the beach for a complimentary cocktail and lunch. All Petra had to do in the meanwhile was wait for Gaston's confirmation that Nziza was at the beach before attempting to join him.

She stared at the television, watching the melodramatic quarrel between two lovers before they ended up in each other's arms to reconcile. What she would give for some true alone time with Kasem, their moments together had been marred by operational planning and debriefing, and discussions on the op, not to mention what they would do if things went south. She shoved the thoughts aside, there was no place for doubts in this stage of the op. They had grappled with whether to trust Kevin, whether what he had told Kasem about the Agency and Nziza could possibly be true, but none of it belonged with her at this moment. Not if today's part of the op was going to go to plan.

Despite her best efforts, she could not quiet the slight pressure in her chest, the weight at the pit of her stomach. It was just nerves, a thread of anxiety at the start of an operation, completely normal, or so she told herself. Still, something felt off, as if the whole thing was about to go completely sideways.

Petra took several deep breaths in a short meditation, then stopped when she heard her phone vibrate on the bedside table.

She checked it and did a doubletake; for a second, she thought that she had to be dreaming, until she read the message again. According to the brief text, Chris was on his way to Burundi. The real question was why. Perhaps he had managed to get some traction with the higher-ups at the Agency? Regardless, he clearly had no intention of explaining until he arrived. The situation struck her as extremely odd—even if the Agency wanted him to liaise directly on the op, Chris wasn't a field operative. In fact, outside of their off-book adventure in Madagascar, Petra doubted that he had been in the field anytime in the last ten years.

Before she could brood on it further, another message from Gaston appeared and with a deep breath, she shrugged off her questions. Petra stood, making her way back to the mirror to do a final check on her appearance. Staring at her reflection, she pushed her reservations aside. It was time.

* * * * * *

Chapter 49

Bujumbura, Burundi

Petra kept her voice steady as she alerted the rest of the team through her com, "Testing, on my way to the beach."

"We read you, kiddo," Carlos' voice came back in response, causing her to wince—it was almost like one of their old interactions, before Kasem's identity as the Ahriman had shattered their friendship.

Without bothering to respond, she adjusted her sarong and reapplied a touch of sunscreen to her face, before leaving the room. She felt oddly naked in the swimsuit and sarong, there was no room for the standard kit she would normally have with her on an op, her Colt pistol or at the very least, a tranq gun. Even with all the improved leg and hip holsters, the only gear that could be successfully concealed in a bikini was her comlink, the small transmitter was attached to and hidden under one of the shoulder straps.

When she reached the lobby, she slowed her pace, making sure to shift her weight between her hips at each step. *The one part the movies might get right,* she wanted to grin, it really did attract extra attention, especially with the bright red of her bathing suit.

She made it out of the lobby and proceeded past the pool area toward the beach, scanning the area in her peripheral vision as she walked. Carlos and Gaston were having a drink at the pool bar with a view of the beach, and Kevin and Kasem were at a table on the opposite side of the pool area. Nziza and his entourage were to her right on the sand. She walked past them, looking around, then turned left toward an empty lounge chair next to where Veronica was sunbathing.

******

The next two hours passed quickly. Petra and Veronica made a show of ordering drinks. Petra made a few trips into the water, making sure to emerge closer to Nziza and his group each time before walking back over to Veronica. By the third time she walked by them, Petra was certain she had caught Nziza's eye, but was debating how to take it a step further. Although they had discussed their options and the different scenarios, this part of the op relied heavily on her instincts. Instincts that were very much out of practice.

She could try a direct approach, ask someone in Nziza's group for a light or something similar, or try another excuse to speak with them. She could also pretend to need help in the water and hopefully would receive it from one of his men. Despite the temptation to discuss it with Veronica, they mostly remained silent, it was too risky to get into something like that out in the open and Veronica was now pretending to nap anyway. Petra watched a waiter bring a large plate of appetizers over to Nziza and decided to go for it, she moved quickly along the beach, pretending to wave at the waiter. She was only a few paces away when the waiter noticed her. "Pardon, monsieur, on peut commander quelque chose?" she asked, requesting to order.

The waiter looked embarrassed and nodded. "Bien sur, j'arrive toute suite madame," he said, promising to be right there. He turned to Nziza and apologized, "Désolé, monsieur."

"Pas de problème," Nziza said, motioning toward the chair next to him. "Vous voulez nous joindre?" he asked Petra— Would you like to join us?

"Merci, mais je veux pas vous déranger," she replied— Thank you, but I wouldn't want to disturb you.

"Pas du tout"—Not at all. Nziza smiled, oozing charm that made Petra want to be sick.

After pretending to hesitate a moment longer, Petra took a seat in the chair next to him which had been vacated by one of his associates. He asked for her permission to order, then spoke to the waiter in Kiruni, the local language. Although she couldn't follow precisely, she thought she recognized the names of a few dishes. Once the waiter disappeared, she noticed Nziza's entourage melt away, taking positions within sight, but remaining inconspicuous. It wasn't a surprise that his men were so well trained, they had changed position seamlessly and an untrained eye would barely have noticed. *Definitely handpicked by the head of the Secret Police.* Pretending not to notice, she and Nziza continued their conversation. His manner reminded her of Jean-Paul Fayet, a French politician she had interacted with during an Agency op, both spoke with natural ease and charm that she found repellent but disarming at the same time.

"Tell me, my dear, how do you like Burundi?" Nziza asked, his deep voice now switching to heavily accented English.

Petra answered this question honestly, describing how open and welcoming she felt the country was. How despite only being there for a few weeks, she felt as if she had been there for months. After that the conversation shifted to what she was working on and she focused on the details of her cover. She couldn't help but notice how little Nziza said about himself.

The waiter returned with a chilled bottle of rosé wine and poured them each a glass. Petra accepted hers and took a half sip, she couldn't afford to dull her instincts. Shortly after that, the waiter brought out some food which she also sampled but kept to a minimum.

"How come you aren't eating?" Nziza asked.

"I'm supposed to meet a friend for dinner later, I want to be able to eat."

"A friend?"

"A colleague," Petra replied.

"Perhaps I am being too forward, but it doesn't sound like you are particularly excited about this dinner."

Petra raised her eyebrows and made a show of being surprised. "Well, he's a work colleague, we'll mostly be talking about that—"

"Come now, have dinner with him another time. You're here, look at this view. Why don't you join me for an early dinner instead? You've barely touched your wine."

Remaining tentative, Petra dragged her feet for a few minutes before finally agreeing, then used her phone to text the team that they were on for dinner. Her com had been active, so they had overheard the conversation already, but she had to keep up appearances.

When she was done, she set the phone aside and raised her glass once more, then took a real sip. The plan was working, but she still had to sell it.

* * * * * *

Chapter 50

Bujumbura, Burundi

Kasem squashed the impulse to wring his hands as he listened to Petra giggling over the com. He was glad that she had engaged Nziza as planned, but the whole set up made him want to hurl, especially the fact that she would have to take him back to her hotel room. He hadn't bothered to voice his sentiments, he had too much experience as an operative not to know that those feelings came from his personal relationship with Petra rather than a lack of confidence in the operation. Still, he didn't like it, and he didn't have to.

The minutes dragged on and he blocked out bits of the conversation, small talk about her cover, where else she had worked, how after all her hard work she had found herself single, blah blah blah. His eyes narrowed staring at the book he was holding, turning the pages as he tried to both pay attention to the op and drown it out at the same time. Kevin, who was seated to his left pretending to watch a replay of a soccer match on the bar television a few feet away, glanced at him a few times as the flirting heightened.

Get me to the end. Kasem's mind wandered, although he continued to listen for Petra's signal. He switched from staring at his book to a feigned nap in one of the lounge chairs by the pool. The waiting that went along with any op was always the easiest part to forget. An interesting contradiction, basic human nature, he stretched his hands over his head and settled back into the chair, glad for the shade the umbrella next to him offered. Many tourists would probably want to bake in the sun, but he had no such desire.

He wasn't sure how much time had passed when he heard Petra mention the signal phrase, "It's been wonderful chatting with you," her voice rang through his com, "but I'd better get back to my room. Thank you for a wonderful dinner. It's already six and I need to check out this evening and head back to town. I have to wake up extra early for a call with Hong Kong tomorrow."

Kasem exhaled slowly, then stretched out as he stood, taking his time to get out of the lawn chair. The sun had drifted lower in the sky, but they still had some time before dusk. He headed inside, giving Kevin a casual wave as he walked by, then made his way through the lobby toward the elevators. Before he got there, he turned left into the bathrooms and locked the door behind him. He retrieved a maintenance uniform from the cabinet under the sink where he had stashed it earlier. Pulling it over his clothes, Kasem paused to check his reflection before heading out, this time in the direction of the service elevators.

As the elevator doors closed, the conversation still going in his com cut out. Nziza had put on a full charm offensive, requesting that Petra stay for another bottle, something especially fancy of course. Kasem welcomed the silence until he stepped off the elevator on the third floor, just as the com returned and he heard Petra agree to stay. "Not for the whole bottle though," she protested, "just a taste."

He reached her room and positioned himself in the closet with a grimace. He couldn't believe that he was actually hiding in his fiancé's closet waiting for her to arrive with another man. The irony was the worst part, the fact that he wanted her to hurry up and bring said man over. Kasem recalled one of his favorite sci-fi action movies *Minority Report,* in which Tom Cruise was part of a pre-crime unit. *Tom Cruise would already have me in cuffs,* he thought with a grin.

"This is Kasem, I'm in position in the closet," he alerted the rest of the team over the com.

"We're ready for you next door," Carlos acknowledged. "Hope you make it out of the closet, buddy."

Kasem frowned, Carlos' attempt at levity felt out of place. Since the start of the op, the silence that had accompanied Carlos' serious looks had been deafening, even with their only limited friendship.

Besides, a six-person team to kidnap a well-guarded war criminal and stop a military coup with minimal backup and equipment? This was one op where they were lucky to have the Ahriman on their side.

* * * * * *

Chapter 51

Bujumbura, Burundi

Petra swayed slightly as she led Nziza toward her hotel room. She was mostly playing up the wine they had consumed at dinner, but she had to admit that she'd had more than her fair share. Despite that, her adrenaline was pumping and her fingers were itching for the needle hidden back in the room. The needle that she would plunge into Nziza's neck.

After her earlier attempt to excuse herself, he had enticed her to stay for another glass, eventually leading to a full bottle of wine. She waited for the sun to set, when the sky turned ablaze in red and orange hues, the reflection shimmering on the surface of the lake. It appeared as if the water didn't exist, as if the world had suddenly been consumed by the sunset. Even with all of the beauty, Petra had to shoulder her continued nerves, the scene felt like she was paralyzed at the center of a volcanic explosion rather than enjoying a beautiful sunset. She was in the eye of the storm, about to follow a group of sirens to her death. She longed for Kasem's presence, to have the op behind them so that they could sail off into the sunset, but she couldn't shake the pressure building on her chest.

She'd had to dig deep to focus on the job at hand. When she attempted once more to make her exit, Nziza had countered, saying that he had ordered them a special bottle of limoncello to top off the evening. Portraying complete surprise, she'd asked to try it some other time. She gave in eventually, but said she wanted to have it while she packed. One thing had led to another just as she had planned, and now he was following her up to her room. At first, his men had accompanied them, one of them even carrying the bottle and two glasses, but once they reached the elevator, she said in a shy voice, "I don't think the room is big enough for all of you to come in."

Nziza had dismissed them immediately, taking hold of the bottle and glasses. So far, it was all going smoothly, she even had her hands free to add to the stumbling tipsy act.

Not entirely an act, a voice in her head added. She would have to be extra cautious; the situation was far from optimal. *At least Kasem's waiting in the closet,* the thought brought her comfort and almost made her laugh.

They reached her room door and she fumbled in her shoulder bag for her key, allowing her sarong to slip slightly at the same time. She let out a peal of laughter and fixed it, then turned her attention back to the door. She purposely took two attempts to slide the key card into the slot, then finally opened the door. "I'm sorry it's a bit messy," she said as she stepped to the side to let him in.

"Not at all."

Petra shut the door and took a deep breath before turning around to face him. He moved across the room to the table by the window and set the bottle and glasses down.

"Let me serve this time," she said with a tentative smile. As she walked past the bed to join him, her fingers grazed the edge of the footboard, the needle was concealed in the folds between the footboard and the mattress. Silently, she cursed the lack of hiding places in a sarong and bikini once again, then took her glass from his outstretched hand.

"Have you had much limoncello?" she asked, placing the bottle in the ice bucket and sliding her hand to the bottom to pick up the small vial concealed there. "Should I go get us some ice?"

"I could ask one of my servants to bring some up."

She shifted, making a show of extreme discomfort. "I'd really rather you didn't."

"I understand, I'll get us some myself."

Petra held onto the bottle and the vial as he grabbed the bucket and disappeared into the hall. She was tempted to say something to Kasem, but decided not to risk it, who knew how good the sound proofing in her room was. Moving quickly, she poured the contents of the vial, a high dose of quick dissolving zolpidem, into one of the glasses, then doled a generous serving of limoncello on top of it and filled the other glass. She heard Nziza's footsteps at the door and hid the empty vial in the back of the desk drawer. It would be less visible there than in the trash bin.

"I'm sorry, I forgot about the automatic lock," she said and opened the door for him.

"That's no problem. Unless you wanted to get rid of me?"

She forced herself to beam at him and returned to the table, holding out the dosed glass. "I took it upon myself to get the first round ready."

He returned her smile as he took the glass, "Thank you, my dear. I didn't answer your earlier question, did I? Too distracted by looking at you."

Petra turned her eyes away, "That's very sweet."

"It's true. But to answer your question—have I had much limoncello. A little, I spent some time traveling in Italy when I was younger."

"Lovely."

"Santé," he said, raising his glass.

She clinked his glass and let herself take a small sip. The first thing that hit her was the alcohol and acidity, followed a moment later by the tart flavor of the sugared lemons. All she had to do now was stall as long as possible while the sedative took effect. Still, she felt off balance, a side effect of all the alcohol she had had to consume to get to this point. *Maybe also because my fiancé is hiding in the closet while I seduce another man.* She was grateful for the needle hidden by the mattress, it was filled with a special catalyst that Gaston had procured, one that would speed up the effects of the zolpidem. Under normal circumstances, such a reagent would never have been needed, she could easily have handled the situation until Nziza passed out on his own, but the backup was comforting. On a "normal" Agency op, she would also have had access to a combined sedative, one that would knock out a target almost immediately, but without Chris' go ahead and their slim timeline, they'd been unable to procure the more top-of-the-line substance. Either way, she was in control now.

She stepped back, flashing a smile at Nziza and taking a seat on the edge of the bed.

* * * * * *

Chapter 52

Bujumbura, Burundi

Petra groped for the needle with her right hand as Nziza's weight descended onto her torso. It had only been a couple of minutes since he finished the glass of limoncello, and she cursed herself for not having administered the sedative earlier at the beach. Even with the risk of his men noticing, she wondered if that would be preferable to having to keep up this act.

Nziza kissed her hard, and she squelched the urge to knee him in the balls, his wet tongue now shoved down her throat. The cool surface of the plastic needle eluded her. The whole thing had seemed so simple in the plan.

She gave Nziza a soft shove upward with both hands, taking the opportunity to slide further back onto the bed. He was hardly fazed and a moment later had resumed the same position, but this time, the needle was closer. The angle was still challenging, she had to twist her wrist backward to get a hold on it, but finally she had it in her grasp.

Without further ado, Petra pressed the release button to remove the protective cap on it and plunged the needle toward Nziza's throat. He sensed her movement and cried out, raising his arm to block her, but he was too late, the needle had already stabbed the top of his trapezius muscle, just below his neck.

He grabbed her around her neck and squeezed. "What did you d—?"

The grip on her neck eased and Petra groaned as his weight fell forward, then heaved him to the side with a grunt. "You can come out now," she croaked. The closet door flew open and she stared at the ceiling, unable to move. *At least my part is over now.*

* * * * * *

Chapter 53

Bujumbura, Burundi

Veronica kept her gaze low as she and Kevin wheeled the massive housekeeping cart out of Petra's hotel room. The cart had been specially designed with a large empty compartment in the center, but even then, getting Nziza's passed out form into it had been an exhausting experience. They reached the service elevator without incident and headed toward the laundry room in the basement.

"How are you doing?" Kevin asked in a quiet voice.

"Fine, just waiting for this to be over."

"I get that, but hey, if this is the only way to get some alone time with you, I'll take it."

The elevator doors opened, and they turned left quickly toward the servant entrance. Carlos had set off a fire alarm on the other side of the building to draw most of the staff's attention, but there was still a risk that they would run into someone. As two Caucasians they would stick out like sore thumbs, even in their housekeeping uniforms.

The warmer outdoor air hit her face as they reached the parking area. Gaston was waiting for them at the van, the back doors already open, with a ramp laid out. Together the three of them heaved the cart inside, securing it in place with two cables on the interior. With his phone, Gaston ran a quick scan for any transmissions that would indicate a tracker and gave them a thumbs up. "Looks like we are clear. Safe drive, see you later."

"Thank you," Veronica said as she got into the passenger seat. Kevin nodded at him as well before jumping into the driver's seat.

"Good luck," Gaston replied.

With a quick wave, Kevin revved the engine and sped out of the parking area. So far, things had gone according to plan, but they still needed to get to the safe house and ditch the van.

They had been on the road about five minutes when Veronica realized that something was bothering her, a foreboding feeling in the back of her mind. They had passed quickly through the service exit, the guard had scarcely given them a second glance.

Too quickly. She knew from experience that when anything was too easy, there was always a rebalancing, as if the universe had to put it right. In a spy movie, that would be the heart of the conspiracy, the betrayal of one of the team members—she shot Kevin a glance. Whereas in reality, it often had nothing to do with that, it just seemed that if enough things went right, that something else would go wrong unexpectedly.

She pushed aside her concerns, especially the ones about Kevin—he had certainly been in the thick of it with the rest of the team today. Despite the attempt to redirect her train of thought, she couldn't help but wonder what awaited them at the other end of the drive.

* * * * * *

Chapter 54

Bujumbura, Burundi

Carlos turned onto the main road outside of the Club du Lac a few minutes behind Veronica and Kevin. He glanced at Kasem in the passenger seat, who had barely said a word since he had sat down. Other than a few bumps on the road, they continued their drive toward the safehouse in silence, both keeping their gaze focused straight ahead.

Finally, Carlos couldn't stand it any longer, although he tried to use more diplomatic language than normal. "Must have been an interesting experience, hiding out in the closet while Petra er, took care of Nziza."

Kasem glanced at him, then turned back toward the windshield, "Nothing I couldn't handle."

Well, you are the Ahriman, Carlos wanted to say. He maintained his self-control long enough to stifle a drawn-out sigh. They reached the central area of the city without any further conversation and Carlos followed their chosen route to avoid one of the central roundabouts. Other than the lake road, which was nigh on unavoidable for all of them, each car had chosen slightly altered routes—the idea was that the other two cars could draw attention away from the van carrying Nziza if needed.

Carlos was debating whether to try another attempt at levity when the com sputtered with Veronica's voice, "Team, tracker activated on target. Attempting to jam."

"Damn," Carlos said. He looked at Kasem, "Can you get us a route that converges on theirs? I know if we turn right up there, we'll be moving in their general direction..." His voice trailed off, kicking himself for not studying the city map well enough.

Before Kasem could answer, Veronica's voice returned, "Signal jammed, but we still may have company."

"I've got you. Turn right up ahead and take the next slight right, that'll take us toward Rwagasore and we can get to their route." He glanced at the map on his phone, "Yup that'll work."

"Veronica, we're converging toward you," Petra's voice came over the com.

"Ditto," Carlos added.

"Roger that," Veronica acknowledged.

Carlos focused on driving as Kasem directed him across the next couple of side streets past the Boulevard de l'Uprona. It had only been a few weeks since he had followed Kevin down that street, but that reality felt like another lifetime. "For all the spy tech in the world, we've got Google Maps to thank for this chase," he muttered as he turned a sharp right on Kasem's instructions.

"Good thing they have it here, or we'd be out of luck," Kasem agreed.

Ever heard of a rhetorical statement, buddy? Carlos was tempted to ask but kept his attention on the road. Perhaps Veronica had jammed the signal fast enough, they might be in the clear.

He clung to that hope until Veronica's voice made his heart sink into his stomach, "Hostiles at our location. We're pinned down, we're going to be taken."

* * * * * *

Chapter 55

Bujumbura, Burundi

Veronica's first concrete warning was a high-pitched beep as they drove along the lake road. Veronica dismissed it initially, but after a few seconds she locked eyes with Kevin. "Please tell me you can't hear that," she said.

"I wish I could." His expression was grim, but he kept driving toward the town center, which they would have to pass through on their way to the safe house.

Veronica glanced backward, Nziza was still in the housekeeping cart and there didn't appear to be any movement. The beep however was almost definitely coming from the cart, slightly muffled by the towels and sheets they had thrown on top of him. She grabbed her phone and opened one of the Agency apps, one that was supposed to jam any and all transmissions. "Now we pray," she said as she activated it. She could only hope they weren't too late. "Team, tracker activated on target. Attempting to jam," she informed the rest of the group through her com.

The beep stopped immediately, and she felt a momentary surge of relief, then turned her attention back to the road.

"Signal jammed, but we still may have company," she updated the com.

A moment later she heard Petra's voice, "Veronica, we're converging toward you."

"Ditto," Carlos' voice came across as well.

"Roger that." She exchanged a glance at Kevin, hoping that they were out of the woods.

They were on the edge of the town center now, with about another fifteen minutes on the road to get to the safe house. She cursed at the group of cars ahead as they pulled to a stop at a traffic light—the intersection ahead of them was heavily damaged because of drainage problems and with the cars ahead it would take a couple of minutes to get across.

"Still way less traffic than it would be in pretty much any other city," Kevin said as if he could read her mind.

"Right," Veronica grimaced. They drove across the intersection, the car weathering the two deep dips in the center slowly, then speeding up as they moved past it.

They had just navigated through the town center when she heard it—a siren approaching from behind. Kevin hit the gas and turned right at the intersection toward the Chausée PL Rwagasore.

Veronica frowned, "What are you doing? We're supposed to take Bubanza."

"If they're tracking us, we've got a better chance on a busier street—"

"No way," she overruled him. She had no intention of trusting Kevin's instincts; even if he had been in the weeds with them on the op, he could just as easily lead them into a trap. "Take the side road as planned. It's faster and closer to the safe house, and we're less likely to be spotted, that's why we chose it."

"I hear and obey." He turned left twice to get them back on course, and soon after that they'd reached the edge of town.

Veronica's heartbeat drummed in her ears and she retained a thread of hope until they turned the corner to head uphill as planned. They sped past the Hotel Belair, along with a couple of small restaurants and convenience stores.

Almost there. They turned into a residential street just a few blocks from the safe house Gaston had set up.

Three massive black Chevy Suburbans were parked ahead, blocking the street. A group of soldiers stood in front of the cars, some with AK-47s raised and ready.

Kevin screeched to a halt and swung the van into a U-turn, one that almost flipped them over onto their side, but it was too late. Two more Suburbans had pulled in behind them, blocking even the slimmest chance of escape.

Veronica tapped on her com, "Hostiles at our location. We're pinned down, we're going to be taken." As the men approached, a lump formed in her throat. Maybe Kevin had been right about the main road.

* * * * * *

Chapter 56

Bujumbura, Burundi

Carlos yanked the steering wheel to the left to pull over onto a side street one block from where the GPS marked Kevin and Veronica's positions. "Hold tight, we're on your six," he radioed through the com. The map on Kasem's phone painted a grim picture, even before they were close enough to have a visual on the other car. The dot that marked Petra and Gaston's car was still several minutes away, having stalled at a crowded roundabout in the town center. Whatever he and Kasem were going to do, they were on their own.

"There's an alley that runs toward them," Kasem motioned to their right as they got out of the car.

"Lead the way." Carlos followed, and they each pulled on a pair of night goggles, the shadows on the dark street changing to bright green outlines as the goggles came online. He had to admit that Kasem had been invaluable on the op, he had researched and prepped more than any of the team, possibly as much as the rest of them put together. He had also actually explored the city, so the map wasn't just a two-dimensional image. It had actual meaning, especially in relation to the different hills that sloped upward from the lake. Without that understanding, it was easy enough to say that two points on the map were close together, only to find out that they were on separate hills, as in the only way to get from one point to the other was to first descend toward town. They certainly wouldn't have been able to navigate to this specific access point so quickly without that understanding.

They reached the alley a moment later. "Some alley," Carlos wrinkled his nose, "incredible scent you've discovered."

"It's the fastest way."

They squeezed into the passage, really more of a spacing between the walls on either side rather than an actual alley. "I bet a cat would have trouble going this way," Carlos grunted and urged his legs forward. Much as he disliked both Veronica and Kevin, they needed help and fast. If they took much longer to get to them, it would all be for naught.

When Kasem remained silent, Carlos asked, "How much further?" The spacing between the wall was jagged and uneven so he could only see a few paces ahead.

"Looked like a quarter mile or so on the map. You doing okay, old man?"

Carlos couldn't help but grin, this was Kasem's first response to his many attempts to inject some lightheartedness into the tension of the op. "Doing fine, thank you very much. Just can't believe I'm squeezing my way through a garbage chute for that bloody Patrushka and the Agency's lead cheerleader. I could have been at a barbecue!"

"Russian doll and a cheerleader, I like it. Time to replace their call signs."

"You get us through this alley, and we can make you the team mascot."

"Aye, aye, captain."

They groped their way through the alley for what felt like another half hour, when in reality it was only a few minutes. Veronica made a few updates during that time, but all they could do was continue toward them. Finally, they reached the end of the passage, a narrow opening onto the adjacent street. From their position they could see what looked like three armored SUVs about fifty feet to their right, just slightly downhill, with the van stopped further down the street and another two black SUVs beyond the van.

Carlos' hand moved immediately to the holster at his waist, raising his Remington to eye level. "I'm going to cross the street for a better angle. You move down this side, see if we can flank them."

"What about Nziza? We might be able to get Kevin and Veronica, but there's no way we get to that housekeeping cart."

Carlos sighed, he was right and they both knew it. Their attempt to stop the coup had failed.

"Babysitting little Patrushka is going to be the death of me. But the team's the priority. We can't even use a fire starter, they'll be too close, and we don't have any small explosives. V grabbed a couple, but they must be in the van," Carlos answered. "Anyway, we'll deal with fallout from the op later."

"Got it."

"Watch out for the fireworks." Carlos stepped away, then turned back, "Hey, buddy—don't get dead."

"You got it, Cap."

* * * * * *

Chapter 57

Bujumbura, Burundi

Petra stared at the three cars stopped in the middle of the intersection, blocking their route up the hillside. Could a minor fender-bender really be blocking them from getting to the rest of the team?

She glanced at Gaston in the driver seat, "Any chance this will clear up quickly?"

He shook his head, "It doesn't happen often, but when it does…"

"Team, we're seriously held up, may not get to you in time. Cut the cargo and run," she said into the com.

"What happened, kiddo? Too busy flirting to get your hands dirty?" Carlos' voice came back.

Petra ignored him and glared at the intersection again. The op had failed and there was nothing she could do. All she had to look forward to was a life on the run.

* * * * * *

Chapter 58

Bujumbura, Burundi

Carlos watched as Kevin and Veronica emerged slowly from the van with their arms overhead. Three black-clad mercenaries joined them from one of the SUVs blocking the road ahead, guns drawn. He lined up a shot at the closest one, wishing that he had his long-range pistol with him. "I've got a shot, K and V, hit dirt in three."

Carlos counted down in his head, then squeezed the trigger.

* * * * * *

Three gunshots flew through the air within a foot of him and Carlos pressed his back against the corner of the wall for cover.

The scene on the street had turned to chaos as soon as he'd fired. At least six more mercenaries had emerged from their SUVs and were inching their way toward his position, but Kasem was laying down cover fire to slow their approach. Veronica had managed to take cover under the van with the ensuing turmoil, but he couldn't see where Kevin had got to. That was probably a good thing, if Carlos couldn't see him, the M.S.S. probably couldn't either.

Regardless, he didn't have time to give it any thought. He had to hold out long enough until Petra and Gaston got there as backup.

Except that they were stuck in a traffic jam. He fired off another set of shots, stopping only to replace the magazine. His perception narrowed, all he could hear were the bullets, along with the feeling of recoil in his wrist as he fired off subsequent shots vaguely in the direction of the approaching mercenaries. A couple more went down from either his or Kasem's shots, but the rest were getting closer.

"Team, take cover," a voice came over the com, cutting through the commotion.

Carlos barely had a chance to react before one of the SUVs exploded on the street in front of him taking out at least four mercenaries and forcing the rest to the ground. For a second, he wondered if they were on a movie set. *How did the kid make that happen?* Or had Kevin broken free and set one of the explosives? Regardless, he didn't have time to dwell on it.

He stepped to the edge of the wall and took aim before firing off another shot, then hit the ground to army-crawl toward an abandoned fruit stand a few paces ahead on the street for a better firing position. The stand would offer some cover, albeit not as good as the wall.

He was almost there when a burning sensation seared through his calf. His adrenaline was pumping so hard he made it to the stall anyway, when he finally looked at his right leg. Blood was spurting from just below the head of the muscle.

Pressing his hands to the wound to stem the flow, Carlos gasped into his com, "I'm hit. Behind the fruit stand."

* * * * * *

Chapter 59

Bujumbura, Burundi

Carlos felt a wave of disorientation hit him as he tried to slow the blood flow. Gunfire continued to split the air around him from what felt like all directions. Dizziness threatened to overwhelm him, but he directed all of his focus toward applying pressure.

The gunshots slowed as two of the mercenaries approached the burning car. Kevin appeared from behind him, seemingly out of nowhere. "You're doing great, keep that pressure. We've got to stop the bleed."

"Swiss army knife... left jacket pocket. And ... tourniquet." The words felt like they came from someone else as the warm blood continued to seep into his hands.

Kevin groped in Carlos' jacket and retrieved the knife followed by the tourniquet. With the scissor attachment, he cut through the fabric of Carlos' pants, stopping a few inches above the wound. He then grabbed the Velcro strap tourniquet from Carlos' pocket and circled it around his mid-thigh. "This is going to hurt, you've got to stay quiet. They don't know where we are yet." He pressed his left hand on Carlos' mouth and rotated the rod clockwise.

Carlos' face contorted with each twist. "Isn't that enough? That's got to be enough," he started to beg. "Come on, babushka... please, it's enough."

"You're okay, but you know I can't stop yet..." Ignoring Carlos' pleas, Kevin continued to twist.

Carlos screamed against the pressure of Kevin's hand on his mouth. Even when he'd been captured and beaten in Madagascar, he had never experienced pain like what came with each twist of the tourniquet. He fought to retain consciousness, Kevin had to turn the tourniquet until the bleeding stopped. Each of the last three twists made him feel like he would rather have been shot in the chest. "We can stop now, babuska."

* * * * * *

Chapter 60

Bujumbura, Burundi

When Kevin finally latched the tourniquet rod in place, a wave of relief washed over him. He released the pressure over Carlos' mouth. "Bleeding stopped. You're going to be okay."

"Don't you think we can loosen that a bit? I'm all right," Carlos whimpered.

"You know the drill." Kevin shook his head, the memories of Agency training still overwhelming him. He remembered all of the anger that he'd pent up, anger which he'd directed toward the Agency as he went further and further down the FSB rabbit hole. Fat lot of good it had done, considering how the FSB ate their young. He'd been cut loose as soon as he tried to stop them from going after Veronica. There had been no discussion of ideology—exposing the FSB's hypocrisy. Kevin had turned away from the Agency because he'd seen them renege on their values time and again, sometimes to serve what they called the Greater Good, and sometimes just to serve selfish government interests. He'd been so naïve to think the FSB would be different.

"Carlos is down," Kevin said into the coms. "Through and through to the calf, looks like a capillary bleed. I used a tourniquet to stop the bleeding."

Another series of shots erupted near the downed car, and Kevin used a button on his phone to trigger a second explosion, this time closer to the set of cars further down the hill.

Carlos groaned into his earpiece, "Veronica, what's your status?"

"Pinned down, under the van. They haven't come looking yet, but they will."

Carlos gestured toward his Remington, "Take it, go."

Kevin hesitated, surprised that Carlos would trust him with the weapon. His earlier request for a gun had been greeted with a flat no, but they were out of options. He nodded, everything had already gone sideways, and they couldn't leave Veronica where she was. "Can you make it back to your car?"

"I think so."

They both knew it was a lie, but it made Kevin feel better. "Cavalry's on the way."

* * * * * *

Kevin propelled himself forward, keeping low to the ground while moving as fast as possible. The sky had turned to dusk, offering some extra cover, especially combined with the distraction that a second explosion Kasem had somehow managed to set off. He reached the other side of the street and made his way back toward the SUVs, staying in the shadow of the boundary wall of the mansion to his right. The lights inside the house had gone off—most likely the residents were taking shelter in their cellars.

What surprised him was that there were no sirens, not even in the distance. There'd been the initial siren he and Veronica had heard before they'd turned down this street, which could have been anywhere in town, but that was all. It had only been a few minutes since the gunshots had started, but the Burundais police ought to be on their way. Unless the M.S.S. ties to the Secret Police could stop that from happening? He wasn't sure if the police arriving would be good or bad—it could really go either way. But if the M.S.S. could stop such a basic response even after a gun fight, the team had certainly underestimated their pull. He refused to dwell on that, police or not, he needed to provide enough cover for Veronica to escape before the mercenaries discovered where she was hiding.

The gunfire had died down since the second explosion, but in the minute or so that had passed, the mercenaries had started to reemerge. Carlos and Kasem had already taken out the four from the first two SUVs, along with the first explosion, but the three further down the road remained intact. Two of the black-clad assailants were now on the road and making their way toward the van with Nziza.

Still on the side of the street, Kevin covered most of the distance toward the van, the continuing fire from the first SUV explosion shielding him from sight. Since the troops weren't looking for him, he was able to move in relative concealment. He was only a few paces from the van when the mercenaries got there.

Kevin came to a halt in the shadows, a deep pressure on his chest. He could cut through the alley and get away, that would be easy enough. From his current position, he could try to take out one of the assailants, but the van was blocking most of his angles, and he would be unlikely to be of much help. If he broke position and ran toward the van for a better shot, he would be completely exposed—which would most likely get him captured or killed. Without night vision goggles, the better angle might not even help him. The gun magazine was almost empty but there was a slight chance he could take out one or two more soldiers before he was completely out.

Rationally, he knew that Veronica probably stood a better chance if he escaped. If he and the team regrouped to find a way to get her out. But there was the small chance that they would kill her before the team could get to her, or that he would be able to help her escape if they were both on the inside.

"They're here, fall back, abort," Veronica said over the com.

Whatever happened, he refused to risk Veronica's safety. Not after everything he had already put her through. Not if there was even the slimmest chance that he could change the outcome.

Kevin broke from the safety of the shadows and into a run. He closed the gap toward the back of van and somersaulted forward, cringing as the asphalt scraped his palms and then the back of his neck. At the end of the roll, he lined up the Remington and emptied the magazine in the direction of the assailants.

He still had no idea if he'd hit anything when the lights from one of the SUVs landed on him.

"*Haut les mains, lache l'arme.*" – Hands up, drop the gun, an amplified voice behind him said in French.

Kevin got to his knees and turned around, his eyes still adjusting. He searched for Veronica, and a moment later, he could just make her out. She was on the ground in front of the van with an A.K. pointed straight at her head.

* * * * * *

Chapter 61

Bujumbura, Burundi

Kasem's heart sank, his mind moving a mile a minute as he processed Kevin's update. What could he do? Carlos was down, and their carefully planned op had now gone completely to hell. From his position in front of the alley, he could see the street stretching downhill in front of him, including the five SUVs and the van in which Veronica and Kevin had concealed Nziza. Carlos was somewhere on the other side of the street, apparently concealed behind a fruit cart. Against the rapidly descending shadows, Kasem could make out something diagonally to his left, a little further uphill, that he guessed must be the cart. The first SUV Kevin had set ablaze was a few paces downhill, and the fire was still roaring, along with the one from further down the street. The fires had provided enough distraction for him to move around, but as soon as the mercenaries had started to reemerge, Kasem had retreated back to his original position for concealment.

Squinting, he tried to guess the distance to the fruit cart. If the assailants were well equipped, he would probably be an easy target since there was no way he could belly-crawl all the way across the unusually wide residential street. Even at a full run, they would have plenty of time to take him out if they looked in his direction. Judging from the direction in which the figures down the street were moving though, their attention was mostly focused on the van. That made sense given their mission would almost certainly be getting to Nziza over anything else.

Which left him with an open opportunity.

Without debating any further, Kasem radioed the team. "I'm going to get Carlos. I'll bring him back to the pin for our car."

"ETA five minutes," Petra said through the com.

"Roger that."

Kasem holstered his gun, his best chance was not to give away his position by using it. He bolted forward, using a diagonal path toward the shadow that he assumed was the fruit cart. Within a few strides he was behind the burning SUV, another several took him past all concealment. As the cart drew closer, he dove forward, rolling over his left shoulder and caught his breath.

He had miscalculated, the shadow that he'd assumed to be the fruit cart was a makeshift auto rickshaw with the back covering missing. From this position, he could see what had to be the fruit cart, parked about three houses down from him. "Carlos, almost there, be ready to move."

A few seconds later, Kasem reached it. Carlos' back was propped against the base of the cart, with his legs stretched out in front of him.

"About time, buddy." Carlos made a feeble attempt to chuckle. "You did some good work out there," he nodded toward the two fires down the street, still going but now starting to diminish.

"You said there'd be fireworks, somebody had to deliver. That was all Kevin actually, I had nothing to do with it."

"Ballsy, when he didn't have a place to take cover."

"Come on, you know we've all got nine lives." Kasem ran his hand over the extended left leg. The tourniquet above his knee was secure, but it would still be a tall order to make it across the street.

"Maybe more. But they're getting their asses kicked down there. You should go, they need help."

"Petra and Gaston will cover them." Kasem squinted as he peered around the corner of the cart. The mercenaries were still approaching the van, slowed by a few shots from the other side of the street that he guessed were Kevin's work.

"They're here, fall back, abort," Veronica said over the com.

"Go," Carlos repeated.

"There's no time. I'm too far, and we're no good to anyone captured. I'm getting you out of here. Think you can walk?"

"Not like we have much choice. You look like you've been neglecting the gym, not sure if you can carry me."

"Right." Kasem threaded his arm under Carlos' right shoulder and braced himself for the weight.

"Besides, check out these shorts. Good old Patrushka shredded up my pants. I can't wait to show off these legs."

They took a step forward and Carlos grunted in pain, then another, speeding up as they moved uphill. Kasem helped push him forward. His com buzzed in a triple-dash pattern—their emergency code to indicate anyone being captured, but Kasem refused to process until they reached cover.

They finally made it to the entrance of the alleyway, and Kasem paused, turning back to survey the street. He was too late to help Veronica and Kevin, who were being loaded into one of the remaining SUVs.

Rather than dwell on it, they pushed on. "Not far now, just another fifty meters or so to the car," Kasem said.

"Meters? Who do you think you're talking to?"

Carlos was dizzy from the pain, but he used the narrow walls for support to hop forward on his good leg since there wasn't enough room to lean on Kasem. They navigated the rest of the way back to the car, and using both the seat and Kasem for support, Carlos managed to get into the passenger seat.

Kasem checked behind them, grateful that no one seemed to be in pursuit and caught his breath over the steering wheel. There was no activity on this street, such a contrast to the danger that they had just been in. He turned on the engine and Petra's car pulled up behind them. Tapping on his com, he said, "I've got Carlos. The tourniquet stopped the bleeding. We're too late for the rest."

"Got it. See you back at the house," Gaston replied.

Carlos looked over from the passenger seat, "Take us home, Kimbo."

Flipping the car around, the hillside disappeared behind them and they sped toward the relative safety of the team house. A third of their team had been captured and they had nothing to show for it: no Nziza and Carlos had been shot. At this point, Kasem couldn't see them getting out of Burundi alive. Even if they did, he wouldn't have much of a life to look forward to.

* * * * * *

Chapter 62

Bujumbura, Burundi

Petra threw her arms around Kasem, overwhelmed by a combination of relief that they were safe and sheer desperation at the plight they now faced. Shortly after their return to the house, Carlos had passed out on the couch, and Gaston had left, citing the need to sleep for at least three days. Petra's brain felt like she was sequestered in a minefield. The thought of Kevin and Veronica in the M.S.S.' custody, even with both of their respective betrayals, was too much to bear. She and Kevin had been friends since Agency training, and her friendship with Veronica had started shortly after she had returned from her first operation. Her fears underscored something that she had always known but was now being hammered home—the unspoken part of her commitment to the Agency, the spy code, so to speak.

Leave no one behind, show up for the people that we care about. Regardless of the consequences.

She looked over at Carlos and clung to the hope that her friendship with him, at the very least, could be salvaged. They were more than colleagues or even friends—Carlos was part of her family, almost as much as Kasem.

Rather than wallowing, Petra attended to the wound. The tourniquet had stopped the bleeding, but the bullet wound still needed to be dressed. The bullet had passed through the muscle, but luckily the bone was intact, so she cleaned it using alcohol from the first aid kit and applied a pressure bandage to cover it. She bit her lip, thankful that Kevin had gotten the tourniquet on so quickly, she shuddered at what could have happened. If Kevin hadn't risked his neck to get to him, Carlos would have bled out on the street.

Once the bandage was in place, Petra strapped a splint around Carlos' calf. The field medicine kit didn't have one long enough to extend above his knee, but she hoped it would be better than nothing when he put weight on it again.

Gaston had made arrangements for an off-book medic, but he wouldn't arrive for a couple of hours. After attending to Carlos, Petra stared out the window. Streaks of lightning were piercing the dark clouds on the horizon. They were at the tail of the rainy season or start of the dry season. She had seen pictures of such storms, but the reality was nothing in comparison, even with the view of the sky limited by the garden wall.

Carlos awoke momentarily then drifted back to sleep, and his guttural snore mingled with the sound of the engine. *Louder than a rhinoceros,* a bittersweet smile crossed her face. She was so grateful that they were all alive, that she and Carlos still had the chance to mend the rift between them. She stepped outside and went out to the bench in the garden, the raindrops covering her face within seconds and soaking through her t-shirt.

Tears rolled down her cheeks, mixing with the raindrops. The shock was wearing off now, and she knew how dire their situation remained, but the flashing storm clouds were mesmerizing.

She wasn't sure how long she stood there watching, her mind turning in a hundred different directions. Would they be able to rescue Veronica and Kevin? What would happen to Kasem when they left Burundi? She had no idea how many people at the Agency knew about Kasem's past as the Ahriman—probably Chris, but who else? She had her doubts as to how much the Agency even knew for sure, Veronica had been so cagey when confronted for any details.

Grant. It had to be. Which meant the Agency wouldn't be able to confirm the accusation.

Petra ran over the conversation that they had had when she had cornered Veronica in the living room two nights earlier. There was no other way the Agency could have figured it out, not at this stage anyway. The more she thought about it, the more certain she became. He wasn't a reliable source, especially with their history. Besides, Grant couldn't have had more than a passing glance at Kasem in New York or D.C.

Petra looked down, noticing that her hands were clenched. She had done everything to avoid contact between Grant and Kasem, but it had all gone haywire. They were just lucky that Grant wasn't a trained agent. If he had been, his word might have been enough to condemn Kasem.

Chris would have hauled him away. She swallowed the bitter pill, if Kasem ever came face to face with him, Grant would figure it out for sure. Despite her best efforts, they were about to drive off a cliff.

The realization was too much for her. A wave of nausea hit her, and she doubled over, barely managing to get to the patio trash bin as she started to retch. Ready or not, the storm was here. The only way out was through.

* * * * * *

Chapter 63

Bujumbura, Burundi

Petra stared at the video projection of Chris, aghast. "You'll be here in a couple of hours, but the Agency won't give us authorization for a backup team—even though you want us to stop the coup, *and* Veronica and Kevin have been taken." She couldn't even believe what she was saying. "Forgive me for saying this, but you're not exactly a field specialist," the words burst from her mouth before she could stop them.

At this rate, we should be grateful we could get a medic to stitch up Carlos' leg and give him a real splint. The thought again hammered home the severity of their situation—luckily, his gunshot wound had been minor, especially since the blood loss had been stemmed by the tourniquet, and all the medic had to do was close the wound. Carlos had his leg propped on the table, with a large splint for support while the muscle healed.

Chris grimaced, "I know, but I'm the best you're going to get. You got any better ideas?"

"Without backup, our only choice is to inform the military here. Let's loop in the government, and they can stop the coup," Carlos interceded.

"No," Chris shook his head, "that won't work, we don't know how many of them are in Nziza's pocket. Besides, the Agency isn't authorized to be on deployment in Burundi in the first place. Aside from the feathers that would ruffle, we don't have enough credibility to convince them it's a real threat."

"So why not go through someone else?" Carlos sounded like he could barely contain his exasperation. "Maybe now would be the time to call in your buddies at the C.I.A.?"

"We already tried that," Chris answered. "You're on your own."

With a sullen look, Petra wished she could spontaneously generate a workable idea. She sighed and shrugged, "Fine, Chris. Then the only way to stop a coup without a military team is to take Markov out of play."

"What are you saying?"

"We kidnap him ourselves. Nziza can't take power if he can't find Markov." The plan made her sick to her stomach.

"You can't be serious?" Kasem said, echoing her thoughts. "That would mean that the Agency is executing a coup—we'd be as good as war criminals."

"Do you have a better idea?"

"Petra, you're onto something," Carlos said before Kasem could respond. "If we take Markov out of play, the coup falls apart, maybe long enough for the Burundais army to take care of the rest. Then all we have to do is release him, and everything goes back to normal."

Petra rolled her eyes. No plan in Agency history had ever come out that clean in practice. "Some semblance thereof, I guess."

"Can you execute on that?" Chris asked. "You'd have to kidnap him from the residence."

"I don't know—we need details on the guards, schematics, numbers." She ran her fingers through her hair, "Even with all of that, it's a long shot. With Carlos out of commission, we're only a three-person team. And even if we can pull it off, we'd have to leave Kevin and Veronica behind, there's no way we could get Markov and rescue them from Blue Bay." As she spoke, she clung to the hope that this would convince Chris to send backup. "We're lucky we tracked the mercenaries that took them to Blue Bay. They're still alive. We can get to them, if you give us a real team."

"I'm sorry, Petra, that's a no-go. I'll see what I can get on the residence, though—we should be able to pull satellite feeds on the guard formations, maybe even some old blueprints from the French or Belgians."

"Fine. We'll see you in a bit." She hung up before he could respond, feeling momentarily satisfied for cutting off the conversation.

Hopelessness descended upon her a second later like the ongoing thunderstorm. The Agency wasn't sending anyone to help. Whatever her issues were with Veronica, she wasn't about to leave her to be tortured in a Chinese prison. She felt a weight in the pit of her stomach, much as she wanted to focus on Veronica and Kevin's welfare, her mind couldn't help but return to Kasem.

What if V gives him up to the Chinese? Petra knew the old spy doctrine as well as anyone. No matter how well trained, everyone broke eventually, and at that point, his secret would be out. She glanced at Kasem, not daring to make eye contact for fear that he would sense what she was thinking. She couldn't bear to discuss it: if she didn't say the words out loud, perhaps they wouldn't be true?

Gathering her composure, her gaze moved between Kasem and Carlos, the silence in the room deafening. "Any ideas?" she asked, focusing on Carlos. If anyone was going to have contacts that would help them, it would be him. Gaston had already exhausted his network and neither she nor Kasem had ever worked in Africa, so they had nothing to draw on.

The silence lingered for several moments before Carlos met her gaze. "I might have something."

Puja Guha

******

Chapter 64

Bujumbura, Burundi

Carlos hung up his phone and turned around to look at Petra and Kasem, still seated in the living room. "They'll be here in a few hours."

"How many?" Kasem asked.

"Five of them. Really solid guys, ones that we can rely on." *A lot more trustworthy than Kevin,* Carlos wanted to add but kept to himself.

"Chris just sent us whatever he could get on the residence," Petra tapped on her tablet screen to project blueprints of the house and gardens above the table. "There's a guard post by the street with two guards, and an additional eight posted within the gardens. I'm not sure how many will be in the house, but there'll at least be his four personal guards. Markov's bedroom is on this side of the house, here," she pointed to the spot on the projection. "He said one of the Agency's tech guys was able to breach the security system, so he can access Markov's personal calendar. This evening he's supposed to be home, having a private celebration with his family."

"We could cross over the wall here at the closest point, from the cliffside, then make for the bedroom. That way, we avoid the guard post on the road entirely. The alarm system is fairly simple—they're relying on the number of guards and the camera system rather than a well-calibrated system." Carlos zoomed in on the wall, "If we take out these two cameras, there will only be two guards within eyeshot of where we'll cross the wall." An idea occurred to him and he considered it for a moment as Petra and Kasem continued to look at the blueprints.

"That's not that many," Kasem said, "five of us could take Markov. One stays at the wall, the other four cross, and one takes position outside after the cameras are out. The last three go in, tranq the guards, grab him, and get out."

"Plus, one more on the outside coordinating and keeping watch," Carlos nodded. "We should split—have a small team who moves on Blue Bay, while the other one goes for Markov." He looked at Petra, "You and I could do it, maybe with one of Tim's guys."

"Look what just happened, and with a similar size team," Petra shook her head. "We can't possibly take Blue Bay with only three people. Besides, you have to take it easy on that leg, so it'll just be two of us. The doc said you'll be fine, but you have to give the stitches time to close."

Carlos ignored her point about his leg and switched out the projected blueprints for the all-too-familiar map of Blue Bay. "We don't have to take the whole resort, just get in and get out." He gestured toward a point on the beach where they had breached the Blue Bay fence. "When we were planning the water entry, we figured we'd go in from here. But the Agency's got a tracker on Veronica—"

"Really?" Petra frowned, clearly surprised. "That's not standard protocol—are you sure?"

"They got the CIA's tech last year—remember the trackers we used in Mada?"

"Okay, so we've got a shot. I'm just glad they deactivated ours," Petra exchanged a glance with Kasem.

"Same here," Carlos agreed. "Anyway, we know exactly where she's being held." He tapped on the tablet screen, and a red dot appeared on one of the huts located in the middle of the resort. "We can access this hut directly, moving down from the road. If we stage an accident up here, further up the road, we'll draw the guards away."

Kasem leaned over and peered at the map projection. "It could probably work, but I'd rather be on the team that moves on Markov."

Petra shrugged, "Fine, I'll move on Blue Bay with someone from Tim's team. We can use Gaston for backup. We can't leave Veronica and Kevin there to rot."

"I'll drive the getaway car," Carlos cracked a grin, but neither Petra nor Kasem appeared to be amused. He scratched his head, wishing that he could wave a magic wand and rid the room of the previous animosity. He'd been so angry he hadn't seen the whole picture. His gaze lingered on Kasem. Without Kasem's off-the-cuff intervention, he too would have been captured alongside Veronica and Kevin.

Or worse.

He was about to acknowledge that, but before he could open his mouth, Petra stood up and placed her coffee mug on the table abruptly.

"We're set for the moment, so I'd rather not sit here because it's awkward. Besides, I'm not really in the mood for jokes," she placed her hand on Kasem's shoulder. "I'm going to our room, come in whenever," she said as she disappeared down the hall.

I guess she's still angry.

＊＊＊＊＊＊

Chapter 65

Bujumbura, Burundi

Kasem drummed his fingers on his leg, the silence deafening as he and Carlos remained in the living room together. *Never thought I'd be waiting eagerly for the Agency to show up,* he thought of Chris' impending arrival. He was tempted to follow Petra, but her dramatic exit had made the situation even more awkward, and he was hoping to ease the tension. Except he had no idea where or how to begin.

The bathroom door slammed, followed by a loud creak as Petra turned the faucet to start the shower. Kasem sighed, he and Carlos were alone for the first time since the start of the op, other than when he had carried the half-conscious Carlos to the car. Pretending to read the book that was open in front of him, Kasem fidgeted—the living room armchair wasn't comfortable under the best of circumstances, but the awkwardness meant that the cushion might as well be made of concrete. He reached for the side table and drained his water bottle, hankering instead for a finger of whiskey. Imagining the smokiness of a glass of Lagavulin, he wondered how many he would need to take the edge off. *At least three or four.*

He felt the weight of Carlos' gaze and frowned, contemplating whether it would do more harm than good to break the silence. Kasem tried again to focus on his book, having restarted reading the same page three times already without internalizing any content.

Kasem had reached the end of the first paragraph when Carlos finally spoke up, "I should thank you—for getting me out of there yesterday. You took a big risk, and you didn't have to. So, thank you. I owe you one."

"No thanks needed, anyone would have done it."

"I don't think so." Carlos hesitated, "You know before Veronica told me who you were—I had this picture of you and your past. I knew you worked in Iran and probably did some dark stuff… but I also knew Petra wouldn't be with you if you weren't a good guy. That, along with everything you did for us in New York and D.C., and then in London and Mada—I thought I knew exactly who you were."

Kasem stared at him, remaining silent as Carlos continued, "All that to say, I knew you were on our side, but then it all came crashing down when I found out that you were—*are*— the Ahriman. But maybe I was too quick to judge—there's more to this story, even if I had my head too far up my ass to see it." He paused, "If you're open to it, I'm ready, in fact, I'd like to hear it, to see the whole picture. I want you to tell me everything. How it all happened."

Gaping at Carlos, Kasem racked his brain. *Could I tell him the truth?* He looked down at the area rug below the coffee table, examining the geometric pattern, still dumbfounded. Petra had always trusted him, she had always relied on Carlos' counsel and friendship.

She would want to trust him. He knew it in his bones, Petra and Carlos were family. After another moment of consideration, he took the plunge.

"There's a lot of detail and a lot of nuance that we don't have time for, but I'll give you the headlines," he started. "When Petra was posted in Iran, we started dating. Initially, she was cultivating me as a source, that's how we met, but she ended up pursuing other assets. We stayed together, and eventually, she read me in on who she was. It all seemed so insane…" Kasem's voice trailed off as he recalled the night she'd told him that she was a spy. "I didn't even know her real name, but she introduced me to another source—hoping that we could help keep each other safe. The whole thing backfired, the government found her other source, and rather than give up Petra, she gave me up instead."

"You were captured?"

Kasem nodded, "Captured, thrown in prison, interrogated—the works. That's when General Majed, a rogue Iranian general, tricked me into working for him. He told me that they had Petra—or Lila, as I knew her back then—in custody, and the only way to buy her freedom was to commit to serving him."

"That's why you did it?"

"Of course, it all turned out to be a ploy—Petra was never captured." Kasem took a deep breath, "But the things I did were real. The people I killed, even under orders. She thought I was dead, and then we came face-to-face on her operation in Kuwait. She told me that she'd never been captured, that the Agency got her out as soon as she realized that I'd been captured. I couldn't believe it, but that was it for me. I cut ties and ran. I don't know if I would have gone through with the op in Kuwait—I'd like to think that I wouldn't have, but I'll never know. Anyway, the Ahriman died in a building fire there, and I've been trying to get back to being Kasem Ismaili ever since."

"So, it's true? You're the Ahriman?"

"I *was* the Ahriman, but not anymore. I can't ever redeem myself for everything I've done, but the Ahriman died in Kuwait—I promise you that." Steeling his expression, he braced himself for Carlos' reaction, also pondering what Petra would say when he told her what had transpired. The secret felt like a weight off his back, and a sense of freedom washed over him—

he could breathe again, having taken someone that he trusted into his confidence.

Whatever happens, it was the right choice.

Before Carlos could respond, a loud creak sounded from outside as the gate to the driveway opened—Chris had arrived.

* * * * * *

Chapter 66

Bujumbura, Burundi

Petra gave Chris a tentative hug—their last interaction in Madagascar had been tense, despite ending the trip on a good note. The group exchanged a few pleasantries but elected to wait on the operational briefing since Carlos' crew would be arriving in less than an hour.

Bad decision, Petra squirmed in her seat, the living room full of elephants that no one wanted to acknowledge. The Ahriman, her history with Kasem, Veronica's blatant disregard for protocol. The fact that they could all barely stand each other. She sighed, the icing on the cake was Chris' presence: that the Agency wanted them to execute the op with one arm tied behind their backs.

They'd rather Kevin and V disappear than deal with his betrayal and how their relationship compromised her.

With a deep breath, she took the opportunity to observe everyone's posture and demeanor—anything to keep her mind occupied while the second hand on the wall clock moved like a ticking time bomb. *Tick, tock, tick, tock,* she could barely check her impulse to remove the clock's batteries.

Chris made some tries at small talk, but each attempt landed in silence. He asked how the last year had been for her; however, since she refused to provide the Agency with much detail on either her cover identity or Kasem's—at least any more than they already had gathered—so the topic was characterized by fits and starts.

"Paris is beautiful and charming," she repeated using a number of different phrases as if that was all that their life there entailed. "I like teaching," she also acknowledged since the Agency already had intel on her post in the public policy program at Sciences Po. *Really personal stuff.*

She was grateful when Carlos took over the brunt of the conversation, telling a story of how he and his wife had visited Athens for the first time a few months earlier. As a history buff, Diane had almost collapsed onto her knees at the Parthenon, repeating, "This is the birthplace of Western civilization!"

Petra chuckled, struggling to picture the poised and proper Diane in that kind of abandon. She caught Carlos' eye, and his grin widened, easing the knot in her stomach. Had the iciness between them begun to thaw? Her gaze moved to Kasem, who sat upright on the couch, his arms slack with his hands on his thighs instead of crossed against his chest. Something had happened while she was in the shower, that much she could ascertain, even if she wasn't sure what. Carlos and Kasem had been alone for a while, she had to wonder what they had talked about.

Chris looked amused at Carlos' anecdote, then turned the conversation back to Petra. She had just deflected another probing question when Gaston showed up. He took on the brunt of the conversation, much to her relief, as he and Chris hadn't seen each other in years.

A few minutes later, Chris changed the subject, "All right, before the military team gets here, a little shop talk. Carlos, could you tell us more about who these guys are?"

"I worked with one of them years ago—Tim, or as we call him now, *The Tim.* He was my contact on an op in Mexico. He's super competent, always comes through in a pinch, and we're good buddies now. He's ex-special ops, and also an ex-cop, but now runs a security training program called The O'Brian Group outside of D.C."

Kasem leaned forward, "A security training program?"

"He and the other guys run training simulations for the State Department and World Bank, and probably other organizations where staff are posted in locations where they need security training. They also run trainings for military personnel—they cover driving, combat first-aid, land navigation, stuff like that. They're all ex-military with different specialties, really a top-notch team. Since we can't get backup from special ops, they're probably our best shot. We're lucky to have them."

Petra caught the expression on Kasem's face and could tell that he was intrigued. Would something like that work for him? Their discussion on his career prospect cycled through her brain, he had been so frustrated at being unable to find something he could be passionate about, and he obviously couldn't go back to project finance in Iran. As Carlos went into further detail on the team's qualifications, she started to dissect the idea until the outside gate sounded again.

Their team had arrived.

* * * * * *

Even with Carlos' explanation, Petra wasn't sure what to expect when the crew walked through the door. She recognized The Tim as soon as he came into the living room, well before Carlos had made any introductions. She squelched a grin, he had a particular swagger and boisterous demeanor. In half a second, he was already unforgettable. Petra recognized him as a kindred spirit. She felt an immediate kinship to the other team members as well, their stance boasted competence without taking themselves too seriously. *Not that they couldn't take any one of us out with their bare hands.*

Carlos introduced them one by one, with Tim last. "And this is the famous The Tim," he said, clapping him on the shoulder.

Petra broke into a smile, their immediate camaraderie amplified by the warmth of his tone and transparency of his no-nonsense greeting. Clearly, she had hung out with way too many spies over the years, the experience was such a novelty. "It's good to meet you, Tim. We're lucky to have you."

Once the introductions were done, they settled on the couches as Chris stood up to initiate the team planning session. "First off, I want to say thank you to all of you for being here. I know this isn't the easiest of circumstances." He turned toward Tim, then scanned the rest of his team, "I know Carlos already briefed you on what happened to two of our team, so I won't bore you with that again. We have two objectives—get them back *and* take out Nziza before he moves on his plan for a military coup. So, two objectives, three teams. Two on the palace, one on Blue Bay." He tapped on his iPad screen, and blueprints of the Presidential palace projected above it.

"We got intel from a source in the M.S.S. that the Chinese are on high alert tonight, which tells me two things. It's Easter, so I would wager that Nziza's troops will move early in the morning, on Easter eve—when most people, including military personnel, will be celebrating with their families. That means our window is closing, and we have to move on Markov this evening. Gaston, does that track with how things work here?"

"Yes. Many people won't even be in Buja this weekend, they're vacationing in other parts of the country. Those that are in town will mostly be prepping for church and other festivities on Sunday morning."

Petra frowned, wondering who Chris' source was. *Why didn't he tell us this before?*

Chris continued, "In an ideal world, we'd take Nziza out instead of kidnapping Markov—"

"We're kidnapping the president?" Tim stared at Chris, then turned toward Carlos, "You did *not* tell me that. I thought we were stopping a coup, not executing one."

Before Carlos could respond, Chris interjected, "If I may—we're not kidnapping him, just taking him out of the equation. We don't have the manpower to stop Nziza's troops without the local military, and we don't know who we can trust. We'll get to Markov, bring him back here, and then the coup will fall apart all on its own."

Tim looked unsatisfied but listened in silence as Chris explained their plan to breach the Presidential Palace and take Markov out of play. Having come up with this plan with Carlos, Petra only half listened. Something about Chris's reply to Tim's point irked her, but she couldn't put her finger on it. His answer had been fine, and it had been her idea to kidnap Markov. Despite her best efforts, she found herself unable to silence her doubts.

She took a long sip of water, thinking back to what Alex, one of her training officers, had said to her years ago: "When something doesn't seem right, it's based on your intuition. Don't ignore it—go back through everything you know, everything you've read. You saw something, dismissed it as nothing, but it's still there, in the back of your mind. That's intuition."

That's intuition.

Petra exhaled slowly, the words ringing through her head. She zeroed in on Chris' face, on his micro-expressions, still unable to figure out what was bothering her. The only thing she could think of was that Carlos should have been the one explaining the plan, it would have landed far better with Tim and his team had that been the case. Still, the Agency had sent Chris in to take over this op, so that was hardly proof of anything. She tabled her thoughts as Chris finished his explanation of their plan to breach the Palace.

"If we manage to get Markov out, then what?" Tim asked. "The troops still take the palace—even if they don't have Markov, they could do considerable damage."

Chris nodded, "It's a risk that we have to take. If they do try to claim that they have the president, he can go public condemning the coup."

"We *have* to get Nziza, though," Kasem added. "The only way Markov can stay credible is if he's managed to capture the coup leader."

The rest of the room turned toward him, Petra included. She was surprised that he had inserted himself into Chris', and as such, the Agency's flow, but she had to agree with him. Despite that, she wished that they could limit their involvement—she didn't want to be part of an op that took Markov out, but making sure that he stayed in power wasn't great either. Regardless though, Kasem was right—Nziza should be on trial in the Hague.

"Gaston, what do you think?" Chris glanced over at his old contact.

"Kasem is right. If Markov doesn't neutralize Nziza, he could just try again in a few months. Given Markov's support, they could go back and forth for years, and the country would be devastated. This is post-colonial Africa, and if a leader isn't able to demonstrate enough strength, the country could degenerate into a one coup per year cycle. I don't want that to happen here," Gaston replied.

Kasem looked around the room, then focused on Chris. "You already said that we don't know how much support Nziza has within Markov's government. We may not know who or how many, but we know that support exists. These ops are all guesswork, based on as much intel as we can find. My guess is that Nziza has someone within Markov's personal guard. So, when we bring him back here, we need to bring his closest guards as well. Somewhere in that group is the key to finding Nziza—the Chinese moved him out of Blue Bay already, so we're too late to get to him there. This is our best chance—we can't just move Markov, we have to figure out who's compromised him."

"I like the way you think," Tim stood up, "but how many guards are we talking about? We can only take out so many."

"We would have to tranq his personal guards anyway, but then we could bring them back here. There's only four in his direct entourage—if there's a mole, it should be one of them." Chris tapped his fingers on the coffee table and looked at Tim, "Can you do it?"

"So, we have to extract Markov, his family, and four guards, all without calling in the national guard?" Tim crossed his arms, "Can your tech guy get us inside the compound? I know we have some schematics that we could use if we scale the wall, but that's not going to work here. I'll also need my whole team—we can't allocate people over to Blue Bay." He gave Petra an apologetic look.

After several moments of arguing, Chris finally agreed. "Do what you have to do."

"Okay," Tim turned to his team and doled out a series of instructions, person by person. Finally, he glanced at Kasem, "You'll come with us in the second car."

"Petra, I'll join you and Carlos at Blue Bay, along with Gaston," Chris said.

Petra let out another sigh. *But you're not even a field agent,* she wanted to protest. She would rather just have Carlos, even if he only had one good leg at the moment. "Fair enough," she kept her tone level, "the plan stays the same. Gaston stages the distraction, then we enter the property from the road, and beeline from the entry point to Veronica's tracker. My hope is that they have Kevin in the same place." *Otherwise, we're shit out of luck,* she neglected to add.

"Great, we move at six," Chris said. "Tim, you and your team, take the palace, along with Kasem, and the rest of us will head to Blue Bay."

Petra sat up with a frown at the words 'take the palace'. Even if kidnapping Markov was their only shot at stopping the cop, Chris' phrasing pulled on her already concerned state of mind. Taking the Palace would be more like the Agency holding Markov hostage, basically, an Agency coup. The possibility stank—but rang true, especially considering the number of coups orchestrated on the part of Western spy agencies.

The Agency can't have sunk that low. She remembered Kasem's conversation with Kevin, and the possibility that the Agency had worked with Nziza. She hadn't wanted to believe it then, and she didn't want to believe it now.

She was still vacillating as to whether she should voice her reticence when Tim spoke up instead, "Just to be clear, as soon as Nziza is neutralized, Markov goes home, no harm, no foul. First, we secure him, then we immediately explain what's going on, why we kidnapped him. Make no mistake, my team and I refuse to be involved in any kind of backdoor coerced recruitment."

A recruitment op, Petra wanted to curse. She trusted Tim's experience implicitly, and the idea set off even more alarm bells. If he was right, how could they get out of it?

"Sorry, I didn't make myself clear." Chris fiddled with the button on his blazer, "We are in no way taking the president hostage, just doing what we must to keep him safe. In doing so, we can make sure he awards the power deal to the American bidder, in the country's best interest, and not to the Chinese."

Petra's frown deepened, she could have sworn that Kasem had said that the Indian power provider would be the most beneficial deal for Burundi's economy.

If it looks like a duck and quacks like a duck... She kicked herself for not studying the deal in more detail. Kasem had been right, there was obviously more going on here than Veronica was privy to. She turned toward Kasem, then Carlos, studying their expressions, but was unable to get a clear read.

Although Tim appeared only partially convinced, he raised no further objections. Petra caught him exchanging a glance with Carlos and made a mental note to broach the subject with them later.

Chris looked relieved, adjourning the meeting with another thank you. A moment later, he slipped away to one of the bedrooms, citing the need to check in with the Agency management.

"I don't know about you, but I could use some shut-eye," Tim stood and stretched his arms overhead. "That's when we make the worst mistakes—when we're tired."

Despite the lightness in his tone, Petra could tell that he still had reservations, as did she. She let out another sigh. They couldn't do this op without the Agency, and they had no choice but to stop the coup.

Somehow, they always ended up boxed in.

* * * * * *

After the team planning session, Petra retreated into the garden to take a moment to herself. Her head was a turmoil of thoughts and emotions, still processing everything that had happened since they'd arrived in Burundi weeks earlier. She hadn't realized how much adrenaline had been coursing through her system, but she was painfully aware of it now, with exhaustion threatening to override all of the skill and presence she would need to move on Blue Bay. Drawing in a deep breath, she sat down on a rock in the sunlight, hoping that it would rejuvenate her.

She remained there for several minutes, taking in the healing energy with her eyes closed, when she heard the back door to the team house.

"There you are, chérie," she heard Gaston say.

Reluctantly, she opened her eyes and gave him a small smile, as he approached her perch, "Hey, how are you?"

"Ça va, I guess. I wish things had gone better so far, but I am glad that Tim and his team are here."

Leaning back against the garden wall, Petra nodded quietly, wishing that she could be alone again. She was fond of Gaston, and they'd become fast friends in their brief time together, but she had precious little alone time. She also knew how much effort the rest of the op would take that very evening.

"Are you all right?" he asked.

"Maybe. I just wish things could be calmer for a while."

"Une vie trop tranquille est une mer morte."

Petra raised her eyebrows, amused at the French saying. "A life that is too calm is a dead sea? I haven't heard that one before."

Gaston bowed his head, "I am happy to provide more. I know many of these old sayings."

"That's okay," she chuckled. "I don't think my life is in danger of becoming a dead sea."

"Mais, of course not," he gave her a look of exaggerated shock. "We did not choose to become spies to sit on our couch

Puja Guha

all day. Although, I did think that when I retired I would have more couch time. I suppose you thought the same."

"I did."

"It's okay, chérie. After tonight, you and Kasem, you can enjoy plenty of couch time together."

"I hope so." Before either of them could say more, the door opened again and Tim emerged from the house, guzzling a gallon-sized jug of water.

"The other retirees," Tim grinned as he approached. "I'm impressed these Agency folk managed to wrangle this many of us together. They've got more pull than I thought."

"Something like that," Petra shrugged.

"Come now, I was just saying how much we need more excitement in our lives," Gaston countered.

"You know, I've been saying that since I got on the plane," Tim agreed. "Seriously though, are you both okay with the plan? There's a lot riding on you and I'm sorry to leave you to take Blue Bay on your own. Too bad Peg Leg Carlos can't be more involved."

Too bad, indeed, Petra thought. "We'll be all right," she said, hoping to convince herself as much as anyone else.

"Of course, we will be fine," Gaston added in a tone that sounded far more confident.

"Good to hear it," Tim said, looking between the two of them. "Sorry if I interrupted anything."

"Not at all," Gaston shook his head. "If only the operation were tomorrow, we could have a bit of a party tonight, help us to relax."

Tim looked amused and took another gulp from his water jug before replying, "I'll have to check out the town some other time."

"You must—Burundi is a beautiful place."

"How long have you been living here?" Tim asked.

Petra let her attention drift as Tim and Gaston continued to converse. Both of them clearly had a better ability to blow off steam than she did, and she smiled to herself, recalling how Kasem had relayed Gaston's comment about stopping to smell the flowers. He was probably right, she and Kasem could certainly lighten up a bit, but now wasn't the time for it. She had an op to get through, whatever way she knew how.

* * * * * *

Chapter 67

Blue Bay, Burundi

Veronica's eyes opened in slits and quivered, attempting to focus on the room around her. Her face smarted from the beating she had taken earlier, and the pain would only heighten as her adrenaline wore off. So far, she'd been able to maintain her cover without telling the guards anything. Still, she knew as well as any other operative that it was only a matter of time— she either had to come up with a convincing lie that would satisfy her captors, or they would push her to her breaking point when she would tell them everything. An overwhelming urge to vomit came over her.

Glancing at the chair a few feet away close to the opposite wall, she cringed, recalling how they had dragged Kevin out after dumping her back in the room. With a deep breath, the fogginess in her head wavered, and she ran through everything that had happened since she'd been captured. They couldn't have been held for more than a day, she assessed with relief. The alternating torture pattern had probably continued since early that morning, but without a window, she wasn't confident in her ability to tell time. She and Kevin were being housed in what looked like an empty storage room. A noise caught her attention, and she quieted her mind to listen.

Waves. The sound was unmistakable.

Both M.S.S. strongholds were at the lakeside, but holding her at the Club du Lac, Burundi's most popular resort, would probably attract undue attention. That meant that she and Kevin were almost definitely being held at Blue Bay. The guards who had spoken to her thus far were Burundais, and they hadn't scanned for her tracker, but she doubted her luck would hold up once Chinese intelligence got involved.

After another deep breath, her training took over, as did a sense of calculating calm. Her recollection sharpened, including details on where she had been taken and what she'd seen, followed by a flood of emotions as she remembered Kevin coming back to help her. Just over a month ago, he had come to warn her about the F.S.B., and now, he'd risked everything to return to the van for her.

What did his actions mean and why did they even matter? The questions plagued her, and she cursed aloud despite the pain searing through her jaw from the beating she had received. She pushed past it and continued the daunting process of unpacking what had transpired in the last twenty-four hours.

She swallowed, their capture of Nziza had been a spectacular failure. They had needed military backup for the van, and the fact that they'd missed a deactivated tracker... Veronica grimaced, recognizing her failure.

Dismissing the train of thought—beating herself up would lead her nowhere—she zeroed in on her current circumstances. The room had a solid wood door a few paces to her left, with a wimpy looking handle and lock. Even if they could get out, they could do little to prepare for who would be on the other side.

Closing her eyes, Veronica pictured the map images of Blue Bay they had studied before deciding to move on Club du Lac instead. She could see the bird's eye view of the beach and the ridge-line to the south as a lookout point. The point would offer both cover and concealment, but only if they had enough time to clear the beach. She winced, consciously recognizing that she had implicitly assumed that she and Kevin would escape together, rather than getting away on her own.

Does he deserve my help? The answer remained beyond her grasp.

Veronica resigned herself to that choice. Regardless of what had happened between them—even regardless of his betrayal of the Agency—she couldn't leave him behind. Carlos had been hit, and Kevin had gone to his aide, then run further into the lion's den for her.

Why didn't he run? Whatever answers there were to that question, they would have to wait until she was free. To get to that point, the first step was addressing the knots binding her wrists to the chair.

The chair was made of wood, reminiscent of her classrooms in middle school, down to the tiny splinter pricking into her right forearm. She twisted her wrist and felt along the back of the seat, searching for the source—if she could widen the splinter, perhaps she could use it to gnaw through the ropes. Tracing the length of the splinter with her finger, she picked at it, and when it gave way, she managed to expose a section on the wood that was a smidge sharper than the smoothed-out edges of the chair and got to work. Eventually, even this dull edge would get through the ropes that were holding her down.

* * * * * *

By the time one of the guards returned with Kevin, Veronica was unsure whether the rope had cut deeper into her wrists, or her so-far unsuccessful attempt at slicing through it had made more headway. Keeping her hands still, she slumped over to avoid scrutiny, all the while observing the guard dump Kevin into the other chair across the room. Once he secured Kevin to the back of the chair, he left immediately without giving her so much as a second glance. The door slammed shut behind him, and her shoulders relaxed, she recognized the guard as the same one who had dealt with her earlier. Given that, she would wager there were only two of them, a thought which brought her a modicum of confidence. The guards were stocky and well-built, but they could take them.

She looked over at Kevin, waiting for him to say something. After several seconds went by, she frowned, "Kevin? Are you okay?"

"I'm fine," he raised his head slowly to meet her gaze.

His face was red, and she could see a shiner starting to form around his left eye, but what concerned her more was the redness around his neck and collar bones. *They treated me like a girl,* she realized that they'd been far harder on him. "What did you tell them?" she asked. Deep down, she even wondered if he was the reason that they had been caught—could he have betrayed them?

It could all be another trick, maybe they had played right into his hands. That possibility was unlikely, he was also being held prisoner, and he had risked his life to save her, but she wondered all the same. His previous betrayal was still raw, and she blinked away a tear as she remembered the moment Chris had first informed her of it. *Was this all part of his plan?*

"Nothing—I didn't tell them anything."

"What did they ask?" This time, despite her best efforts to retain a hard edge, her tone was gentler than before.

"Who I work for, who else is involved, what our plans are. Standard stuff, what you would expect."

Veronica sighed, everything he was saying sounded reasonable, and in all likelihood, he was telling the truth. Especially since the same suite of questions had been posed to her as well. Yet, he had fooled all of them for years. "I mean it, Kevin. Did you tell them anything?"

"Did you?"

"I wouldn't betray our team." The words left a bitter taste in her mouth, but she couldn't stop herself.

"I never betrayed *you*."

Veronica clung to her anger while continuing to rub the rope binding her wrists into the slivered edge of her wooden seat. Although it had finally started to fray, she still had a long way to go. *Get free and leave him behind,* she told herself. She couldn't afford to have someone with her that she didn't trust.

"I know you don't believe me," Kevin said in a softer tone, "but it's true. I never betrayed you. I couldn't do that, no matter who asked me. I swear on my father's grave."

On your father's grave? His words resonated deeply, she knew how close he had been to his dad, who had raised him as a single parent after his mom passed when he was eight. *That can't be a lie, it can't be.* She found herself unable to challenge him, processing what he had said. "No matter who asked you? What do you mean? The F.S.B.?"

"Of course."

"Why are you talking about them as if you're supposed to serve them unconditionally? They aren't some gift to the world, God's gift to humankind. You were doing black ops. Do you realize you almost blew up half of D.C.? How many innocent people would have died?"

"You're right, at least about D.C.—I let myself be blinded. But you're not right about everything. The F.S.B, the Agency, they're the same. What's the difference? Look at you, do you really think I don't know you blackmailed Petra into being part of this op? Don't pretend that you weren't willing to burn all your friends just to bring me in. I may not know what you have on them, but I know what you did. All in the name of what? Some greater good? Some illusion that will never be real?"

His words stung, and she was taken aback, confronted by her hypocrisy. "Fine, you're right, I put them on the line to bring you in. I had to, I already let you go once." She paused as his words sank in further. "When did they recruit you?" she asked after a protracted silence.

"On my second posting—a long one out in Vietnam, the first one after Nairobi. I developed this asset, a young guy, only a little older than me. We became buddies, real friends. He brought in tons of intel on the M.S.S., he'd been with them a couple of years already, rising quickly through the ranks, but got disillusioned when they sent someone he knew on a suicide mission when they could have saved him. I worked with him for over a year before he asked me for a favor—his grandfather was sick, and there was this clinical trial in Sweden he wanted to get him into. I told him that I'd do my best, that I was sure the Agency would come through for him after everything that he'd already done for us…"

"What happened?" Veronica could hear the weight in his tone, riddled with a sense of loss. What had the Agency done? Part of her didn't want to know, but she couldn't look away, as if she was approaching a wrecked car, complete with black smoke and occupied gurnies.

"They told me they'd look into it, then they came back with these insane demands. They would only get his grandfather into the trial if he could give us even more intel—if he broke into his superior's safe, regardless of the risk."

A lump formed in her throat, she didn't want to believe it, but she knew exactly what had happened. "Go on," she whispered.

"I told him what they said, I even convinced him to do it. That we would pull him out immediately if there was a sign that things were going south. I think I even believed it, I certainly made him believe it." He paused, "But then it all went haywire, and he got caught. I wanted to extract him, but the Agency wouldn't sanction it, they actually wanted me to burn him. So, I went for it on my own. Nothing worked, and he was going to be executed."

"I'm sorry."

"He was going to die, and I asked the Agency to at least honor the deal, to get his grandfather into the trial, but they said no, that he wasn't worth wasting any more resources on." Kevin's voice trembled, "He was my friend, and they acted as if he was just a pawn on a chessboard. That's when the F.S.B. approached me. One of their operatives had been trying to recruit me for months. Really, we were both trying to recruit each other, but I don't think he ever expected to make any headway. We just pretended to be buddies, like we were playing a game of chicken. When I couldn't get Hahn out, though, I let something slip, then I went for it, asked if they could help me. I told him that if they helped me get my friend out, I'd work for them."

Veronica tried not to think about the number of times she had exploited similar vulnerabilities to force someone into spying for the Agency, risking their life to become an asset. "Did you get him out?"

"We did. After that, they let things go dormant, said they'd activate me when they needed me. Things started a couple of months later, a favor here, another one there. Small stuff really at first, things that didn't seem to matter much."

And before you knew it, you were in way too deep. Veronica nodded, she'd seen it more times than she could count, the process of reeling in an Agency asset past the point of no return. The Agency would ask them to do something seemingly insignificant, not a huge transgression, but something that would get them in trouble if anyone found out. Then another, and then another, until there was no going back. "Where is he now?"

"They got him a new identity, and he has a life now. I only got to see him one more time, just to say goodbye."

"What about the clinical trial?"

"By the time we got him out, his grandfather had already taken a turn for the worse. He wasn't eligible anymore."

Veronica let out a long sigh, wishing that there was something that she could say to change what had happened, to lessen the blow Kevin had suffered at the Agency's behest. "I'm sorry," she whispered, for the first time starting to understand why he'd done what he had.

"I did what they asked because they saved my friend, but after a while, I followed orders without thinking about it. That's when things got darker, but I was too far gone to take a stance. When I realized they wanted to go after you, I couldn't go through with it anymore."

"What about D.C.? The attack? You would have gone through with that."

He looked away, turned his gaze to the ground. "I was in a dark place, and I didn't start to come back until we were together. I want to believe that I would have stopped…"

Despite her better instincts, his words rang true. Veronica refused to go down that path, it didn't matter, he had still betrayed them.

But I can't leave him here.

"I've been working on my ropes, but it's slow going since I can't see them. Think you could move over so you can talk me through it?" The redirected focus felt necessary—even if she now knew that he had, or perhaps even did, really love her, she couldn't possibly grasp what that meant.

* * * * * *

Chapter 68

Bujumbura, Burundi

Petra fastened her holster around her waist, then positioned her Colt pistol, a Swiss Army knife, and tranq gun in their respective spots. Try as she might, she couldn't shake the foreboding feeling in the pit of her stomach.

We should abort. She was still questioning her gut—would the Agency be willing to interfere in a government's decision on who to award the power deal to? Despite her best efforts to convince herself, she remained unsure if she could trust Chris under these circumstances. He had always come through before, she recalled how he'd shown up in Madagascar to help with Carlos' extraction.

He was her friend, she knew that much. She just couldn't say the same for the Agency, a question that she now wished she had taken the opportunity to discuss with Tim and Gaston when they were in the garden earlier.

Petra grimaced, regardless of how apprehensive she felt about the op, they could neither allow Nziza to take over the Burundais government nor could she let Kevin and Veronica be tortured in a Chinese prison.

We're stuck with this op, she reluctantly acknowledged to herself for the umpteenth time. *But I don't have to like it.* She made a mental note to keep a close eye on Chris. Whatever the Agency was up to, he was at the center.

Kasem walked into the room and put his arms around her waist as she leaned her head back onto his shoulder. "I'm really glad you're here," she whispered, planting a kiss on his cheek.

"Nowhere else I'd rather be," he grinned. "Well, maybe a few, like sunbathing on the beach with you at Blue Bay, or maybe skinny dipping."

We could get married there.

"I can think of a few other things I'd like to do with you on the beach at Blue Bay," Petra chuckled, letting him think she was alluding to more adult activities. There was something she wanted to say, but she didn't know where to begin. For some time now, she had known that her future would be entwined with his, regardless of what that meant, but she hesitated to broach the subject. She had turned him down so many times, but there was a chance that the op would go sideways. How much longer could she wait?

"What is it?" he asked. "There's something on your mind. What Tim said? I hope it won't come to that, but if the Agency's trying to take Markov hostage, we won't let that slide."

"That's part of it, I'm definitely worried about that."

"Wait, before that. There's something I have to tell you. I got us a safe house here when I was out the other day, just in case. No one else knows, Gaston introduced me to a couple of people and I widened the circle from there." He leaned over and whispered in her ear, explaining where it was and how to access it.

"Wow. I didn't realize…"

"If things go to plan, we won't need it."

She nodded slowly, the air heavy between them. If things did go well, they wouldn't need it, but how often did that happen? Her earlier hesitation fell away and she decided to take the plunge. "We'll deal with whatever we have to. I'm worried about the op, but that's not what I was thinking of. I know I've been reticent about our future—I turned down your proposal once in Japan, and this time I accepted, but with a lot of hesitation because of where we are as a couple. Because of what this life together entails for you, and the sacrifices that you've had to make for me."

Kasem opened his mouth, and she motioned with her right hand to stop him from responding, "Just let me finish." She exhaled, then continued, "We might not know the answers now, but I'm ready—ready to commit to figuring it out with you. Ready to take that step. Things aren't perfect, but we'll manage it together."

"What are you saying?"

"If we make it out of here, I don't want to wait any longer. I want to marry you."

* * * * * *

Chapter 69

Blue Bay, Burundi

Carlos peered out of the backseat window through his binoculars, then glanced at Petra in the driver seat. They had driven up a side road and parked along the ridgeline above Blue Bay resort, concealed by several bushes. He shifted and cringed, even though the gunshot wound to his leg was minor and required only rest and cleaning to allow the stitches to heal, the area was still painful when he moved. His leg was propped up and stretched over the seats, and he had to twist in the opposite direction to look out the window, a position that made use of all the yoga his wife had made him do for the past several years. Nevertheless, he was uncomfortable, although he would rather bear it and be part of their operation than stay home and rest. Despite his continued anger at her for cajoling him into this op, Veronica was one of them.

Glancing at Petra once again, Carlos opened his mouth for the third time. He had to say something, had to tell her that he felt differently than when he had confronted her back in Paris, but the words eluded him.

I know it was more complicated, and I shouldn't have been so quick to judge. It all seemed so simple, but that statement felt empty rather than conveying how sorry he was. Kasem might be the Ahriman, but he'd still done a lot of good. At the same time, Carlos understood why he had reacted in that way, while recognizing that he should have given her the benefit of the doubt. Therein lay the crux of the issue, that he had jumped to judgment despite all of the years that he and Petra had known each other.

And everything that they'd put on the line, everything that they'd done for each other. Carlos sighed, Petra was part of his family, and he missed that camaraderie, but he wasn't sure if she would accept his apology. *Would I?*

Her gaze remained fixed on the entrance to Blue Bay, she had avoided one-on-one conversations with him since he had blown up at her in Paris. They waited for Chris to get into position on the road below in silence. After waffling for several more moments, Carlos finally said, "Kasem and I talked earlier today before Chris got here."

"I know." Her eyes landed on him for a second but then returned to the entrance.

"I should have heard you out—I'm sorry, I was wrong. I was too quick to judge."

"Thank you for saying that." Petra gave him a slight nod, but her tone remained cold, "I appreciate it. We both do."

"I mean it, I shouldn't have judged you. I should have given you a chance to tell me everything." He stopped there, resisting the urge to ask the question that nagged at him. Would she have ever told him the truth?

The iciness in Petra's posture thawed, "It was a big thing to find out." She hesitated, "Especially since I didn't tell you myself. Maybe I should have, maybe I even would have, but it was Kasem's secret, his story to tell." She met his gaze, "There were times I wanted to tell you—especially with how much you encouraged me to trust him again. I love him, even knowing what he's done, and it took me a long time to get here. A big part of why I decided to trust him again is because of you."

Carlos exhaled, relieved to hear her acknowledge the immensity of the secret. He reached out and squeezed her shoulder with his left hand. "It's your story too, he thought he was protecting you."

"It was my fault..."

"I understand now why you said that. He'd already done more for you than you could possibly ask." Carlos remembered a conversation they'd had a few years earlier in New York. "I get it—why you were so afraid to bring him in, to speak to him after thinking he was dead and running into him on that op in Kuwait. He loves you, there's no question about that. I'm glad you two managed to put the pieces back together."

"I never got the chance to tell you that we're engaged."

"I kind of jumped the gun when I chewed you out after I saw the ring. Anyway, he's a lucky guy, don't let him forget it."

"We both are."

Before Carlos could respond, his com crackled, and Tim's booming voice echoed through their ears. "We're in position, cowboys. Ready to go."

* * * * * *

Chapter 70

Blue Bay, Burundi

Tim glanced at the rearview mirror to look at Kasem, who was seated in the back. The car ride had passed mostly in silence, and now that his team was in position, they had to wait for twilight before making a move on the palace. Based on his read, Tim could tell that Kasem wasn't military, and his accent was mixed—mostly American, with a hint of something else in the back. *Maybe Arab? Iranian? Afghan?* Carlos hadn't shared much about the team, and Tim had sensed the tension between Carlos, Petra, and the man seated behind him.

"What's your story, cowboy? You ex-Agency too? How'd you get stuck with my buddy Carlos?"

Kasem shrugged, "It's a long story."

"All the best ones are," Tim nodded, "and they mostly have to do with a pretty lady—even when you get older, kid."

"Really?"

"These days, most of my stories have to do with my two little girls. You got any kids?"

"No."

"Well, Kasem, I pray that if you have kids, that you have some boys to balance out the girls. I have daughters, and I will tell you, they take over your entire life. Man, my two little girls—they're not so little anymore now—they've been driving me up the wall since they were yea-high." Tim gestured at his waist and shook his head. "One time, I was trying to get my daughter ready to go to her grandma's house, and she said to me, 'Dad, this doesn't match.' We tried six different outfits before I could get her out of the house—I was standing around holding up tops, being like, 'What about this one? What about this one? Honey, we have to go.' That went on for almost an hour, and I tell you, it's been like that ever since. She was only four back then."

The picture of someone like Tim being beholden to a four-year-old was priceless. "I like that story," Kasem said when his laughter subsided. A moment later, he sat up straighter. "What is it exactly that you do? Carlos didn't tell us much, just that you're all ex-military. He said you run some kind of training facility?"

"Yup, exactly. State department employees, NGO staff, people like that, they all need training for more dangerous postings. We run a three-day program that helps prepare them for that, but we also do more in-depth stuff for the military."

"Sounds pretty cool, let's you use all of those old skills in a less intense setting."

"It works out," Tim agreed, "except when we have to do favors like this for old friends." He shrugged, "Nah, I'm just playing, I'm glad we could be here. It's lucky we were so close by."

"Of course."

"You interested in a job?"

"Er, yeah, maybe," Kasem said, clearly taken aback.

"When you get back stateside, you give me a call." Tim reached into his pocket to pull out a business card and handed it over to Kasem. "We can always use another good man, and I know Carlos wouldn't trust you if you didn't have a good head on your shoulders."

Kasem looked like he was about to speak, but changed his mind, then accepted the card and stuffed it into his pocket. "Thanks."

"Somehow, I think you've got more to say, but we'll work on that later. I'm serious about the job, though. It's yours if you want it, at least as a trial."

******

Chapter 71

Blue Bay, Burundi

Petra watched the sun descend over Lake Tanganyika in an array of pinks, reds, and oranges in stark contrast with the azure water. The reflection of the red and orange hues shimmered, encompassing the water and making it look like it didn't exist, as if the whole world could be consumed by the sunset. Even with all of the beauty, Petra shuddered, the scene made her feel as if they were heading straight into a volcano, albeit a stunning one.

"Holy crap, this place is beautiful," Carlos said, echoing her thoughts.

"Too bad we're never in places like this for fun."

"Don't ever tell Diane how amazing these places are, she'll start to say that I never take her anywhere."

The side of Petra's mouth crinkled, the moment was bittersweet; her past interactions with Carlos were characterized by such banter. Despite his earlier apology, she remained unsure as to whether they could return to that type of relationship. She was still hurt and angry, although they were on a better path now. She wanted to forgive him, part of why she'd agreed to Gaston and Chris driving down to Blue Bay separately. "Sure," she nodded and turned back toward the sunset.

"Are you ready for this, kiddo? Seems like your mind's elsewhere."

The concern in his voice brought down some more of the wall she'd put up between them since the operation had started. "I'm ready, but I can't help think about what we'll do—if Kasem's identity ever comes out. How do we go on? What do we do…?" her voice trailed off. "Don't worry, I'll be focused on the op when we move. You know how it is, the rest of the world disappears."

"Of course." Carlos hesitated, "For what it's worth, I don't think they have any proof. If they did, Kasem would already have been arrested." He shrugged, "Or who knows, it's the Agency, they might have tried to turn him, to use him to capture General Majed."

Petra fidgeted. Would they do that? It was the Agency, and they had already used Kasem to impersonate the Ahriman once.

"Sorry, kiddo didn't mean to alarm you. I'm sure it'll be okay—you're doing this op, and V promised you a way out. Besides, like I said, I doubt they have proof."

I hope so. "How do you feel about this op?" she asked to change the subject. The pit of her stomach was becoming a massive knot, and talking about Kasem's fate made her want to be sick. She didn't want a life in the shadows, but she couldn't imagine a life without him.

Damned if I do, and damned if I don't.

Carlos clapped his hand on her shoulder, clearly sensing her concern. "It'll be all right, kiddo. We'll make sure of that."

His offer to help reassured her slightly, and she nodded, then repeated her question, "How do you feel about this op? Something feels off—I don't understand why Chris would say that the government here needs to support the American bidder on the power deal. I could have sworn that wasn't in the country's best interest—the Indian JV was offering a better price."

"There might be other factors—other concessions. The Americans did offer to provide solar panels to the airport at no additional cost."

"That's true," Petra said, still unconvinced. The calculations that Kasem had shown her—albeit back of the envelope ones—had indicated that even if the government had to pay for the installation of panels at the airport, the Indian joint venture was still offering a better deal on the development. "Kasem ran the numbers, and his calculations said that the Indian deal offered a twenty percent cost-saving for a similar level of quality, even with the airport price included." She shook her head, "It's like what Tim said, we're not in the business of blackmail. I'm telling you, Carlos, something's not right."

* * * * * *

Chapter 72

Bujumbura, Burundi

Tim watched the perimeter of the presidential palace through his binoculars, first with simple nighttime vision to observe the wall exterior, and then with the heat sensor attachment to keep track of the guards on the inside. The Agency's technology-enabled him to add an extra layer to the image, seeing past both the exterior wall and into the house itself. So far, everything seemed as expected, but he had been on too many operations to take that for granted. The number of guards that appeared through his heat vision sensors was far less than they would have expected, there were only four total in the entire garden, when their intel had indicated there should be eight. If the whole family was inside the house, then he only counted four inside as well.

Tim sighed, dusk was just starting to fall, but the night sky would offer more cover if they waited a half-hour longer. He would have preferred to wait until true darkness, but Chris had overruled him.

Seems like a decent dude, Tim thought of Chris, *but the op guidelines are wrong.* The Agency had no business meddling in this power deal, and he'd wager that all of them, including Chris, knew it.

"I've accessed the security system, coordinating with the Agency's tech," John's voice came over the com.

"Copy. Proceed with the plan."

Tim's eyes narrowed as he surveyed what he could from his limited low-ground vantage point. Normally, they would have had this place under observation for days before an op like this. He also didn't love having Kasem as an addition to the team, although Carlos had insisted on it. "He has great combat training," Carlos had said, "you might even want to give him a job."

A job is easier than having an unknown on your team. Tim caught a glimpse of Kasem in his peripheral vision to the right and reassured himself: if Carlos said he was good, then he was. What he was really worried about was Chris' agenda, and there was nothing he could do about it.

* * * * * *

Chapter 73

Blue Bay, Burundi

Kevin breathed a sigh of relief as Veronica was able to get through the last strand of ropes binding her hands. With her hands free, it was quick work to release her legs from the chair, and a few moments later, they were both on foot. Kevin threw caution to the wind and put his arms around her, pulling her in close. They hadn't been this close since before he'd betrayed her and the Agency, and the loss of contact had been even harder on him than he'd anticipated.

He had always known letting go of real connection would be the hardest part, but somehow, he'd ended up completely falling for her. He drew in a long breath as Veronica wriggled from his grasp, grateful that she had let him hold her for a moment. If they didn't make it out of there, at least that would be their last memory together. His eyes moved upward, searching for the sky, glad that the universe had granted him that boon.

"We have to get moving," Veronica said as she took another step back. She picked up the chair that she had been bound to, raising it over her shoulder as she positioned herself by the door. "I'm going to call for help," she readied herself to attack.

Kevin gave her a quick nod and slumped in his chair as she bellowed at the top of her lungs. "Somebody help! He's having a seizure! Help, we need help!"

A few seconds later, Kevin watched with his eyes open a sliver as Veronica slammed the chair on the guard's head when he came barreling through the door, knocking him out. Jumping up, Kevin joined her at the doorway, where she handed him a pistol from the guard's shoulder holster. For herself, she grabbed the revolver from his hip holster and slid the utility knife from his belt into the back of her waistband, then stood up.

Veronica glanced back at Kevin before stepping into the hallway, pointing the revolver ahead of her. "Watch my six."

* * * * * *

Chapter 74

Bujumbura, Burundi

Kasem could hear his heart drumming through his head as they maintained position, parked in a field down the hill from the president's residence, about a thousand yards below the patio from the Belvedere restaurant. The contrast between the hopping restaurant, blasting old 90s music remixed with house beats, and the stillness of the residence was eerie. Kasem grimaced, although he was grateful for the extra concealment the high volume would provide, the mix of Celine Dion and electronic music didn't seem right.

He watched the residence through the Agency's app, which showed the few satellite images of the palace that they had been able to get. Although he would have liked to have more time, he was reassured by the fact that the satellite feeds aligned broadly with the intel that Chris had shared. The feeds came from the same source, so there was no reason for them to be different, but Chris' behavior screamed conspiracy.

Was the Agency going to try to hold the government here hostage? A wave of disgust washed over him.

Greater good, my ass…

Kasem caught Tim's gaze in the rearview mirror, still surprised by the earlier job offer. That type of job would use his spy skills without being on actual operations, and it might even be fun.

Returning to the op at hand, Kasem considered what he should do if the Agency was indeed trying to blackmail the Burundais government. He wiped his hand across his brow, not wanting to consider the possibility.

If he went against the Agency, any chance of getting away from his past would be gone. He knew it in his bones, yet he couldn't sit right with what his gut told him was about to happen.

You don't know that. Besides, it wasn't his business. He bit his lip, if he could just follow orders, then he and Petra ought to be home free in only a few days. They could get married, have a life together. All he had to do was stick to the plan.

"Team two is in position," John said through the com. "We found cover on the other side of the house, past the Kiriri Garden hotel, on the right side, further up the hill. What now, boss?"

"Hold your horses, I'm thinking."

"I should record this moment—the Tim is *speechless*," John chuckled.

Tim shrugged, "No one will believe you anyway, recording or not."

"I bet your daughters will, I know they've succeeded at it. Probably the only ones in history who've gotten the job done."

Kasem opened up the city map on his phone and scanned the area, making sure that he had properly memorized the street map around the residence. Since they didn't have adequate weaponry to stand up to a full-scale assault from either Markov's or Nziza's men, every detail mattered even more than it otherwise would have. Every route they could use had to be mapped out since, inevitably, the op was unlikely to go completely as planned.

The minutes until twilight dragged out, each of the two teams watching the perimeter wall from different angles, with

278

occasional updates on the movement of the guards. With the Agency's heat-sensing binoculars, they were able to toggle between a direct view of the wall, red images of the guards against the backdrop of the garden, and finally, the same type of images for the inside of the residence.

Kasem used his finger to rotate the map and zoom in on the point where they had decided to scale the wall. That side backed up against the west end of Kiriri Garden hotel, extending further down the hill, meaning they could access the residence compound without going through any of the nearby streets.

The sky turned reddish with the hues of dusk, then moved into the light gray of twilight. "Team two, standby," Tim said, watching the compound for another moment. "You're a go, we'll be right behind you."

* * * * * *

Kasem crouched next to Tim in the hidden compartment underneath the backseat of the car, watching the exterior through the heat vision sensors on his goggles as they moved toward the gate of the presidential compound. Dave, one of Tim's team, was driving their car, dressed as an upscale chauffeur, with Ian in the passenger seat as a bodyguard escort. John and Ben were leading up the other car. *Why didn't Tim and I split up?* he wanted to ask, shifting in an attempt to find a more comfortable position.

"Now, these are close quarters. Sorry, we couldn't split up since there's no compartment in the other car." Tim winced, looking over at him, "Carlos owes me big time, I am way too old for this sh—*stuff*."

Kasem nodded, amused at the reference to Lethal Weapon but not sure what else to say.

"How long have you known Carlos?" Tim asked, breaking the silence.

"A few years," Kasem answered, keeping his answer as vague as possible. He had no idea what Carlos had or would share with Tim, and he had no intention of inadvertently getting caught in a lie.

After a moment of silence, Tim gave him a quick nod. "I get it, you know. Your past is your past, but it doesn't have to define your future."

"I hope you're right about that."

"Did you hear the story of how I got my nickname, *The Tim*?"

"No, I haven't. Do tell."

Tim chuckled, "We've got a few minutes until they reach the wall, so why not? I was working in Kabul a few years ago, training a team of local border police. We had intel on some insurgent activity a few hours away and set up a convoy to neutralize it. Before we headed out, I spent some time studying the map—making sure I knew where we were headed and how to navigate. As an aside, I'm a big fan of real land navigation, not relying too much on these damned little boxes that control our lives these days," he removed his phone from his pocket and gestured with it, then placed it back in his jacket. "An hour after we dispatched, I noticed we were going over a bridge, crossing a river, and that set off some alarm bells. Based on the map, I knew that we shouldn't be passing over any bridges, so I mentioned it to the local commander."

"What did he say?"

"He said, 'Tim, Tim, don't worry about it, we're fine, nothing to worry about,' but I wasn't buying it. So, I insisted that we call in our position, and it turned out we had crossed the border into Turkmenistan. Without realizing it, we had somehow gotten across the border, no checkpoints or anything.

We turned around and headed back towards the base. As soon as we got back across the bridge, we set up a checkpoint so that wouldn't happen again, then went on with the rest of our mission. When we were back at base, that commander started calling me *The Tim, the one who reads maps.* Eventually, the nickname got shortened, but it stuck, no matter how many times I told him it was just Tim."

"That's a good story." *Quite the character.* Kasem could see why Tim and Carlos were such good friends.

"Turkmenistan," Tim scoffed. "Don't worry about it, Tim, we'll be fine, we can't possibly get lost… crossed a whole river and expect to end up in the same place? Turkmenistan, my ass."

Kasem reigned in his laughter, turning his attention back to the gate. The car stopped as the convoy presented its paperwork at the guard station. "If only we could hear through these things," he said, glancing at his goggles. He could see the two heat signatures move within their station, one coming out to meet the first team's car.

He waited with bated breath, then watched as the guard walked slowly around the first car. "Looks like he's checking the underbelly with a mirror," Kasem said.

After completing a full circle, the same figure moved toward their car, and Kasem's muscles tightened further.

This had better work.

He let out a sigh of relief several moments later when the guard returned to his station; the black and white image of the gate in his goggles started to open slowly.

Kasem's stomach did a flip as the convoy drove slowly into the compound.

* * * * * *

Chapter 75

Blue Bay, Burundi

Petra caught Carlos' gaze as he motioned down the cliffside toward the beach. They waited a few more minutes as dusk rapidly turned to twilight.

"All right, kiddo, this is all you," Carlos said. "McLaughry, Frenchie, what's your status?"

"I'm in position, concealed in the brush, due northeast, sightlines on the house with Veronica's tracker. Petra, I've got you covered, so whenever you're ready."

"All set up, and the exit's clear," Gaston added from his position covering the road back to the city. "Is it too late to tell you that I really hate that nickname?"

"Acknowledged. And I'm Switzerland, I'm staying out of any nickname debates with Agent Puppy," Petra said with a grin.

"How could you?" Carlos replied in a melodramatic voice. "I thought we were friends."

"Agent Puppy? Frenchie does not sound so bad anymore," Gaston chuckled. "Puppy, are you sure you're old enough to lead this op?"

"Back to the op, children." Petra took a deep breath, reviewing her path to the hut. Carlos would remain at the car to keep watch, and Chris would provide backup with sniper rifles. Gaston had staged a car crash on the hillside above the road and was covering their backup exit at the northern edge of the Blue Bay property, just in case they couldn't make it back up the hillside to where Carlos had stashed the car. The hillside route offered more cover and used a side road that would completely bypass the accident site but was longer. Making it to Gaston's car would be faster, although less viable if the guards were in heavy pursuit.

Since neither Chris nor Carlos was field ready, and Gaston had been out of the game for some time, they had modified the plan so that Petra would go in on her own, albeit with their backup. More people inside meant more liabilities—a point she had stressed to them, not wanting to have to extract them as well if things went sideways. Now she was questioning that decision, she should have pushed to have Kasem or someone from Tim's team as her backup.

Make a beeline for the beach house, that's all you need to worry about right now. Just thread the needle through the fence.

"Goodbye, *old man*," she said to Carlos, then into her coms, "it's a go." She scrambled out of the car, imagining Carlos rolling his eyes as she moved down the slope.

She kept to the ridgeline for as long as possible as the bushes would help to conceal her, especially if the guards below had similar night vision gear. When she reached the point at which continuing along the ridge would increase the distance considerably—and have her reach the road far off from the designated entrance point—she turned course to move quickly down the hill. She kept as low to the ground as possible but favored speed over concealment. At the back of her mind, she had a small hope that they could extract Veronica and Kevin fast enough to back up Tim and his team. *You never know what could make the difference.* That said, if they hadn't grabbed Markov in the first few minutes, the whole thing would have gone haywire anyway.

Although those thoughts flashed briefly through her head, the only thing to focus on was the next stride forward. Within just over a minute, she reached the road and sprinted across the street, grateful for the lack of streetlights. She made it to the entrance point and crawled through the brush into the resort.

Here goes nothing.

* * * * * *

Chapter 76

Blue Bay, Burundi

Veronica searched for the exit to the beach house, resisting the urge to sprint forward—she didn't want to alert any guards to their escape. As they continued through the house, she frowned, searching for the other guards. She scanned the upstairs landing along with the two bedrooms adjacent to the storage room where she and Kevin had been held, then peered down the stairwell. After a moment of hesitation, she sped downstairs, but she still couldn't see anyone.

If they're already gone, then Nziza is moving on the Palace... tonight.

A shiver ran down her spine. She'd told herself that she didn't care about the government here, that she could ignore the Agency's higher purpose if it meant capturing Kevin, but she now had to recognize that it was a lie, at least in part. Despite her best efforts to ignore the larger mission and focus on Kevin, she refused to let the current government fall.

I can't have that on my conscience, the words echoed through her head, resonating in a way that she would never have predicted. How had she let this happen? She'd been so caught up in her own story that she had set them all up for a catastrophic fail. In the same vein, she wondered if she should let someone suspected as the Ahriman go free. She tabled that train of thought, she couldn't afford to get into her head right now.

Veronica approached the main door and pressed her back against the wall to remain out of sight as she peeked out of the window. "Just one guard on the porch, two more on the sand below," she whispered at Kevin. "I'll take him, you follow."

Before waiting for his answer, she burst through the door, slamming the butt of her pistol into the guard's head. He slumped to the ground, and she groped for his gun. As she grabbed it, a bitter taste ran through her mouth—the back of his head had hit a protruding plank, and blood was seeping out onto the porch.

The realization that she had killed him slammed into her like a steam roller. She had only had to do it three times, but taking a life never got easier.

You didn't have to kill him. She moved toward the staircase leading to the beach, Kevin only a few steps behind her, when she heard two gunshots.

"Take cover," she hit the deck hard, squinting in an attempt to pierce the darkness. *Where had the shots come from?*

******

Chapter 77

Blue Bay, Burundi

Petra saw two figures appear on the porch alongside the guard stationed there, but before she had a chance to react, she heard the shots from Chris's rifle. The guards outside the beach hut fell, and she had no choice but to make her move—hopefully, his shots would keep the porch guards pinned down until she could take cover under the entrance staircase.

She ran forward out of the brush, not bothering with concealment anymore—speed was now her best weapon. "It's incredibly hard to hit a fast-moving target," one of her Agency's trainers used to say to egg them on to move even faster during training drills. She cleared the perimeter pathway and pulled her night vision goggles down. The metal thumped against her collar bones, but she didn't let up until she hit the ground behind the staircase, unsure if she'd been spotted.

"At the hut," she radioed to Carlos. "Any movement from the fence line?"

"Nothing outside—looks like you're in the clear, kiddo."

"I'm going in." Petra holstered her Colt pistol and retrieved her tranq gun from her pack, she couldn't risk a stray shot hitting Veronica… *Or Kevin,* she begrudgingly admitted. She had to believe that at least part of their friendship had been based in truth, despite his betrayal of the Agency. Her thoughts flickered to her relationship with Kasem and the other assets that she had worked with, relationships that had all started because of a lie. Those relationships were still real, even if they had only started because of the Agency, a reassurance that was comforting. Even if he had been working for someone else, some portion of Kevin's interactions must have been grounded in reality.

Petra moved cautiously up the staircase, the two heat signatures she had seen through the goggles were nowhere to be seen. When she reached the top, she pressed up against the house wall and sneaked a peek around the corner. She caught sight of the porch guard splayed on his back. She stepped toward the body, checked the pulse to confirm he was dead, and then approached the front door, crouching beneath the window. It looked like the blackout curtains were drawn, but she didn't want to risk being seen.

She inched forward and reached for the doorknob with her left hand, keeping the tranq gun at chest level as she opened the door a crack. The hallway inside the beach house was dark, and she pulled the night vision goggles back up from her neck before proceeding further. A quick glance told her that one side of the hallway was empty, but before she could step far enough inside to clear the other side, she felt the cool metal of a gun against the back of her head.

Raising her hands above her head, Petra cursed under her breath and let the tranq gun roll back over her wrist.

"On the ground, asshole," the person said from behind her.

Petra's shoulders relaxed as she recognized Veronica's voice, "V, it's me." She leaned forward to set the tranq gun on the floor, then pulled the night vision goggles off of her face since they rendered her unrecognizable. Squinting without the aid of the goggles, Petra caught Veronica's outline stepping toward her and pulling her into a hug.

"Thank you for coming."

* * * * * *

It took Petra several moments to extract herself from Veronica's awkward embrace. She and Veronica had been friends once upon a time, but being blackmailed into joining the op hadn't won her any favors. When Petra wriggled free, she could see Kevin hovering in the background, and for a moment, they locked eyes. Petra gave him a brief nod, not sure what other greeting he should merit.

"What she said," Kevin took a couple of steps toward them.

Petra nodded again, then tapped on her com, "I have both packages. Moving out to extraction point."

"I'll keep your path clear," Chris acknowledged.

The line crackled as Carlos chimed in, "Hostiles are quiet. Frenchie, hold position and watch for movement. I'm heading to the pickup point."

* * * * * *

Chapter 78

Bujumbura, Burundi

Kasem reacted on instinct when the cars finally came to a stop on the driveway in front of the president's residence, releasing the access panel so that he and Tim could move from the hidden compartment in the backseat and take position under the car.

They had just scrambled out when John and Ben emerged from the first car and sent off two shots each in quick succession, tranquilizing the four guards stationed in the garden. "Team 1, moving in now," John reported as Kasem watched his and Ben's feet disappear toward the house residence.

"Team 2, follow," Tim said, and Dave and Ian sped off after them. "It's just you and me now, bud."

Kasem glanced back at Tim, "Heading to my post now, boss." He took off toward the boundary wall, grateful that they had already looped the security feed, so he didn't have to worry about being seen.

A couple of minutes later, he hoisted himself onto the top of the wall, careful to clip the barbed wire before getting into his lookout position. The place they had chosen was underneath a large overhanging tree, so it would be hard for anyone to spot him, but high enough that he had almost a full view of both the garden inside the compound to his left and the access street and cliffside on his right.

Making sure to scan the area often, Kasem focused his attention on the house itself—the goggles didn't allow him to identify the heat signatures, but he could guess which ones were part of their team as they moved through the ground floor toward the stairwell leading to Markov's bedroom and office.

* * * * * *

Chapter 79

Bujumbura, Burundi

Kasem turned to survey the outside of the compound, which looked like an eerie array of black and white outlines through his night vision goggles. He looked around slowly, trying to absorb as much detail as possible. *You never know what could save your life.*

The next few minutes dragged on as he split his attention between the house and the interior of the compound and the quiet street and cliffside on the exterior. As it grew even darker, he could see the heart of the city below, with interspersed lights against a starry backdrop. He checked his phone, wondering how Petra and Carlos had fared at Blue Bay.

When he looked up, he saw distant movement on the street. Adjusting his goggles back to the binocular setting, he zoomed in, trying to discern what it was.

Is that a—? As the picture came into focus, he straightened up, tweaking the settings further to confirm. He tapped on his coms, "Team, there's a military convoy approaching from down the hill. We've got maybe twenty minutes," he guessed based on the distance and the winding street patterns to get up to the residence.

"Roger that," Tim responded. "Inside team, status update?"

The team remained silent for several moments until John's voice came over the com, "The package is secure, extraction in process."

Kasem felt a modicum of relief, at least one part of the op was going to plan, but it was short lived. A screech blared through his ears, one of the guards must have set off the alarms. After what felt like an eternity, the alarm stopped, and John provided another update, "Alarm system has been neutralized, moving to extraction point."

Kasem watched with his stomach in his throat as the convoy got closer, their only chance was to get out of the compound before it arrived. He racked his brain for options. There were only two roads leading up to the residence, the larger one which they had used—that passed by the Belvedere restaurant and the Kiriri Garden hotel—and the other, a small residential street. Which should they choose? He found himself dumbfounded and took a deep breath.

Which would the Ahriman choose?

As soon as he gave himself a moment to think, the answer was clear. The convoy would set up a roadblock on the smaller street and approach from the larger one, creating as much chaos as possible for any police or troops that might try to come to the president's aid. That was how Nziza would have planned it.

Almost like clockwork, he saw part of the convoy split off onto one of the residential streets—based on the map he had studied, Kasem knew that it offered a roundabout route to the residence. "The convoy has split, the main contingent is using the larger road to get here, the other group is moving toward us from the other side," he radioed to the team.

Kasem glanced at the equipment he had on hand. Where was Carlos and his magic jacket when he needed it? Carlos was a regular Mary Poppins when it came to spyware, something that had come in handy on their previous ops.

An idea occurred to him, and Kasem considered it quickly, determining that it was their best shot. He waited and watched as the two Humvees pulled over on either side of the street about a block and a half away. He resisted the urge to spring into action, his Remington pistol would hardly be able to make the shot.

Where's a bazooka when you need one?

Three militia hopped out and removed several large barricades from the back of one of the Humvees, then proceeded to set it up across the street. When they were finished setting it up, two of them hopped into the other vehicle and headed toward the main road, presumably to join the main convoy.

"Convoy has barricaded the side street," Kasem clenched his jaw. "I'm taking care of it." The Ahriman versus a Humvee, his greatest conquest yet.

Shifting forward, Kasem turned around and lowered himself down the wall with his hands. When his arms were fully extended, he released his left hand to descend a little further before he let go. His feet hit the bushes below first, then the ground, and he crouched into a squat before twisting sideways to roll onto his shoulder. The bramble stung against his skin, but he was grateful for it—the bushes had both broken his fall and likely kept him out of sight. He caught his breath and watched the Humvee for a few seconds to be sure he hadn't been seen, then crept through the bushes toward the exterior wall of the neighboring property.

Once he reached the second house, he paused to count, there were four more properties between him and the barricade. He kept moving, belly-crawling through the shadows as needed, thanking the stars that Nziza's men did not have the Agency's tech.

He continued until he was two houses away from the barricade and extracted a fire starter from the Agency's pack.

Carlos, this is for you. He flicked it on and tossed it toward the other side of the street. The year before in Madagascar, Carlos had used a similar device to help free him from capture, so it only seemed fitting.

Kasem crouched even lower, pressing his back against the wall behind him. *Three, two, one,* the starter exploded, bursting into flames that rose nearly a story high.

* * * * * *

Chapter 80

Blue Bay, Burundi

Carlos' gaze darted over to Petra in the passenger seat, he could feel the tension emanating from that side of the vehicle. "Keep your shirt on, kiddo, we'll get there."

She gave him a tight nod, then glanced toward Kevin and Veronica in the back seat. "You two all right?"

In the rearview mirror, Carlos saw Veronica shake her head and answer, "We're fine, just bruised. They roughed us up, but it could have been a lot worse."

My ass, Carlos thought but chose to remain silent. He and Veronica had never been close, but the history in the car was a bit too much for even him to make light of. *Even I have a filter... sometimes,* the corners of his mouth turned upward, but he forced himself not to grin. He checked his phone, noticing another text update from Tim that the two teams were inside the presidential compound. His expression hardened as the traffic light turned green. They were still an hour away, but at least Tim had the best team for the job. Carlos hit the gas, and they sped on toward the city, Blue Bay resort disappearing into the background.

* * * * * *

Chapter 81

Bujumbura, Burundi

Kasem ran forward toward the Humvee, using the distraction provided by the fire to his advantage, and stopped in front of the house adjacent to the barricade. "Team, what's your status?" He wanted to wait to take out Nziza's men until the team was already on their way—otherwise, the Humvee might radio the main convoy for help before they could get Markov and his family past the blockade.

Kasem recognized Tim's voice, "In the car, leaving the compound now. Do you have a safe exit?"

"Exit through the side street." Kasem attached his silencer and lined up the shots, the three combatants had emerged from the Humvee. About to take out the first one, his index finger froze.

I'm not the Ahriman anymore. He holstered the Remington and retrieved his tranq gun instead. Taking a deep breath, he squeezed the trigger.

* * * * * *

297

Chapter 82

Bujumbura, Burundi

Chris stopped at a traffic light on his way back to the city and reached for his phone. His mouth fell open as he read the message that had just come in from Edward, one of his superiors at the Agency. They couldn't be serious, things had already gone too far, he wanted to bang his head against the dashboard. The light turned green, and he moved forward then pulled over, glad that Carlos and Petra had driven on ahead. After a deep breath, he looked at the message again, wishing that this was all part of a bad dream.

"Do whatever you need to do to save President Markov, but afterward, I want to personally remind him where his best interests lie—to award the deal to the Americans. Make sure you have an insurance policy ready for this."

Edward's message was abundantly clear, an insurance policy meant that Chris should order his team to take Markov's family hostage as soon as they had secured him from Nziza's men.

If they had his family in custody, Markov would fall in line, Chris had no doubt about that. He shook his head, recalling the team's reservations about instituting a military coup—somehow, Edward had set this whole thing up so that the Agency wasn't doing that, but was still manipulating the outcome of the power contract.

Chris was debating what to do—part of him wanted to pretend that he never received the order—when his phone rang. In his gut, he knew that the call had to be from Edward.

I have to convince him he's wrong, he decided, that couldn't be what the Agency did here. Besides, he wasn't even sure the team would follow that order, his stomach did a flip at the possibility of a mutiny. Most of them weren't even Agency, so they would have minimal recourse if anyone refused to comply. What did the Agency even have to threaten them with?

He shuddered but kept his voice steady, "This is Chris."

"Chris, Edward here. Do you have a status update?"

"Our boys are inside the compound, moving to get to Markov."

"Did you see my message?"

Chris swallowed, "I did."

"I assume you don't need me to tell you that that's an order. We have to make sure that Markov complies."

Chris knew it was a last-ditch effort, but he had to try. "Isn't that what the Chinese were trying to do here? If the Americans have the best offer, why not let Markov come to that on his own? The more we interfere, the less likely they are to work with us in the future—"

"I'm not even going to bother responding," Edward cut him off. "There's one additional point that I didn't mention earlier. If the team is able to capture Nziza, I want him taken into Agency custody. He can't be put on trial in Burundi."

"But Sir, capturing Nziza would cement Markov's authority. He would need that after an attempted coup."

"I'm afraid we can't take that chance. Nziza has too much power in Burundi, we'll have to take him into custody. Besides, he's too much of a loose cannon, but never mind that."

Chris frowned, processing what Edward could mean by loose cannon. "Are you sure? Again, the more we interfere, the less likely Markov will want to be accommodating—"

"I hoped it wouldn't come to this, but I'll be relieving you of your command," Edward interrupted.

"What are you talking about?"

"After we spoke, I made plans to join you in Burundi. I just landed and will meet you once your team has neutralized the threat. I thought it would be a formality, in fact, I was sure you could handle this on your own, especially after all your years of service. It's clear I was wrong—this entire op has turned out to be bollocks, quite the catastrophe, really. I expect your team to take custody of the president and his family, and I'll see you at the safe house. If the team is able to locate and move on Nziza, you have your orders."

* * * * * *

Chapter 83

Bujumbura, Burundi

Kasem coughed, the smoke from the now dissipating fire grating his throat. The adrenaline from taking out Nziza's men was starting to wane. He grappled with one of the barricades, turning it perpendicular so that the team's cars would be able to pass. When he'd made enough room, he crouched to the side, praying that they would be able to get clear before Nziza's convoy realized that Markov had been extracted.

"Leaving the compound now," one of the team said through the coms.

"Pick me up by the barricade," Kasem replied. *Come on, let's move.*

Moments later, Dave pulled over next to him, and Kasem rolled into the car before they sped off.

* * * * * *

They made it inside the team safe house, where Tim had the awkward task of explaining what had transpired to Markov and his family.

Kasem watched from the sidelines, his adrenaline still pumping. He could hardly believe that they arrived at the team house without incident, he had kept glancing behind him the entire way, sure that another Humvee from the convoy would break off to tail them. Luckily, the onslaught on the residence had occupied the convoy's attention—Nziza's men were too busy scaling the residence walls and breaching the gate to realize that Markov and his family were no longer there.

We stopped the coup. They had made it. Now, all they had to do was make sure that the Agency didn't do anything fishy.

* * * * * *

Kasem let out a long exhale, seeing President Markov with his family was triggering and brought up a similar moment from Iran. Under General Majed's orders several years earlier, he had been part of the team to take a Commander Derderian and his family captive—Derderian had opposed General Majed and had paid the price. Kasem sighed, the way in which Markov's wife held her two daughters bore a disconcerting similarity to that memory, one which had already been brought to the surface by his most recent nightmare.

Except for the result, Kasem reminded himself. Markov and his family were safe, not captives. He shuddered as he recalled how the general had ordered him to execute Derderian in front of his family, then left the entire group to die.

"Thank you for helping us," Markov said from behind him.

Kasem turned around, shifting his weight between his feet, "We did what anyone would do."

"I doubt very much that that's true—but thank you."

Kasem nodded before retreating into the hallway, the images of Derderian's family and their execution flashing before his eyes, threatening to overwhelm him, to override their current victory. He had not expected to have any direct interaction with Markov, and he had to fight to stop the memories from overpowering him. Stumbling back toward his bedroom, he shut the door behind him and pressed his back against the wall, a sharp weight on his chest. He lowered himself to the ground, speaking a single phrase under his breath.

"The Ahriman is gone."

* * * * * *

Chapter 84

Bujumbura, Burundi

Tim reached for his phone after he was done briefing Markov and his family to call Carlos. "The president and his family are secure. You were right, the kid did good."

"I told you he has what it takes. Any word on Nziza?"

"No—but we'll see if Markov's guards know anything. He must know the coup failed by now, so I imagine he'll try to go into hiding again."

"How did Markov take the news?" Carlos asked.

"As well as can be expected."

"So, not well at all."

"Can't be easy to hear that you would have died if we hadn't kidnapped you."

Carlos grinned, "If I had to hear it, I'd want to hear it from you."

"Amen, brother."

"We'll be there in a few."

* * * * * *

Chapter 85

Bujumbura, Burundi

Kasem took several minutes to compose himself before he pulled himself to his feet and ventured back toward the living room. They had separated Markov's guards, securing them in different corners of the house, including Carlos' room and the storeroom where they had held Kevin.

Based on his gut, Kasem headed toward the storeroom. The guard that they had deposited there was younger and seemed more likely to be vulnerable to promises of money and glory, while the others were older and more seasoned, having worked with Markov for several years including prior to his election. The young one was a recent replacement when another member of the president's personal guard had retired.

On his way, Kasem grabbed himself an apple from the kitchen, then stepped into the storeroom. He stood in the corner without making eye contact, drawing out and slowly chewing each bite. Forcing your target to anticipate what you were going to do was an interrogation tactic that he had learned in Iran, one that was quite effective without too much effort. When he was finally done eating, he wrapped the core in a tissue and tossed it to the ground, then glanced at the guard as if he had only just noticed his presence.

Kasem observed the guard in silence. He was just a kid, couldn't be older than twenty or so. Now that they were alone, he could identify what had drawn him to this room in the first place—there was a look in the guard's eyes, something that screamed fear and pain instead of anger.

"Would you like one?" Kasem squatted on the ground and motioned toward the apple core.

The guard nodded, and Kasem retrieved another one from a shelf in the storeroom, then stepped back while he took a few bites.

"Do you speak any English?" Kasem asked a few moments later.

"A little." The soldier shot him a glare, then his eyes fixated on a line of water bottles on the shelf behind Kasem.

Kasem grabbed one and unscrewed the top, and handed over the bottle, careful to place it into the soldier's grip—with his hands zip-tied together in front of him, holding the water bottle would be tricky.

Once he had gulped down several mouthfuls, Kasem spoke again, "What's your name?" In the back of his mind, he could recall his training, how to spot a mark, how to connect with them. Kasem grimaced, he couldn't tell the difference between genuinely wanting to connect with a kid who had probably been conned or blackmailed into working for Nziza and his spy training.

When the soldier remained quiet, Kasem repeated the question and waited in silence, looking at him expectedly. Another few seconds of awkwardness followed until he finally answered, "Simon."

"I'm Kasem. Sorry to meet you under these circumstances. Do you like working with President Markov?"

"Yes."

"How long have you had your post? How did you get hired?"

Kasem and Simon went back and forth in a series of basic questions about his employment with Markov and relationship to the family. Kasem continued on instinct, maintaining a fast pace with his questions, never acting aggressive, but letting the speed of his queries keep Simon off balance. He continued in this manner for almost ten minutes before diving in head first, "When did you start working for Nziza?"

Simon attempted to backtrack, to deny the accusation, but Kasem remained on the offensive, acting as if he already had confirmation that Simon was indeed their mole.

"We're not after you, but we need to get to Nziza." Kasem included this statement alongside his questions a couple of times, noticing a change in Simon's expression.

The tactic was working.

"Why did you do it? Do you not like President Markov? Do you hate his family?"

The spree of questions took only a few more minutes before Simon broke. "I have a family to support…" he cried out. "They threatened me, said they would take my sister away if I didn't cooperate—"

The pressure on Kasem's diaphragm eased with the confirmation that his instincts had been correct. They spoke a short while longer, Kasem asked for further detail on Simon's background and how he had been recruited before moving on to what he was really after. If they'd had time, Kasem would have waited a few days to broach Nziza's location, but he had no choice but to push forward.

"If you help us find Nziza, we'll take care of you and your family. All we need is his location. No one else has to know."

******

Chapter 86

Bujumbura, Burundi

Tim frowned as he hung up the phone, debating whether he should be suspicious of the discussion he'd just had. Edward, one of the senior Agency officers, wanted to speak to President Markov in private, now that he had been secured.

Something was shady, he could no longer ignore his intuition. Why would such a senior officer come all this way? And why have a meeting in private? He had always been good at sniffing out duplicitous orders, especially those that crossed ethical lines—his skills had been even further honed by dealing with his daughters' attempts to pull one over on him when they were teenagers. They were both grown up now, but he'd lost count of the number of times he had caught them either attempting to smuggle a boy into the house or sneaking out after curfew between the ages of fourteen and seventeen.

If it smells like a rat...

He sighed—even if he acknowledged that something was afoot, what could he even do about it? He couldn't go rogue and arrest Edward, especially not just for having a conversation. Pursing his lips, Tim set his concern aside to update his team. It wouldn't do for the team to tackle Edward by mistake, although he had to acknowledge the temptation.

As he turned down the hallway, Tim almost ran smack into Kasem. "Whoa there, buddy, we're not in a horse race! Watch yourself," he said in a mocking tone.

"I spoke to the guard in the storeroom, the kid. I can get him to talk—we might be able to find Nziza," Kasem replied, in rapid breath.

"Okay, what are we waiting for? Carlos undersold you, bud." Tim clapped him on the shoulder.

"All he wants is for his family to be taken care of—we can get them out of the country, into witness protection or something, right?"

"I certainly hope so, but you know who you need to talk to about that? That Agency lead Edward, and I think Chris too, will be here in a few minutes. You should run it by them. I can't imagine getting a 'no,' but these spy types are a crazy bunch."

"If we wait too long, it might be too late. What if Nziza gets away? How long till they get here?"

"Not too long, maybe an hour at most." Tim nodded, "You do what you what you have to, what you think is right." He paused, then added, "We can't let a war criminal get back into power here, these people deserve more."

"You thinking of something in particular?"

"Too many to count, or at least I'd rather not." Tim shrugged, "You worked in Iran, you know what I mean. I can't stand it when our government puts their pocketbook over innocent lives, gives national security a bad name. My father died for the coup in Iran, and where did that end up? Nziza's no better than the Shah."

Kasem shuddered, "We're not going to let that happen here. I'm going to make the deal."

Before Kasem was out of eyeshot, Tim called out, "You know, I was serious about that job offer. It's yours if you want it, kid."

* * * * * *

Chapter 87

Bujumbura, Burundi

Petra gritted her teeth as they reentered the outer limits of the city. The Burundais police force had finally reacted to the raid on Markov's home and had set up roadblocks all over the place, stretching their hour drive to almost two hours. She listened to the news, which was spouting a story about an attack on the presidential residence, but that the perpetrators had gotten away. She only barely contained the urge to slam her fist onto the dashboard.

"I bet Nziza wasn't even part of the raid. We have to find him, take him down, otherwise this will all be for naught. He'll just try again in a few months." She focused on Nziza because there she had some control, unlike the image that plagued her in the back of her mind—Kasem being hauled away to an Agency black site.

"We'll get him, kiddo. Tim's trying to flip one of his men," Carlos said.

"Here's hoping." She glanced at the back seat once again and caught Veronica's eye. "Did you update Chris?"

"Yeah, he'll be waiting for us at the team house."

Great. Petra once more tried to repress her concerns about what Chris would do to Kasem once the operation was over. The image of the black site materialized in her mind again, and she shook her head, snapping herself back from that dark place. They had done everything they were supposed to, it was out of their hands now.

After this, no more Agency, no more ops.

Before she could go any further down the rabbit hole, Petra's phone rang. "Kasem?" she said as she picked up.

"Babe, I've got a lead on Nziza. He's posing as a low-level Kenyan diplomat, Hotel Belair, room 208."

******

Chapter 88

Bujumbura, Burundi

Kasem hung up the phone with a triumphant expression, although the operation had started out dire, it now seemed solidly on the upswing.

There might be life after this, he thought, especially as he recalled Tim's job offer. It would have been better if the opportunity was in Paris, but it still meant that he could have a real career, that he wouldn't have to hide his past.

At least not all of it. The Ahriman would have to stay buried.

Tim and his team had moved Markov's guards into the central bedroom and were enjoying a well-deserved snack in the dining room, leaving Markov and his family in the living room at the front of the house. Kasem slipped away from the group and walked outside, taking in the night sky and basking in the light of the perfectly centered full moon, shedding light across the garden. He couldn't help but feel it was a good sign. Even his concern about how Petra would react to the new job offer was nothing in comparison to what they had been grappling with only a few days before. He'd been so sure that they would never be able to have a life because of the Agency, and because of Veronica.

But here we are, and she said that she wants to marry me. He had never been more certain of anything that he wanted. They

Puja Guha

would build a life together—a life without lies, or spy craft, or missions.

He sat down on the back patio, enjoying the calm after the frenzy of the last few days. He had not realized how much he missed that feeling of contentment, being able to be still. If nothing else, the abundant free time in Paris had taught him that.

Kasem heard the sound of the front gate opening and peeked around the corner of the house, watching as two cars pulled into the driveway. A moment later, Chris emerged from the first car, and a middle-aged man, who he assumed was Edward, emerged from the second. A gentleman, Kasem surmised. There was no better description—the man was wearing what looked like a three-piece suit and holding a long cane. The only item missing was a monocle.

Kasem moved back behind the corner to remain out of sight. Tim had mentioned that they would be coming to meet Markov—he hadn't thought anything of it earlier. Now that he did, his fears about the Agency's potential involvement in a coup returned.

He watched as they disappeared into the house. Making sure to keep his distance—they were trained spies, after all— Kasem followed, stopping outside the main door, and peered in through the porch window.

They made their way down the hall, but a minute or so afterward, Chris reemerged, looking even more nervous than before. Kasem resisted the temptation to take him aside and confront him, they weren't on good enough terms for that to yield any useful information. Stepping into the living room, Kasem moved quietly past Markov's wife and kids, who were deeply engrossed in some kind of board game spread out on the coffee table. He waited until Chris went toward the dining room before sidling down the hallway to the door behind which Edward was speaking to Markov.

Kasem pressed his back against the wall, placing his right ear as close to the door joint as possible without making it obvious that he was eavesdropping. At the same time, he opened the kit Tim had given him before the op and grabbed one of the listening devices, a small earpiece that magnified directional noise. *So much better than those giant directional mics,* he recalled from his training in Iran.

It took a second to focus the device properly using the mini remote from which he'd extracted the earpiece, but the audio sharpened when Kasem found the right setting.

"Would you mind if we spoke in English?" a nasal voice said, which Kasem recognized as what had to be Edward's British accent. "My French is only just passable."

"Of course," Markov answered, "although I doubt my English is much better than your French."

English is good, Kasem agreed. There would be no point in listening if he couldn't follow what they were saying.

"I very much doubt that," Edward replied with a chuckle.

Kasem rolled his eyes, he had little patience for these sorts of pleasantries. Was Edward recruiting Markov as an Agency asset? Or at least an informant? From Edward's position, Kasem could see how that was desirable, yet he doubted that Markov would agree to provide the Agency long-term access to the internal workings of the government. There was no way he would pass on classified intel, so becoming an asset was probably a no-go. Kasem considered other possible scenarios, wondering whether Markov would occasionally be willing to share off the record information.

After a short pause, Markov continued, "I can't thank you and your team enough for what they did here today. My family and I are so grateful, as our country would be too if they were

314

Puja Guha

privy to what happened. I do, however, wish we could have been informed in advance."

"We were just doing our job, but I'm quite content that we got to this outcome. We were lucky—things could have easily gone sideways," Edward said. "We have a team attempting to capture Nziza now—we'll update you on their progress. Hopefully, we'll have him in our custody soon."

"If you do capture him, I would like you to turn him over. He should stand trial for his crimes here, my people deserve that," Markov stated.

"Are you sure you'll be able to hold him?" Edward questioned. "He must have support from within your government, otherwise, how could he have gotten this far?"

"You said he had the support of the Chinese," Markov countered. "With their backing, financial and otherwise, they wouldn't need much support from within my government. What's that American saying? Money talks?"

Kasem straightened up against the wall outside, recognizing Markov's tactic of flattery and pretending he wasn't familiar with things that he clearly was. Markov was smarter than he'd let on, along with the fact that he spoke perfect English.

"It certainly does," Edward agreed, "but that said, Nziza wouldn't have had a chance of taking over without internal support. It might be wise for him to be taken care of."

"What do you mean?" Markov asked.

Kasem's hand went to his mouth, remembering his conversation with Kevin. There was only one reason that the Agency would want to hold Nziza. He had dirt on them, which meant he had indeed been an Agency asset.

"It wouldn't do for him to escape custody again. Besides, you're going to need allies going forward," Edward said in his sickeningly smooth voice.

315

"I see. Are you referring to someone specific?" Markov's tone sharpened.

"I believe having the Americans on your side is of particular importance when it comes to dealing with the Chinese. I know you might be considering other partners, but I want to emphasize how much it's in your best interest—yours, your family's, and your country's—to work with the Americans on this."

Kasem's jaw almost dropped as his worst suspicions were confirmed. Not only was Nziza a former asset, the Agency was holding Markov's family hostage to ensure that the power plant contract was awarded to their preferred bidder.

"And if I choose a different direction?" Kasem detected the slightest tremble in Markov's voice.

"I don't know, I won't be responsible for the consequences. I can only ask you to heed my advice."

I can't let them get away with this.

Kasem stood frozen outside the door. He recalled the jabs Carlos had made at the Agency, and it all made so much more sense now. Not that he had doubted Carlos, but the hypocrisy had seemed abstract, surreal—after all, what he'd seen in Iran was far worse, so having a few doubts about the Agency's motives never seemed like such a big deal.

Until it manifested in something like this. The Agency was threatening Markov's family, holding his children hostage...

Kasem took a deep breath. He remembered his family's stories about the Shah. The secret police, the kidnappings and the murders... and then the revolution, all of which were equally terrifying. Burundi had already been through its own horror in the Civil War.

He knew in his bones what he had to do. He only wished that he could talk to Petra about it, to give her a warning of the grenade he was about to throw into their lives, but there wasn't time. Kasem glanced around, seeking out Tim or anyone from his team, perhaps they could help him, but at that moment, he couldn't see anyone he could trust.

He could no longer be the man who followed orders blindly. The Ahriman had done that. That life was behind him, now and forever.

Kasem reached for the door handle, if he was going to take action, he had to move now.

* * * * * *

Chapter 88

Petra glanced at her reflection in the passenger seat mirror and ran her fingers through her hair, attempting to give it a semblance of order as they drove toward the Hotel Belair. Ten minutes later, Carlos pulled to the side of the road half a block away from the gated entrance.

"It'll have to do," she shrugged at Carlos, then turned to the backseat. "V, you're coming in with us, a friend who's going to have a drink at the restaurant." Petra hesitated, her gaze moving between Kevin and Veronica, the question of whether to trust them weighing on her. She caught Carlos' eye, and he nodded.

We don't have a choice, kiddo, she could hear him saying. Chris had gone straight to the team house, and she'd asked Gaston to go along as well—she didn't trust Chris' intentions with the op, but she did trust Gaston. "Kevin, I want you on surveillance from the street. Text Carlos if anyone goes in or out," she tossed her phone over to the backseat.

Carlos handed Kevin a pair of night vision binoculars from the driver's door, then said, "Let's do this."

Petra and Veronica followed him on foot to the hotel gate, through the small parking lot inside, and up a ramped entrance to the hotel lobby, all illuminated by a series of lanterns. Outside the lobby was a large, covered patio, Veronica took a seat on the far right so that she could keep an eye on both the lobby and the parking lot, along with several of the hotel room balconies which overlooked the patio. Petra waved at her as she and Carlos approached the receptionist.

"Why don't you go sit down, babe," Carlos motioned to his left where there was extra seating in the lobby. "I'll get us a room."

"Thank you." Petra sat down and observed the space while he spoke to the receptionist in broken French to get them a booking for that night. There were elevators to one side, and no security guards were stationed in the interior—at least none in uniform. Still, she was certain that wouldn't be the case when they got close to Nziza's room. The question was how many guards he'd have posted—he wouldn't want to draw too much attention, but he would want to be protected. She also had to hope that they would be different guards than the ones who had seen her at Club du Lac. Although her appearance had been different, with the wig and colored contacts, a trained eye would certainly be able to recognize her, but it was a risk they had to take. In all likelihood, Nziza would have dismissed the guards that "allowed" him to get captured.

Petra continued to take in the space, noticing a staircase heading upstairs on the far side of the elevators. If it had access to all floors, it could be a good exit option.

Several minutes later, Carlos joined her, planting a kiss on her cheek to keep up the illusion that they were a couple. "Sorry about the wait, sweetie," he said, "I got us a room with a view of the city, come on." He showed her the envelope that contained their key card, with the room number 206 written on it, and led her to one of the elevators.

When the elevator doors opened on the second floor, Petra noted two security guards at the end of the hallway on their left. A flood of relief hit her, they were a different pair of guards than the ones she had interacted with at the Club du Lac.

Exchanging a glance with Carlos, they walked down the hall in that direction to test if the guards would bother them or not. Carlos exaggerated his limp so that they could take their time and watch for a reaction. As they got closer, Carlos grabbed her arm and said, "Babe, I think we passed it, oh it's this one." He stopped in front of their room, and she giggled as they went inside, keeping up the show.

Petra shut the door behind her. "Just the two guards, so that shouldn't be too much of an issue. Did you see any cameras?"

"Nope, but it's not like we had a lot of time for recon. Our best advantage is surprise, let's move fast." He extracted a tranq gun from his shoulder bag and handed it to her. "You're the better shot."

"Yes, I am," she grinned. She pulled a shawl out of the bag and draped it over her shoulders to conceal the tranq gun, keeping it pressed against her chest. Before they headed back into the hallway, she tapped her earpiece to update Veronica and Kevin, then looked at Carlos. "You ready to move, old man?"

He grumbled in indignation before stepping back into the hallway. Petra moved into position behind him, and as he stumbled forward, she caught him under the arms. "Babe, you shouldn't have had so much to drink." She fired off the first tranq dart from under Carlos' armpit before she finished the sentence, with the second one off a moment after that.

They covered the few steps to Nziza's door quickly, then pulled the guards back down the hallway and dumped them in their room. Carlos panted, his breathing labored as he leaned forward with his hands on his knees. "I thought Diane had whipped me back into shape, but I clearly need more training."

"More training and a time machine," Petra winked at him. "You okay, grandpa? Do you need a nap—"

He straightened up with a loud grunt, "Let's move."

Petra picked up the welcome basket the hotel had set up in their room—pretending to be room service when they knocked on the door would be their best option. "Good thing they don't wear uniforms here," she said with a shrug.

"And that everyone's a night owl."

They ventured back down the hallway. Petra's heartbeat drummed through her ears—this was their chance to take a murderer out, to end this operation. And settle Kasem's debt to the Agency once and for all...

This had better work.

When they reached Nziza's room, Carlos took position to one side, opposite the hinges so that he would be close to whoever opened the door, even if they only opened it a sliver. Petra held the welcome basket up in the middle, as close to the peephole as possible, and flashed a beaming smile. At the same time, she positioned her right hand underneath the basket, lining up the tranq gun so that she could neutralize the person on the other side. "*Bonsoir, service de chambre,*" she said in a chipper voice while Carlos rapped on the door. "*Compliments de l'hôtel.*"

Her left hand trembled slightly as she held the basket steady, the stakes of the operation felt as if they were growing with each passing moment. Although she could hear some movement inside, along with a couple of voices, she couldn't make out any of the words.

They were out of luck: no backup or intel, and the only hotel in Burundi with good soundproofing.

Before she had a chance to think any further, the door opened.

* * * * * *

Chapter 90

Bujumbura, Burundi

Kasem rushed into the room, raising the pistol that Tim had given to him and pointing it at Edward. "I'm afraid your plan here isn't going to work. Hands up." He resisted the urge to add the word asshole followed by a series of expletives. He turned to President Markov, "You can ignore all of that—feel free to award the contract in a way that's most beneficial to the people here. I won't let him hold you and your family hostage." He looked back at Edward, "You will not hold this country hostage."

Markov took a step backward in obvious shock but remained silent as Kasem approached Edward. Using one of the zip ties that Tim had supplied prior to the op, Kasem wrenched his arms behind his back and fastened his wrists together.

As Kasem pulled Edward to the side of the room to secure him to a chair, he met Markov's gaze. "The team outside, they'll get you and your family somewhere safe…" Kasem's voice trailed off—he was willing to bear whatever the Agency threw at him for disobeying their orders, but Tim and his team shouldn't have to pay the price.

"I'll get my people to help," Markov whispered before Kasem had to explain. "I said it before, but it means even more now—thank you."

Kasem nodded, then motioned toward the door to hurry Markov up.

"Are you sure you want to do this, young man?" Edward turned his head back to glare at Kasem. "Actions have consequences, you know."

"I'll take my chances. President Markov, you're free to go."

Markov sidled out of the room, and Kasem picked up his phone. "Tim, the President would like to be moved to a secure location. Edward was trying to set an Agency trap for him, so let's make sure he won't have access to him again. If one of you can take over holding Edward, I'll help you make sure Markov's family is secure." Kasem swallowed, thinking of the safe house he had set up with Gaston's help—he had wanted Petra and him to have an option if they needed to run. That safe house was now Markov's best option, leaving him and Petra out of luck.

"Got it, cowboy. I'll get the family together, and John will be in to relieve you."

A sense of relief washed over Kasem, at least his plan might actually work. His gaze landed on Edward. *Whatever the consequences.*

"This is your last chance," Edward looked at him again. "I know exactly who you are and what's at stake. Get Markov back here, and I'll forget all of it. You can have the life you want, with the woman you want—free and clear. If you don't, I'll take you into custody. If you run, the Agency will expend all of its resources to track you down. I'll make sure the manhunt for the Ahriman is the biggest priority for every intelligence agency in the world."

"I've been on the run before, and the Agency didn't catch me. I can handle myself." Part of him wanted to be selfish, to turn Markov over so that he and Petra could have a life. He could pretend that he hadn't had a choice, end the saga of the Ahriman once and for all. But his integrity was no longer for sale and he could not compromise. Not this time, not anymore.

"It wouldn't just be you we'll be hunting. Do you think for a second I believe that Petra doesn't know exactly who you are? She'll be a known accessory. There's nowhere the two of you could hide. Once we find you, you'll spend the rest of your lives at an Agency black site, separated and alone."

"She can hold her own—we've both stayed hidden from the Agency when we wanted to," Kasem's voice cracked. He didn't want to believe that the Agency would do that to one of their own operatives. They probably didn't even have proof that he was the Ahriman, let alone that she knew about it.

"Did you think we don't know about your time in Kyoto? To be fair, not everyone knew, but I certainly did. We keep tabs on our former agents, even if we let them have the illusion that we don't know how to find them."

"But you wouldn't—you wouldn't put her in a black site. She was one of your operatives—" Kasem trembled, realizing what he had to do. He couldn't run—even if Tim would help him escape, Petra would bear the cost, as they all would. He hesitated, wavering, it wasn't too late to pretend none of this had happened.

He stood on the brink of that decision, then shook his head. He had looked for redemption one too many times. Petra had believed in him, but he could only be the person he was in her eyes if he followed through now.

I have to pay for what I've done.

"My dear boy, Petra will pay for her crimes. My bet is that she let you go instead of taking you into custody in Kuwait, kept your real identity a secret. If you let Markov go, you'll both have to face the piper. Separately, of course, we couldn't have a lovers' bond helping you to make it through. And do you think those men out there, Tim and his team will get through this free and clear? We'll find a place for them too, don't you worry. They can't defy the Agency without consequences, even if they are independent."

"No, they were doing us a favor, the Agency wouldn't even send a team." Kasem choked on the words, unable to continue. *I can't let this government become an Agency pawn,* he wanted to scream.

"Ready to move when you are," Tim's voice rang through Kasem's earpiece.

Kasem's shoulders sank, a combination of relief and despair. His window to back out of helping Markov was closing rapidly, and his fate would be sealed, but he was relieved that the selfish choice no longer seemed viable. "This conversation is over."

"They will all pay for your crimes, Carlos, Tim, Petra—all of them." Edward's nasally tone was calm and calculated, he seemed entirely unphased that his plan had gone haywire.

"There has to be something, another way—"

"I can offer you a deal. The Agency won't pursue Markov or anyone on this team. We'll chalk it all up to a botched operation, brush it under the rug, so to speak. But in order to do that, we need a win."

"A win?"

"I doubt this will surprise you. The Ahriman is a bigger prize than any Burundais power deal, or an asset in the government here. You, my dear boy, are a legend. Turn yourself in, and I'll let them be."

An image flashed in front of Kasem's eyes, the memory of General Majed using the threat of Lila's capture to hold him hostage. He'd had to do it then, and he had to do it now. There were no other options. He took a deep breath, solidifying his resolve.

The story of the Ahriman ends here and now.

******

Chapter 91

Bujumbura, Burundi

Kasem ran into Gaston in the living room and they waited together while two of Tim's men took Markov and his family to the safe house that he had set up just outside of the city. Originally Kasem had planned to go with them, but instead he'd chosen to give them the information and stay at the house on the slim hope that he might see Petra before Edward took him away.

"Are you all right?" Gaston asked. He'd mostly been silent since arriving at the house a few minutes earlier, taking in the situation without any overt reaction.

"No, but I did what I had to."

"This is what you meant when you said the stakes were everything."

"It is," Kasem nodded. "Thank you for your help with the safe house."

"Of course. I didn't know that's what you were trying to do." Gaston paused, "We could get you another one, you know. Somewhere to help you both get away. It doesn't have to go this way—I don't know what you did, but you don't have to turn yourself in. You can find a way out, I'll help you."

"Thank you, but no, there's no point. It's no life for her, for either of us. A life on the run, always looking over our shoulders. I was hoping that by doing this op, we'd be clear of my past, but I was wrong."

"But you could disappear, that's what you trained for," Gaston countered. "Go, live your life. There will always be risks, but you can't let that stop you."

Kasem gave him a small smile, touched by Gaston's kindness, "I can't let her pay for crimes, I can't let any of you. If I go free, the Agency will come after all of you."

Gaston sighed, "Maybe I should be thanking you. I don't know what you're paying for now, but we've all done things. Hopefully for the right reasons, that's all we can ask ourselves." He stood and disappeared into the kitchen, returning with the remnants of the bottle of Auchentoshan-12 single malt they had drank the night before they moved on Nziza, along with two glasses. "It's all that's left," he said as he poured them each two fingers.

"It'll do," Kasem picked up one of the glasses. "Cheers."

"La vie est un combat, perdu d'avance," Gaston raised the other glass with a solemn look. "Life is a battle that we've already lost," he translated. "We all have our time. I hope this isn't yours, but if it is, my friend, what you've done here is commendable. I'm honored to know you."

The words were so poignant and the saying so appropriate, all Kasem could do was nod. He didn't trust himself to speak, words couldn't convey all the different emotions running through him. They spent the next few minutes in silence, prolonging each sip of the whiskey. The wait felt like an eternity—the team was staying off their phones in case the Agency attempted to trace the other safe house—until Tim reappeared at the doorway. "They're clear, cowboy. You did good."

It's time.

"Thanks, Tim." Kasem looked over at Gaston, "Tell Petra I love her." In a way, this was better, he wasn't sure he would be able to leave if he saw her first.

"Why not hold off for a few more minutes? Maybe give her a call? You should at least say goodbye," Gaston said.

"There's no other way. If I call her, I don't know if I'll be able to..."

"I'm telling you, we could find another way."

"Thank you, my friend, but I can't let you risk that," Kasem shook his head. "They'll come after all of us with everything they've got. I could chance it on my own, but...no." Kasem remained steadfast that he wouldn't take the rest of the team down with him.

"You sure you want to make that decision for her? She deserves more than that," Tim frowned. "Let me tell you—I know from experience that strong women do not take kindly to men taking decisions for them, and that Petra, well she's as strong as they come."

"She'd want to run, to do anything we have to, but that's no life. If this is how I settle my debts, then so be it."

"I'll just be keeping my distance when she finds out," Tim shrugged, obviously trying to lighten the moment.

"You and me both," Gaston agreed.

"You're a good guy, no matter what dear old Mr. Darcy thinks." Tim held out his hand and Kasem shook it.

Kasem couldn't help but chuckle at the Jane Austen reference as he glanced back at Tim. The moment left a bitter taste in his mouth. He had been so close to a real career, perhaps a real future as Petra's equal. Despite that, any doubts he'd had were gone now, his decision was set.

Kasem glanced between Tim and Gaston, two people who he'd known for such a short time, although it felt like they'd been friends for years. "I'm going to release Edward. Once he's free, Tim, I want you to take me into custody." His life would be over, but at least she would never have to look over her shoulder again.

She'll have a better life without me. Petra would dispute that logic, she would be angry that he took this decision out of her hands, but he saw no other way.

"All right. If you find a way out of this, my offer—it still stands," Tim said.

"You can always come back to Burundi," Gaston added softly. "I know many places to hide."

Kasem reached into his pocket to retrieve his Swiss Army knife. He headed back into the room, nodded at John, who'd been keeping watch, then moved forward to slice through the zip tie holding Edward's wrists together. Stepping back, he set his pistol on the ground. "I'm all yours."

Edward snarled, "On your knees, you piece of scum."

* * * * * *

Chapter 92

Bujumbura, Burundi

Petra pulled the blackout curtains across the glass doors that led out onto the balcony and glanced back at Carlos, who was positioned with his pistol pointed at a now gagged and bound Nziza. She took his place and fired off a tranq dart at Nziza's chest.

"Just to be safe," she said nonchalantly.

Carlos nodded as he dragged the unconscious bodies of the two security guards who had been stationed inside Nziza's suite to opposite corners of the room.

Looking over the scene, her shoulders finally started to relax. *It's over,* she thought, despite a nagging feeling in the back of her mind that they had wrapped it all up far too easily.

"You thinking what I'm thinking?" Carlos asked.

"I hope not—that would show I really had aged." From his tone, she could tell that he shared her doubts, but before she could bring up her concerns, the sound of his phone vibrating interrupted them.

"Hey Tim, I was just about to call you. We've got him—"

Carlos' face turned to alarm as he listened to what Tim was saying, and Petra's felt a weight descend onto her chest. What had happened?

A moment later, Carlos hung up and looked at her with a dazed expression. "Kiddo, I've got some bad news."

* * * * * *

Chapter 93

Bujumbura, Burundi

Petra stared at Carlos, unable to comprehend what he was saying.

"I'm so sorry," Carlos said in a soft voice. "I can't imagine how hard this must be."

The truth started to sink in.

The Agency has taken Kasem into custody.

The thought reverberated in her mind, echoing back and forth as she grew weak in the knees. She fell forward toward the dining table in the hotel room and caught herself on her hands, lowering herself to the floor. It took several moments of staring blankly at the ceiling before she was able to struggle to her feet.

Carlos' arm helped pull her upright. "Let's get you out of here."

The next few minutes went by like a blur—they made it to the car somehow, even pretended to be a normal couple venturing out on the town. With each step, her feet grew heavier, as if she was walking through quicksand, sinking further every second. Carlos radioed Veronica, and she and Kevin took over watch on Nziza while they waited for confirmation that President Markov had been taken to safety.

Petra kept her eyes focused on the road, dazed, still trying to process the situation. "How did this happen?" she whispered.

"I don't know, kiddo, but we're going to find out. Chris must have informed Count Hoity-toity about Kasem's past, I can't think of anything else."

She drew in several deep breaths. "We were supposed to pay our debt with this op, and it would be over. Veronica promised me—I trusted her, I thought Chris would honor that deal. I can't believe I trusted them." The shock of Kasem's capture was starting to wear off, and she gritted her teeth, on the edge between denial and anger.

She imagined confronting Chris, and her jaw tightened further. *I'm going to kill him.* "Let's go," she said in a cold voice. "Chris and I have some talking to do."

* * * * * *

"Where is he?" Petra glared at Tim, only just able to contain the urge to punch him.

"They left about a half hour ago. I'm sorry, he told me to let that prissy Mr. Darcy take him."

She looked between Tim and Gaston, a feeling of hopelessness passing over her. She'd trusted them both implicitly, but they'd let her down. "How could you let this happen?" she whimpered.

"It was his choice to make, chérie." Gaston's voice sounded hollow, but she knew he was right.

"We should go," Carlos said to her softly. "Gaston, they could use your help at the hotel to extract Nziza."

"All right," Gaston replied.

When he was gone, Carlos placed his hand on her shoulder. "Markov and his family are gone now, there's nothing more for us here. Let's pick up our stuff, and we can head to the airport."

The airport, the mention of it broke her out of the trancelike state she'd been in. "That's it, we can still stop them. Where else would Edward take him?"

Carlos sighed, "Kiddo, you know we can't do that. It's not like we could take Edward into custody. If he knows about Kasem's past, it's too late. Once we get back to New York, we might be able to negotiate—get the Agency to release Kasem on condition or hold him in house arrest instead of at a black site."

She knew he was right but clung to the possibility that there might still be a chance. "I want to know how he found out. We need to find Chris. Do you know where he is?"

"He's in the last bedroom—"

Petra marched down the hallway before he could finish the sentence.

* * * * * *

Chapter 94

Bujumbura, Burundi

Petra caught sight of Chris on the far side of the room. He opened his mouth, but before he could say a word, she bridged the distance between them. Without hesitating, she grabbed him by the shoulders and shoved him backward into the wall, followed by a body hook with her right hand. Her fist made contact and he doubled over, a wave of satisfaction washing over her. She was about to deal out another one when Carlos pulled her away. Breaking free, she shoved Chris to the ground and pressed her shin on top of his chest, resisting the temptation to strangle him.

"Petra, stop," Carlos cried out for the third time, his words finally starting to sink in.

"Please," Chris whimpered. "Petra, I didn't do this. It wasn't me."

She wanted to punch him again, to dole out head hook after head hook, to take out all of her anger and anguish on him. Even if he wasn't the only one to blame, he was in front of her, accessible.

But that wouldn't get Kasem back. She met his eyes, then released him from her pin hold. "How else could he have known?" she remained on the floor, her voice quavering.

"I don't know, but I can promise you, I didn't tell him."

Petra glanced over at Carlos. *You've got to let him talk, kiddo,* she could read his expression. "How else could he have known?" she repeated after another deep breath.

"I don't know, I did everything off-book. I wanted to be sure before I slimed his reputation or did anything else to mess with your life."

Looking at his face, Petra knew deep down that he was being sincere. Even when he had screwed her over, Chris hadn't lied to her. Every part of her body ached, she longed for an outlet—any outlet—for her grief.

It took several moments to regain composure, to force herself out of the anger spiral. She stared at the ceiling, considering all of the different pieces. Chris had run his investigation off-book, but Veronica had found out about it, used it to help them get to Kevin. "Who else knew?"

"Just me and Grant, I swear, Petra, that's it."

"And Veronica," Carlos added. "You, lover boy, and Veronica."

She wouldn't have. Veronica had blackmailed them to come here. She'd said she didn't care about Kasem's past. But she'd also said that she would do anything if it meant taking Kevin in.

The sting of her friend's betrayal hurtled into her like a gut punch. *Even if it meant ruining my life.*

* * * * * *

Petra remained huddled on the floor, unable to move for what felt like hours. *What do we do now?* she asked herself more times than she could count. At some point, Carlos sat down next to her and put his hand on her shoulder. When she looked at him, she remembered what he'd said, that they would never be able to stop Edward without leverage.

Her gaze landed on Chris, and she knew what to do, she pulled her Colt pistol from its holster and pointed it at him. She had leverage now, and she wasn't afraid to use it. "Call Edward and get him to let Kasem go. Don't test me, I don't care what it takes. I'll do what I have to."

* * * * * *

Chapter 95

Bujumbura, Burundi

Veronica brought the car to a halt at a traffic light, a sinking feeling in her chest. She wondered if she'd made the right call, going over Chris' head to report the investigation into Kasem. Part of her also wished that she wasn't about to turn Kevin over.

She looked over at the passenger seat to where he was seated. "Thank you for your help with the op." She wanted to say more but couldn't find the words.

"You're welcome."

The light turned green and she moved through, her mind a chaotic combination of debate, regret, denial, and apprehension. Edward had already taken Kasem into custody based on the information that she'd provided him a few days ago. All she'd said was that Chris was investigating, that she thought they should do more work, not that she knew anything for sure. After all, he'd be freed if the investigation showed that he wasn't the Ahriman, and if he was, then he deserved his fate. That logic had held up for a while, but now she questioned it—she knew how often the Agency went back on its word, what Petra had done for her in the past, and what Kasem had already done for the Agency. Even if he was the Ahriman, had he redeemed himself?

Yet she had told Petra that she didn't care. The same way she'd told herself she didn't care about turning Kevin in.

"You're doing the right thing," he said in a quiet voice.

"What?" She hadn't said anything about what would happen to him. How did he know?

"Come on, when you turn Nziza over, you'll be turning me in too. It's okay, it's time to face the piper. I thought the Agency was just a bunch of hypocritical bureaucrats trying to cover their asses, but I got too caught up with what happened to see the real deal. I may not agree with all the orders, but they still stand for something. We did what was right here. We stopped a coup."

"We did."

"I have to say though, I'm surprised Markov doesn't want Nziza to be put on trial here. It would have done a lot for his image," Kevin added. "Maybe he's just worried about whatever support he has in the military here. I guess I can see why it would be better to make sure he's well and gone."

"Right." Veronica's throat went dry. Markov had indeed wanted a public trial in Burundi, but Edward had overridden that possibility. "That must be it. I guess it's more likely Nziza will give up his allies if he's in Agency custody."

"I doubt that's why the Agency wants him."

"What are you talking about?"

Kevin frowned at her, "I thought you knew. The Agency had me evaluate him as a potential asset. I told them they shouldn't touch him with a ten-foot pole, so I doubt they ever used him. It would be bad if that got out though, the fact that they even considered it."

The Agency used Nziza as an asset. The thought screamed through her head and she had to focus all her attention on keeping the car steady as she processed it. Edward's support for stopping the coup had nothing to do with keeping Markov in power. It was only about the power deal and tying up a loose end in Nziza.

They couldn't have. She wanted so much to believe it. But why else would Edward want Nziza in Agency custody? Especially after all the effort they'd gone through to keep Markov in power?

Veronica looked out at the street. The Agency was sure to put Nziza away so that the secret would never get out. She glanced at Kevin again, then back at the road. What would they do with him?

They were almost at the airport, only a few minutes to go. There were hardly any cars on the street now that they were past the roadblocks closer to the city.

This is my only chance.

She veered sharply to the right and pulled over, slamming on the brakes. "Get out."

"V, what are you doing?"

"Just go, before I change my mind."

He looked like he was about to protest, then unclipped his seatbelt. He got out of the car and turned back to look at her. "Thank you for trusting me here. I really do love you."

Then he disappeared into the night.

* * * * * *

Chapter 96

Bujumbura, Burundi

Veronica stopped the van next to where Edward had parked and hopped out, still reeling from her earlier decision.

"What happened?" Edward frowned. "Where's Kevin?"

"He overpowered me when we were stopped at a light on our way here." She slumped over, pretending to be ashamed. "He's gone."

"Unfortunate, unfortunate indeed. Well, at least we have the real prize, thanks to you."

She caught his reference to Kasem but simply nodded. Behind Edward, she could see a shadow in the passenger seat of the car.

"You do still have Nziza?"

"Of course." Making her way to the back, she tapped on the car button to open the trunk. Inside, the still-unconscious Nziza was secured to a stretcher. They had extracted him from the Hotel Belair with Gaston's help, much the way they had originally planned to capture Kevin at Café Gourmand.

"Good." Edward tapped something onto his phone, and a man who Veronica didn't recognize emerged from the private plane parked on their right. When he reached them, Edward motioned toward the stretcher. "Take care of him, then get the body inside."

"Yes, Sir." The man approached the stretcher, extracting a syringe from his pocket.

"Are you extending the tranquilizer?" Veronica asked in surprise. "He should be fine for a while longer."

"Not quite, my dear. The threat he posed to Burundi has been neutralized, so it's time we take care of other loose ends," Edward answered. "It's very slow acting, in about ten hours, it'll just look like had an aneurism, nothing that anyone could have predicted or prevented."

"I understand." Veronica contained a shudder. She had hoped it wasn't true, but here it was, clear as day: the confirmation that Nziza was once an Agency asset. Confirmation of how low they had stooped.

The man loaded the stretcher, then reemerged to escort Kasem from the car into the plane as well.

"You did good work here, agent," Edward said. "Feel free to come on board. I imagine you still need a ride home."

"Thank you."

She followed him up the staircase, each step more laborious than the last. She now knew in all certainty that she shouldn't have reported Kasem. Her one consolation was that she had saved Kevin, but her guilt overrode any comfort that would have brought. Nziza would be dead soon to cover the Agency's ass, and they would revel in the win of having captured the Ahriman. Nothing would be said about what Kasem had sacrificed, and the Agency would never have to face the music.

The bitter taste of regret filled her mouth. Would Kasem see the same fate as Nziza?

She stepped onto the plane and braced herself. Whatever awaited them, it was too late to do anything about it. She'd made her bed, now she had to lie in it.

* * * * * *

Chapter 97

Bujumbura, Burundi

Petra was having an out-of-body experience as she kept her pistol trained on Chris in the back seat while Carlos drove them to the airport. The SUV was moving so fast they hurtled through several potholes, but her grip remained steadfast. A voice in the back of her mind wondered if she had gone insane. She would never be able to use the gun on Chris, but she ignored it. For now, there was nothing else to do, she had to be prepared to follow through.

He's your friend, the voice nagged. Even if they'd had their issues.

Both Chris and Carlos remained quiet for the first part of the ride, Carlos seemed to have given up on trying to convince her to let Chris off the hook.

Or at least to behave reasonably, she recognized her temporary insanity. The adrenaline, the crazy, right now that was her asset, the only thing that might prevent Kasem from being dumped into an Agency hole.

"Could you let this go if it were Diane?" Petra had shouted back at Carlos' last attempt.

Instead of answering, he'd simply responded, "All right, I'll drive."

Chris broke the silence, turning toward her instead of continuing to stare out the window. "I'm not sure how many more times I have to say it before you'll believe me. I did *not* do this—I didn't tell the Agency about Kasem. I never had proof anyway, we couldn't confirm that he was the Ahriman, even if we couldn't confirm that he wasn't."

"You didn't tell the Agency? You are the Agency. Besides, when have you ever needed proof of anything?" she shot back. Her gaze landed on Carlos, and her fury thawed for a second before she pushed it aside. *I can't trust anyone.*

As if he could sense her doubts, Chris pressed on, "Come on, Petra, I know we've had our history, but I wouldn't betray you like that. You know me. I would at least have the guts to tell you to your face, to own it. Don't misunderstand me, I don't see why you would be with someone who has such a dark past, but I wouldn't do this to you."

"Because you've been so considerate of me? Sending me back to Kuwait when I wasn't in field ops anymore, hunting me down in Paris because you needed my help. What about my life? My needs? When have you ever cared about that?"

"I know those things hit you hard, but I never lied to you. When I needed your help, when I had to push you, I owned it. Let me prove it to you. Put your gun down, and I'll still help you. If we can get to Edward in time, I'll help you get Kasem back, even help you to get away."

Petra hesitated. He was right, much as she didn't want to admit it. She looked down at her gun, vacillating, but before she could decide, Carlos sped past the public parking lot at the airport. "Moment of truth, kiddo," he said, "we'll be at the private runway in two minutes."

Taking another deep breath, Petra's gaze moved from her pistol to Chris, to Carlos, and back to the pistol.

Sometimes you just have to trust...

They turned left into the runway parking lot, and she lowered the gun. "I'm going to choose to believe you. Because I have no choice, and because for almost ten years, we showed up for each other. If Kasem and I have a chance to get out of this, we need your help."

* * * * * *

Chapter 98

Bujumbura, Burundi

Kasem looked out the window of the charter plane as the heard the engines start to whir. He wasn't sure what he'd witnessed through the tinted car window, just that Nziza had been loaded onboard. Whatever the consequences, at least they had stopped the coup.

His gaze moved from his hands and ankles, both bound with zip ties, to the plane itself, as luxurious as the jet the CIA had chartered on his last operation in Madagascar. The seat was wide, covered with plush microfiber that enveloped him. Under other circumstances, he suspected that simply sitting down would have sent him into a deep sleep. Instead, memories from Madagascar rushed over him—the epic fight he'd had with Petra, and the view of the beach and how it had seemed so bittersweet superimposed on their imploding relationship. Thankfully, they had come back stronger—the memory seemed both far away and recent at the same time.

Whatever had happened, it was out of his hands now. At least this way, she would still be able to have a life. She could move on. His jaw trembled, Petra could have a life with someone else, someone without all of his baggage. A life absent of ops, without any more blackmail.

He cringed as Edward sat down in front of him; the smug, superior expression that never seemed to disappear made Kasem want to gag. *No wonder Tim calls him Mr. Darcy.* Kasem resisted the temptation to roll his eyes.

"My boy, you must be regretting your decision now. I'm afraid it's too late, a life in a cell awaits you, but at least you didn't make it even worse for your beloved. Her only crime, after all, was falling in love with you and anything that followed. It will be hard enough for her never to see you again, but to do that and spend the rest of her life in a black hole, now wouldn't that be worse? I must say, I had a moment of mercy—I considered letting you see her, even considered having you work for me instead of going to prison."

Kasem straightened up, he refused to beg, but he longed to see Petra one last time. His earlier conviction that he would be unable to go through with this if he saw her now felt idiotic. How could he disappear without saying goodbye?

"That got your attention, didn't it," Edward smirked. "Too bad you have nothing to offer, not at this point. After all, you said you would never talk, that all you would do is turn yourself in. It's a shame really, I can't imagine how much valuable intel you must have. In fact, I'm quite shocked we didn't try to use it earlier. It shouldn't surprise me really, that's what comes from letting someone as soft as Chris run you in New York." He raised his eyebrows, catching Kasem's gaze. "Oh, you thought I didn't know about that, my dear boy, nothing escapes me."

The plane started to taxi down the tarmac, and Kasem looked out at the runway again, refusing to engage with such a pompous ass.

"Settle in, this will be the most comfortable place you have to sleep for the rest of your life."

* * * * * *

348

Chapter 99

Bujumbura, Burundi

Petra fell to her knees as they ran out onto the empty tarmac. Their attempt had always been a long shot, but the thought brought her no solace. She touched her cheeks, damp with tears.

It was over, Kasem was gone. The last thread of hope dissipated, and she fought to breathe. They had lost their last chance.

"Come on, kiddo," Carlos held out his arm to help her up a moment later. "This isn't the end, we'll find a way to get him out. There's always something."

Petra brushed herself off and glared at Chris as she stood, clinging to what Carlos had said. "Will you help? He's not that person..." *Not anymore.* "There's more to him than your intel file."

Chris met her gaze, then looked between her and Carlos. "You've both come through for us when we needed you, even though you've been trying to give the Agency a giant middle finger for years. And Kasem, well he saved our asses in New York, and I know he put a lot on the line in Madagascar."

"This has to stop. We've burned so many assets, people who risked everything to help us. Enough is enough, this can't be what the Agency stands for." Chris glanced down at his hands, "The greater good is one thing, and collateral damage is part of that—but not willy-nilly as if we can't see what people have put on the line. What the Agency wanted to do here, how Edward was willing to hold this government hostage over an energy contract... That can't be what we do, that can't be what *I* do. Not now, not ever."

His jaw set. "I'll help you."

349

******

Chapter 100

New York, USA

Petra drummed her knuckles against the cool aluminum surface of the table, attempting to stare down the young man on the other side. "How much longer is this going to take?" She raised her eyebrows and gestured toward the polygraph machine.

He ignored her question and finished attaching the sensors to the index and middle fingers on her left hand.

"What's your name? Baldwin? You know you look like him, right? Alec Baldwin? Maybe he's before your time." Petra maintained her detached demeanor despite the fact that her emotions were on fire.

This is Kasem's best chance... his only chance.

Chris had provided her with Kasem's intel file, and based on what he had gathered, the Agency had nothing definitive to prove he was the Ahriman. In fact, she was their best possible source for an investigation—the only person who'd had extended contact with the Ahriman in Kuwait. She was his best chance unless they could prove that she was compromised.

Petra shoved those thoughts aside. She needed to be completely focused on the polygraph to get through it. While the Agency had taught her how to handle a polygraph as part of her training, she'd never had to put that into practice. Her stomach did another flip, and she exhaled, keeping her breaths slightly shallow. The machine would detect changes in her readings, so the best option was to keep all of them murky.

Baldwin—she couldn't be bothered with his real name—started with some basic questions, each with yes or no answers. She confirmed her name, her citizenship, place of birth, then moved on to her status as a former field operative and research lead. From there, the interviewer returned to basic questions. Clearly, he wanted to establish a strong baseline by asking where she had lived and about her parents. Focusing on her breathing, Petra kept her heart rate high but level, maintaining her attention on the answer to each specific question.

The Agency's method of fooling the polygraph meant that when she was asked the question that would require her to lie, she had to focus on the answer to another question. Although she had been quite good at making up stories as needed during training, this moment was different—this one had real stakes. She refused to dwell on that as she said, "Yes," to answer the question that she was the daughter of Dr. Danielle Thomas.

Under the table, she pushed her thumbnail into the tip of her middle finger, another technique that she'd found to be effective. The extra pressure kept her attention focused at least partially on her hands and helped keep her grounded.

The interviewer paused, and she could sense they were getting to the meat of the session.

"Is the man Sir Edward took custody of in Burundi Kasem Ismaili?"

"Yes."

The interviewers face didn't betray any emotion as he watched the screen on his side of the table. "Is he the international assassin known as the Ahriman?"

Petra resisted the urge to breathe deep, her entire future rested on this lie.

He isn't the Ahriman anymore. She zeroed in on that thought with all her might. *Not now, not ever again.* She met the interviewer's gaze. "No."

* * * * * *

The next morning, Petra woke up early after a restless night of tossing and turning. Her bed had never felt so empty without Kasem, despite the fact that she'd often complained about how he hogged the covers and often took up two-thirds of the bed with his wide sleeping postures. She had gotten so used to it she restricted herself to a small corner even though he wasn't there—what she would give to be able to shove him over to make more room.

She had just gotten up when her phone buzzed, and she reached for it. "Hi Rachel."

"Petra, I've got an idea."

Any grogginess in her eyes disappeared. There was no doubt that Rachel was referring to the situation with Kasem, but Petra scarcely had a moment to process before Rachel spouted the idea.

When she hung up a few moments later, Petra sank back into bed. Could it work? The idea was a long shot, but a real one. If it did, they could get him out, once and for all.

* * * * * *

Epilogue

Kasem stretched his arms over his head and stared upward—for the first time noticing the deviations in the pattern of the textured off-white ceiling. While the Agency was figuring out what to do with him, this tiny room had become familiar, if not something of a sanctuary, at least relative to the interrogation room where he had spent much of his time.

He was grateful the Agency had dumped him here instead of a prison cell, and he had managed to pass much of the time dozing in between interrogations. Despite their best efforts to break him, he had stuck to his story—the one that he had used during his first Agency operation. He maintained that he was a former Iranian operative who'd had contact with the Ahriman but most certainly was not the Ahriman.

"I worked with him, but I don't know where he is or if he's still alive," Kasem had repeated until his jaw hurt. He was surprised they refrained from any more persuasive tactics, but while they had slapped him around a few times, he was relatively unscathed, at least so far.

He shifted his position, the cot felt like it was made of cement rather than any kind of mattress, but it was still far more comfortable than any of the sleeping arrangements he'd had while being held prisoner in Iran. Small mercies.

Another day another dollar, the expression came to mind, something his friend Jamal had used to respond when people

354

asked him how his day was. The lack of enthusiasm in the phrase certainly applied to this moment, but Kasem's situation was even worse. There wasn't even a dollar involved.

He got up and walked over to the adjacent bathroom to brush his teeth. While he ought to be thankful for these provisions, all he wanted was to talk to Petra. To see her flash a smile at him, to assure her that he was all right. To tell her that she should move forward with her life. He returned to bed a few minutes later, contemplating how to pass the time when he heard the door unlock.

Kasem raised his eyebrows as a middle-aged woman in a suit entered the room. "I've already told you everything," he pre-empted the same questions they had gone through the day before.

Ignoring his comment, she said, "Get dressed."

After pulling a t-shirt on and a pair of jeans over his boxers, Kasem followed her out of the room and down the hall to a separate interrogation room, different from the one where he had been taken earlier.

"Wait here," the woman said and shut the door behind her.

Kasem rolled his eyes, there were obviously so many places he could go.

Five minutes later, he frowned as one of his former team members, a CIA operative named Rachel, sat down across the table from him. Kasem shifted in his seat, waiting for her to take the lead, wondering if he should pretend not to know her.

"Hi Kasem, it looks like the Agency is having a hell of a time proving whether or not you're the Ahriman."

He gave her a blank stare. *So? You want me to help?*

"But I'm not here about that," she continued. "Honestly, I don't care whether or not you're the Ahriman. General Majed may have made him into a legend, but I believe the Ahriman was just a man doing his bidding, following orders."

Kasem raised his eyebrows, still at a loss. "Why are you here?"

"Ahriman or not, you worked in Iranian intelligence under General Majed. He captured you, threatened and tortured you, then forced you to serve."

Kasem fixed his gaze on the wall behind Rachel. He refused to give anything away, not until she told him what on earth she wanted. Even if that was the story they had used during the Agency op in New York.

"In fact, one might argue that General Majed ruined your life. Before him, Kasem Ismaili was a go-getter financial analyst with a bright future. Isn't that right?"

"What are you getting at?"

"I have a proposition. If you help us, we'll get you a new identity, whatever you need to start over and wipe the slate clean. We'll destroy all of the files linking you to the Ahriman, and any ongoing or past investigation will be suspended and closed for good. You'll be free and clear, able to live your life however you want, with whomever you want."

Kasem detected her subtle reference to Petra and nodded, "I'm listening."

"I'd like you to help us take out General Majed."

* * * * * *

THE END

Dear Reader,

I'm so excited that you read my book. It still feels kind of surreal, that I have readers who actually read my books! Thank you so much.

I would love to hear what you thought of *Reckoning from the Shadows*. Would you mind posting a review on Amazon, Goodreads, or Bookbub?

Word of mouth and reviews are critical for any author to succeed. I would be so grateful if you would post a review! Even if it's only a line or two, it would be a tremendous help.

If you'd like to stay in touch, sign up for my mailing list here: **http://smarturl.it/PujaList**

I'll let you know about new releases, contests, and more!

Thank you again!

With all my best,

Puja Guha

ACKNOWLEDGMENTS

Somehow, I find myself always putting off writing my Acknowledgments, no matter how many books I've written. I should take it as a given now, but I suspect I'll remain stubborn for the rest of my writing career. So many people have supported me and contributed to my work and development as a writer, something that continues to humble me to this day.

Most importantly, I want to thank you, my reader. Thank you for joining me for another one of Petra and Kasem's stories. I was originally planning to close their journey at three books, but I'm now planning another one in addition to *Reckoning from the Shadows*. A huge part of extending the series is thanks to your wonderful reception and support.

To my editor, Tanya Besmehn, thank you for helping me to continue to grow as a writer. You always push me and even if I resist, I couldn't do this without you.

To John Besmehn, thank you for all your efforts working on my cover design and graphics.

Finally, to my friends and family—thank you for all your love and support. Over the last three years, I've moved to Colorado, been traditionally published, weathered a global pandemic, and endured a year of recovery including three surgeries and far more doctor visits than I could have imagined. I could never have gotten through any of that without you, and I certainly wouldn't be moving ahead with more books.

- To my husband Brendan Collins Snow, it's too cheesy to use phrases like "You're the wind beneath my wings," but that's the sort of emotion that comes to mind when I think of your support.

- To my parents Pradip and Jayashree Guha, I realize more everyday how much you've given me. Thank you.

- To Jessica Glombick – Thank you for listening to me talk about everything under the sun anytime. I'm so lucky we were both in the Parc computer lab at the same time.

- To Tracee Hollman and Gunnar Steden (and Brody and Libby) – I didn't realize we would find a whole new family when we got to Colorado. I'm so glad that Sally and Brody are twins, otherwise we might never have met!

- To the rest of my Colorado family, I was apprehensive about moving here and now I may never leave! A few shout outs, but this list is far from exhaustive and not in any particular order: Joanne Collins, Grace and Ryan Mccombie (and Fernie and Kenzo!), Bruce and Kristin Snow, Shandrika Lee and Alexis Verbin (and Loki), Allison Boening, Brian Forth and Paula Costelo (and Chuck), Paul, Henry and Mabel Glombick, Aaron Cole, Kellie Cushing, Emily Freeman, Kara Hermanns and Casey Wolverton. You mean the world to me.

- And finally, to our dog Sally – I knew that that human bond with pets, but I only understand how much now.

I notice all the ways you take care of me and my mental health. I couldn't do any of this without you.

About the Author

Puja Guha grew up and has worked all over the world, something which she channels into her writing, incorporating settings from New York to Madagascar to Iran. So far, she has published four spy thrillers, an international family drama and a psychological thriller. Her spy thriller series *The Ahriman Legacy* is an Amazon international bestseller and has been recommended by the US Review of Books. The series follows a former spy and assassin on their adventures together, and in the most recent book *Reckoning from the Shadows* they become embroiled in a power struggle with Chinese intelligence that begins in Paris and culminates in the African Great Lakes region. Her recent psychological thriller *Sirens of Memory* was named one of the best crime fiction books of 2021 by Diverse Voices Book Review.

Connect with Puja Guha

Email: pujaguha@pujaguha.com
Follow me on Twitter: http://twitter.com/guhapuja
Friend me on Facebook: http://facebook.com/puja.guha
Google plus: https://plus.google.com/106961837703326951468
Connect with me on Goodreads:
http://www.goodreads.com/user/show/21394716-puja-guha
Connect with me on Linkedin:
http://www.linkedin.com/in/pujaguha
Webpage: www.pujaguha.com

Made in the USA
Las Vegas, NV
06 January 2024

83980416R00203